EX LIBRIS

VINTAGE CLASSICS

T0315636

THE WILD SWAN

Margaret Kennedy was born in 1896. Her first novel, *The Ladies of Lyndon*, was published in 1923. Her second novel, *The Constant Nymph*, became an international bestseller. She then met and married a barrister, David Davies, with whom she had three children. She went on to write a further fifteen novels, to much critical acclaim. She was also a playwright, adapting two of her novels – *Escape Me Never* and *The Constant Nymph* – into successful productions. Three different film versions of *The Constant Nymph* were made, and featured stars of the time such as Ivor Novello and Joan Fontaine; Kennedy subsequently worked in the film industry for a number of years. She also wrote a biography of Jane Austen and a work of literary criticism, *The Outlaws of Parnassus*. Margaret Kennedy died in Woodstock, Oxfordshire, in 1967.

OTHER NOVELS BY MARGARET KENNEDY

MARGARET KENNEDY

The Wild Swan

VINTAGE BOOKS
London

Published by Vintage 2014

2 4 6 8 10 9 7 5 3 1

First published in Great Britain by Macmillan & Co in 1957

Vintage
Random House, 20 Vauxhall Bridge Road,
London SW1V 2SA

www.vintage-classics.info

Addresses for companies within The Random House Group Limited
can be found at: www.randomhouse.co.uk/offices.htm

The Random House Group Limited Reg. No. 954009

A CIP catalogue record for this book
is available from the British Library

ISBN 9780099589754

The Random House Group Limited supports The Forest Stewardship
Council® (FSC®), the leading international forest-certification organisation.
Our books carrying the FSC label are printed on FSC®-certified paper.
FSC is the only forest-certification scheme supported by the leading
environmental organisations, including Greenpeace. Our
paper procurement policy can be found at
www.randomhouse.co.uk/environment

Printed and bound in Great Britain by Clays Ltd, St Ives plc

TO GORDON WELLESLEY

PART I

The Wild Swan

He long survives who lives an hour
In ocean, self upheld.

Cowper

1

May Turner was a retired school teacher. For forty years she had lived and laboured in a smoky industrial town. In old age she betook herself to the village of Upcott, near Beremouth, where she shared a cottage with her friend, Alice Budden. They kept bees, made themselves useful at the Village Institute, and won medals for the best cottage garden in the district.

Busy with her spray or secateurs, May pretended not to hear the admiring comments of passers-by. But they pleased her, all the same. It was agreeable to be praised for something, and her life work had been taken entirely for granted. Her children were now scattered all over the world; if any of them had turned into prize blooms, no medals had ever been pinned upon May's neat shirt waist. She was now merely remembered as a vague, reassuring figure with a sharp nose and a brisk manner, who had presided over their infancy. Flowers were more rewarding.

One fine afternoon in early spring, while she was staking hyacinths, a passer-by paused and stared over her garden gate. She took no notice until a familiar voice exclaimed:

"All in glorious Technicolour!"

At which she jumped and turned round. A lean sandy-haired young man was laughing at her over the gate.

"Hullo, Auntie?"

It was Roy Collins, her favourite nephew, whom she had not seen for some time and over whom she had worried for twenty-five years.

He pushed the gate open and came into the garden. His clothes were terrible, as usual, but he wore quite good shoes.

"You're fatter," she decided.

With an affectionate hug he retorted, "So are you. In fact, I couldn't be sure it was you. All I could see was this nice fat bee-hind. Thought it might be Alice."

"But where have you sprung from, Roy? It is nice to see you. But what are you doing in Upcott?"

"Actually I'm in Beremouth. On a job."

"A job? That's nice!"

She glanced again at his beautiful shoes.

"Exclusive, aren't they?" he said, sticking one foot out.

He beamed at them and shed the best part of twenty years. For a moment he was the freckled shrimp for whom she had bought extravagant presents, in order to watch him undo the parcel. Nobody could be as happy as Roy when everything went right; but that did not happen very often.

He raised his head and the innocent glee evaporated. His thin face became wary and secretive.

"Actually," he muttered, out of the corner of his mouth, "I'm getting along very well. Only . . ."

Only don't tell anybody was the unspoken injunction. Whatever he was doing he had clearly learnt that conspicuous success can be dangerous; it is seldom welcome news to fellow climbers and may engender hostility in those above. He's in some big firm, working with a lot of people, she thought. He's had some bad knocks. He's learnt not to trust anybody. Oh dear! I do hope it's respectable, whatever it is.

"Your mother must be pleased," she ventured.

Roy gave her a black look and shook his head.

"Nothing I do could please Mum, or Dad. I don't ask them for money. They don't ask what I do. I say, Auntie . . . could it be time for a cup of char?"

"Char!" cried May affronted. "No. Char's for tramps. I'll give you *tea* . . . if you'll stop pretending to be more common than you really are. It's very silly and all put on."

She led the way into the house and left him in the sitting room while she went to prepare the meal.

It was a pity that he should have broken so entirely with his parents, but her sympathies were on his side. Mr. Collins was a prosperous undertaker in the Midlands. That Roy, the eldest son, would join the family firm had always been assumed, although they should have known better, for he had never concealed his distaste for such a profession. The storm had burst when he finished his military service. And he ought not, thought May, as she plugged in the kettle, . . . he was wrong to tell them that he couldn't care less for stiffs. That was unkind. It's work that somebody has to do, and we should all grumble if it wasn't done nicely.

That taunt was still unforgiven, although it had all happened five years ago. Roy took himself off to London. That he could be up to no good there was a matter of dogma with everyone save May, who still persisted in the belief that he had something and that he might surprise them all one day. He would end, she confidently prophesied, right on top. Very seldom, in the course of forty years' experience, had she thought this about a child, for the top is sparsely populated. But she had never felt it without subsequent justification and she had felt it once or twice about children believed by their families to be daft.

Roy was not daft, and to be continually called so had not improved his temper. There was one episode in particular which could still rack May with compassionate indignation. When he was about twelve years old he developed a passion for earning and saving money. All his holidays, all his hours out of school, were occupied with chores. He cut grass. He ran errands. He even looked after babies. His parents, at first inclined to commend all this thrift and industry, grew restive; baby sitting, they felt, was unsuitable for the child of well-to-do business people. And then, without consulting anybody, he spent all his savings on an enormous complicated camera which he was seldom able to use because he could not afford to keep it up. Everybody laughed at him without mercy; he was never allowed to hear the end of it. The memory of his stolid little face, of the stoical silence which he offered to a mocking world, sent May scuttling into the larder to open a tin of salmon. He might be getting along very well, but he still looked as though he needed to be fed better.

When she took the tea tray into the sitting room she found him absorbed in a picture which hung over the fireplace.

"I like this sailor's wife," he said. "It's new, isn't it?"

"Oh that belongs to Alice."

"Oh? And where is Alice, all this time?"

"Miss Budden," she said, with a look which had quelled generations of cheeky children, "is at a Whist Drive."

"Cheers!" said Roy, unquelled.

"And why do you call it a sailor's wife. *Girl Reading a Letter* happens to be what it's called."

"Map. That big map thing on the wall behind her. Meant to make you think of voyages and all that. It's nice, that map. The right size for the picture. Got her hair done a queer way, though."

"It's an Old Master. A reproduction."

At this information his face fell.

"Old Masters," he said, taking the tray from her, "are types I can definitely do without. Is she supposed to be the Virgin Mary?"

"Don't be irreverent," counselled May, going back to the kitchen to see if the kettle had boiled.

Never in a hundred years, she thought, would he ask who the Old Master was, which was silly of him, because he had quite a feeling for pictures. At one time she had wondered whether his longing for a camera might not be connected with this. But whenever they went together to the cinema he was so caustic, he seemed to like so little of what he saw, that she had been obliged to give up the dream that he might get to the top in the film industry. Yet she was sure that his visual capacities were uncommon. As a little boy he had been fond of telling her long stories and she had been struck by the narrative form that he preferred. 'And what do you see next?' he would demand. 'You see him creepin' up . . . and creepin' up . . .' Most

7

children, in her experience, would have said: 'And then he crept up', or, in some cases, 'and then I crept up.' But his imagination, which was strong, depended upon some visual stimulus, which he seemed to be anxious to share. He had never taken to books, and, as he grew older, developed a kind of suspicious hostility towards culture of any kind, as though he saw in it some threat to his inner freedom.

The kettle boiled. She filled the tea-pot and returned to the other room. He was still occupied with the Sailor's Wife.

"I remember now," he said, "I have seen it before. In shops and places. The hair is the only old world touch. That little blue coolie coat she's got . . . that's quite up to the minute."

"Have you decided what's in the letter?" jeered May.

"Nothing to upset her. He says he's O.K., wherever he is, and he hopes she's O.K., and love to Mum and how's the dog? It's that roller thing the map's on, going right across the picture. That tells you the kind of girl she is. She has a sort of ruler in her life. She's sensible. She doesn't like him being away so much but she's sensible and knows it can't be helped."

May studied the girl's faint smile, the calm content with which she devoured her letter, and agreed.

"Poor thing," she sighed. "He might be away for years. Their voyages went on so long in those days."

"Let's hope he hasn't been gone more than nine months, or he'll get quite a little surprise when he comes home."

"Tut-tut! Could you eat an egg, dear?"

"Well . . . thanks . . . I don't really think I could.

We get an awful lot to eat at this hotel where I'm staying. The Queen's, on the Esplanade. Very classy."

"The Queen's! But that's——"

"Madly exclusive," agreed Roy complacently.

"Don't say exclusive when you mean expensive. They aren't the same thing at all."

"How right you are!"

"Surely, dear, you could find somewhere more reasonable?"

"Don't say reasonable when you mean cheap, Auntie. It's all right. I was told to go there. Expenses paid."

He accepted a cup of tea and for a moment looked as if he meant to tell her no more. Then he took pity on her.

"I've got a job," he said, "with Blech Bernstein British. In the script department."

At these words May heard a burst of synthetic music. She saw curtains parting on an empty screen. An aeroplane streaked across the clouds, writing, in huge words:

BLECH BERNSTEIN BRITISH PRESENTS

They always did that before every B.B.B. picture.

"The films!" she gasped. "You've gone into . . . after all . . . Roy! The script department? Does that mean . . . ? Not *writing*? Surely?"

"Umhm!"

"But you can't spell for toffee."

"Don't have to. A lot of people in Scripts can't spell. We give it to a girl called Mamie and she puts in the spelling. She knows everything. She told the most highbrow writer we've got that there's no i in portentious."

"I should think not! There's no such word."

"That's what Mamie says. Why should we worry when

we've got Mamie? A script isn't meant to be read, you know. Not like a book. It's more . . . more like the instructions on the tin, if you see what I mean."

"So that's what you've always—But, Roy, how did you get this job? How did you ever get started there?"

"I got started by sweeping floors," said Roy. "And then I got some camera work, on stills. And I wriggled along, and I made friends, here and there, and now I'm in Scripts."

"And next?"

"I'm hoping to get into the cutting room. There's going to be a vacancy, sometime soon, and I've got a friend there, Ed Miller, who's rooting for me."

And where, after that? she wondered, but did not like to ask.

"I always thought those studios were in London," she said.

"They are. Well, in Herts. But I'm down here to help a girl write a picture. You see, B.B.B. have bought this play—*The Wild Swan* it's called. It was a great success; ran two years. And this girl who wrote it, Adelaide Lassiter, insists that she does the screen version. Of course, she hasn't a clue, so they sent me along to write it for her."

"Quite young is she?" asked May anxiously.

"I wouldn't know. About your age, I should think."

"Why do you call her a girl then, for goodness' sake?"

"To make you jump, old dear."

They both laughed and May asked what Adelaide Lassiter was like, at which he looked dubious.

At last he said, "Got a mink coat. Spent her royalties on a lovely pen and ink!"

"That doesn't tell me much."

"Should do."

"Sounds a silly way of spending money."

"You get my meaning then."

"And what's her play like?"

"Lousy. Period stuff. Crinolines."

"Ah! You never did like historical pictures."

"And never shall. They're all phoney. But why we have to come down here is because Adelaide claims she needs to drink in all the atmosphere, while she's writing it. There's an old house in these parts, Bramstock, where it's supposed to have happened."

"Why . . . that's where Mr. Harding lives."

"That's right. We're changing the title. It's to be called *The Bramstock Story*. Kitty Fletcher wants to be Dorothea Harding. That's why."

"Dorothea Harding? You mean . . . that writer? That Victorian writer?"

May found it difficult to believe. Dorothea Harding, the great aunt of the man now living at Bramstock, had been in her day an immensely popular novelist. She wrote very moral romances with historical or classical settings, but her vogue was long since over and all her books were out of print. Her literary reputation, such as it was, now rested upon some poetry, discovered and published after her death, which had at one time created a considerable stir and which still commanded a few adherents.

"I never heard anything so ridiculous," exclaimed May. "She never did anything to make a picture about. She never married. She just lived here all her life and wrote those books."

"I couldn't agree with you more."

"Kitty Fletcher? She won't look a bit like her."

"She'd better not. I've seen a photo of D. Harding. Definitely not box office. The poor girl had a nose as long as Southend Pier. But that could be bad camera work."

"I just can't see where the story comes in. I used to like her books when I was a girl. I cried over them. But you couldn't get children to read them now. She was so goody-goody."

"Auntie! And you say I'm ignorant! You *are* behind the times. Goody-goody she was not. There's a diary been found, and a lot of poetry. They were"—Roy searched his limited vocabulary for a word which should not scandalise his aunt—"they were sizzling. D. Harding wasn't all she'd been cracked up to be. She led a double life. She was a naughty girl. That's the story."

A spasm of impatience and disgust flickered across his face for a moment and he added, "It's supposed to be very dramatic. Here's this spinster lady, so very prim and proper, living in the dear Vicar's pocket and writing prissy books for kids. And all the while, behind the scenes . . . it was her brother-in-law, as a matter of fact. He was her boy first, and then her sister grabbed him and married him, and then she grabbed him back. Just Kitty's cup of tea; madly sultry for six reels and then the voice of conscience begins to yap, and the dear old parson takes a hand and tells her it's not nice the way she's going on. So she renounces the boy and he staggers out into the night, and we get a U Certificate because really it's a moral picture. Mean to say you didn't know about all this?"

"I believe now I did hear something about it," said May sadly. "Didn't somebody . . . some critic . . . write a book?"

"That's right. Alec Mundy. He's a poetry critic; he explains what poets really mean and how they get to write their poetry. He got hold of this diary and wrote a book proving that D. Harding was only able to write poetry because all this happened to her. Adelaide read this book and thought what a lovely play it would make. And Kitty saw the play and thought what a lovely picture it would make. And that's why I'm here."

"But the family, Roy! They're living here still. How terrible it will be for them."

"The family," he told her drily, "can't wait to cash in on Auntie's shame. They're getting £500 for allowing the exteriors to be shot on location. That's a packet, but some advance publicity got out about it before their contract was signed, which gave them a chance to bargain. Oh yes! The family are doing very well out of it."

May thought that this was dreadful and said so. Mr. Harding, she wailed, was such a nice man, a gentleman, and he read the lessons in church. How could he?

"A lot of people on this picture," said Roy, "are holding their noses and taking the cash. Mundy now . . . he's on this script too. All our pictures are supposed to be a hundred per cent accurate and somebody tipped off B.B.B. that accuracy isn't Adelaide's strong point. So they thought they'd better sign up Mundy to put the accuracy in. And if there's one thing in this world makes Mundy throw up it's the thought of Adelaide and her corny play. So wouldn't you think he'd tell B.B.B. where to put their contract? But no. He's right there with us at the Queen's, holding his nose. And believe me, it's one long dog fight. Everything Adelaide wants, he says: No. It's the wrong date. She flaps her hands and says: Dates mean nothing to me, Mr. Mundy. (She's dead right there). All I care for is the *human* angle, she says."

"And you, Roy? What do you do?"

"Nothing, at this stage, except keep a straight face. When they've finished their script, I'll make a shooting script which its own father and mother won't know it, but it'll be something you can go on the floor with. I shall scrap all Adelaide's corny Victorian dialogue. You know. *'Do not, do not* speak of this again, because I *cannot* listen to you.' Which I don't believe was the way anybody ever talked, even then. What I put won't be quite O.K. But I'll get Mamie to look it over. She'll see that I don't turn in any Herods."

"Herods? What's that?"

He laughed and offered her a cigarette.

"Herods," he said, lighting a match for her, "is a name we have, in our department, for dialogue mistakes so bad that even the audience would notice. You see we had a writer once who thought he knew better than Mamie. He was working on *Pontius Pilate*. Mamie didn't like the line: *I'll refer Him back to Herod*. She has these hunches; she isn't highbrow, you know, but she has a lot of experience and she knows the sort of line the critics will make such fun of that the public gets to know. She turned out to be quite right. And since then we've called that sort of brick a Herod."

"Mamie?" murmured May, in fresh anxiety.

"Married-to-a-camera-man-in-S.P.I.-and-going-to-have-a-baby," rattled off Roy, giving her a reassuring pat. "She's supposed to be the Script Supervisor's secretary, but she really runs the whole department. She tells us all off.

14

She says I've got a shocking accent. Have I, do you think?"

"Yes," said May. "And I can't think why, for you were brought up to talk nicely."

"I suppose it's a reaction from listening to Dad being tactful with the bereaved. Well . . . a million thanks for the tea. I think I ought to be getting along. Actually I'm supposed to be calling at Bramstock to find out if Adelaide can't come out there one day and drink in atmosphere right on the spot. She never bothered to, when she was writing *The Wild Swan*, because it was only a single indoor set."

"Why did she call it that?"

"Because of some poetry D. Harding wrote. It seems she renounced him in a swannery in the middle of the night. Big emotional scene. Any other girl would have called it a day. But not D. Harding. She didn't even scream for an aspirin. She went right home and wrote a piece about it. *The Swan went west*, it says. Adelaide is sold on this swannery. Wants to have swans zooming all over the set."

"I believe I remember that poem," exclaimed May, getting up and going to the bookcase. "It's in a book Alice has—*Minor Victorian Verse*, or some such name. . . ."

"Where we part brass rags," said Roy, "is what happens next. In Adelaide's play, this Grant, he goes off and breaks his neck on purpose. Mundy says that wasn't so. He merely fell out of a dog-cart, by accident, three years later."

"Here it is. It's called *The Answer*."

May had taken down a book and now she read from it:

> "I fear now to wander in the meads
> By the grey river.

The swan flying low above the reeds
Cries: Never! Never!"

"I never read a word she wrote," said Roy, "or any of
the books about her. Look through Adelaide's play, that's
all I've done."

He went and read over her shoulder.

"Miserable old bird!" he commented. "Everything
she asks, it just says *Never*."

"Here's the line. *Westward the wild swan went. Her
wings cried never!* I thought it couldn't be the swan went
west."

"Same thing. It went west. That's the way it went. So
now we know. How do I get to this Bramstock? Is it far?"

The directions which she gave him were so complicated that his face fell.

"Sounds like a whole day hike," he complained. "Well
. . . bye-bye! Be seeing you." Hugging her, he added,
"Ah river derchy."

"Whatever's that?"

"Portentious way of saying bye-bye, be seeing you."

She went with him to the door and watched him as
he marched off down the path with that purposeful air
which he always had. Her heart was sad. All this jubilant
flippancy had not deceived her. That was his way too,
when dejected. She knew that he was inwardly dissatis-
fied. So much must have been faced and endured, during
these five years, and his reward, apparently, was to be doing stupid work which he despised.

At the gate he turned and ran back.

"I'm a meanie not to tell you everything," he said
hastily. "Actually I felt a bit shy. I'm getting on a bit bet-

ter than I said. I've sold a little screen play. Nothing important. A featurette."

"Roy! Something you wrote yourself? And it will be made?"

"It's been made. Brickhill Studios. Dorman and Fisher —one of these three-reel featurettes they've been making. They're friends of mine; they were in B.B.B. before they started their own company."

"But has it been shown? Where? I'd like to——"

"I wouldn't know. It'd just be used to fill up programmes. It couldn't be less important. But it was good experience to see it made. Only I didn't direct it myself. I wish I had."

"Oh!" Light broke on her. "That's what you really want? To be a director?"

"Of course," he said, as if surprised that she should not have known this. "And make my own pictures."

Now that she knew, she wondered that she had not guessed years ago. A great number of clues fell into place.

"But what's it called, this picture? What's it about?"

"It's called *Every Wednesday*. It's about . . . about a kid and a Punch and Judy show. But it's nothing really. Only I had to tell you because you were looking so disappointed. Forget it. When I do something I really want you to see, I'll send you a telegram."

2

The stile at the end of the village led into a huge pasture sloping downward to the river, where a faint footpath wandered away over brownish winter grass.

For a country dweller the scene might have held some charm, but Roy found it bleak. He liked verdure and a profusion of wild flowers. Trees and hedges should, he thought, have leaves, nor could he feel much enthusiasm for the celandines which he spied here and there. He believed them to be primroses and wondered why people made such a fuss about them. His exclusive shoes hurt him; in any case, he was not fond of walking.

The effort of putting a good face on things to his aunt had drained his vitality and flung him back into a miasma of depression which had hung about him ever since he came to Beremouth. He wished that he had not mentioned his one small success, for it had been overclouded by a growing sense of disappointment, the extinction of a desire to get into the Brickhill Studios and work with his friends, Dorman and Fisher. They had lately changed their policy. Having skirted some dangerous financial reefs they were now in clear water; they had discovered a line of their own which the public was willing to accept. Their pictures were far better, far more enterprising and original, than those of B.B.B. which nowadays had no policy at all save to capitalise the inexplicable popularity of Kitty Fletcher. But they had taken to repeating themselves. In picture after picture they served up the same dish, with new garnishings. Roy would not have said that these pictures stank, but they had ceased to excite him, and he felt that they would ultimately stink, as all art must which is not perpetually growing and changing. He had come to the conclusion that it would be better to stay on in B.B.B., which was the last stronghold of corny tripe, but where he had a chance of getting experience in the cutting room.

Even the cutting room, however, had now less glamour for him. He could not be certain that it would lead him to his final goal, although it was a step towards directorship. Merely to be a director was, in itself, nothing, so far as he was concerned. If he was not to direct his own pictures, conceived, composed and written by himself, the whole journey would have been in vain. It was with this end in view that he had swept floors, and, if he was never to reach it, he might as well sweep floors for life. But it was only lately that this doubt had come upon him. He had swept floors in the sanguine belief that directors can do as they like. The gradual subjugation of Dorman and Fisher had been a melancholy eye-opener. They were not, he knew, doing what they had set out to do when they left B.B.B.

With every step up the hill he got a clearer view of the fetters, the compromises, awaiting those who achieved the summit. The prospect daunted him so much that he sometimes wondered whether more genuine freedom was not enjoyed by the jungle prowlers at the bottom. In the dog fight waged down there, the feasibility of compromise was seldom debated. Disappointment, frustration and success were all treated with the same embattled cynicism. Each man got away with as much as he could, and gave his best to the picture in hand, never doubting that it would ultimately stink. Some fraction of that best might survive—a minute, unrecorded victory. The greater part was certain to evaporate in the turmoil of production. The responsibility falling upon Roy and his fellows was so microscopic as to trouble them not at all. They were not sticking their necks out. They did as they were told, with much virtuous bustle. In conference they never spoke but to agree. On propitious occasions, when they had learnt how to work under cover, they did as they liked.

Upon Roy's inward eye, as he climbed a second stile, there flashed a vision of Elmer Simpson, who was to direct *The Bramstock Story*. When last they met, Elmer had been going on like a mad thing about a railway station. An efficient, if old-fashioned, director, he was famous chiefly for the fantastic obsessions to which he periodically fell a prey. These were a fearful joy to everybody working for him. Almost anything could be accomplished, by astute subordinates, so long as the bee in Elmer's bonnet was held sacred. Story lines could be completely remodelled. Miles of film could be slashed by Ed Miller in the cutting room. There would be no murmur from the besotted Elmer unless somebody was mean enough to squeal. Such treachery was rare but not unknown, and intrigues of all sorts abounded until Elmer, suddenly dispossessed, began to take notice.

Such a crisis was raging now. Elmer, while ruminating over this new assignment, had visited a picture gallery where he saw Frith's *Railway Station*, and had forthwith gone crackers. It gave, he announced, the period in a nutshell. He wanted it all, an exact reproduction—the crowds, the old ladies with bird-cages, the bearded soldiers kissing their babes farewell, the honeymoon couple entering one compartment whilst, in another, plain clothes officers arrested a fugitive from justice. Roy must see to it that this script furnished him with a great big railway station.

Roy agreed fervently that it was a wonderful idea, but he had not, as yet, done much about it because he thought that it could not last long. The cost would be prohibitive, and nobody was sold on the idea of a railway station except poor old Elmer, in whom it was, perhaps, a reflex gesture of defiance, the remnant of a pipedream that directors can do what they like. Elmer's inspiration, in boyhood, had been a picture called *Intolerance*. To handle huge agitated crowds was his sole ambition, but, for some reason, nobody had ever allowed him to do so. Having reached the top of the hill it was apparently his fate to direct Kitty Fletcher until the public grew tired of her. Roy and Ed might detest *The Bramstock Story* but they would probably, if they were lucky and artful, secure a few moments of satisfaction out of the job. For Elmer it was merely a fresh sentence to the treadmill.

It might, reflected Roy, be as well to ring Mamie and find out if this perishing railway station was still top priority. If so, Adelaide and Mundy must be given their orders, since it was he, not they, who would take the rap if Elmer failed to find it in their script.

Until he got back to Mamie and the studios he would

never, he feared, shake off this melancholy mood. Solitude and leisure did not suit him, and at Beremouth he got too much of both. His companions, much as they disliked one another, were united in their resentment at his inclusion in the team. They thought him an illiterate barbarian and were convinced that he could contribute nothing to their script. Left to himself, with no resource save to wander about on the sands, he had little defence against thoughts which, elsewhere, he kept at bay.

Life at B.B.B. might be a rat race but it was strenuous. So much was always going on, about which he, for his safety, needed to know. To be holding his own was no mean achievement. At any moment somebody might pinch his credit titles or his biro, unless he kept a sharp look out, and there were so many people after that job in the cutting room that even a short absence might endanger his chances. He had his disconsolate moments, but crises of all kinds kept cropping up to distract him. Some long hatched plot might mature. An opportunity might occur to score off an enemy. A change of patron might become advisable. He had taken to intrigue as some people take to drink, as an anodyne against frustration. Frequently he would adopt it for its own sake, for its excitement, rather than for any personal advantage to be gained. He would take a devious and crooked path when straight dealing would have served him just as well. To regard himself as exceedingly tough was reassuring, and he had not yet perceived that the toughest characters in a rat race are those who have least to conceal.

At the end of three fields he came to a valley full of reed beds, running from East to West. Across the river, hills rose from a blanket of brown woods. Gusts of wind fretted the water and rattled the reeds. His aunt had mentioned a footbridge but he could not see one. He plodded on from nowhere to nowhere, while the sun sank into stormy clouds.

Two large birds flew past him towards the sad sunset. The rhythmic beat of their wings arrested his attention before he could decide what birds they were.

Never! Never! Never!

Swans! he thought.

D. Harding was right. They did say *Never!* She must have been here too.

The fact that she must have been here took him so much by surprise that he paused and stood still. Hitherto he had always seen her as Kitty Fletcher, capering in a crinoline. But he now perceived her as a real person, and wondered, for the first time, what kind of person that was.

He remembered the photograph, the long nose, the sunken cheeks, the scanty hair screwed up under a little cap which sat on the top of that gaunt head like a dab of meringue. The clothes were bunched and frowsy looking; she wore a bustle, not a crinoline, and she stood stiffly beside a potted palm on a bamboo stand. It was a parody of everybody's great aunt, in the family album, and it must have been taken when she was old.

That poem about the swan had been written years earlier. Mundy had said that she wrote no more poetry after the death of her lover. It had been a young girl who walked here once and heard the swans. He could not picture her save as a solitary being, walking alone as he now walked, and hearing in these wings some premonition of the future. That dramatic parting, Adelaide's big emotional scene, had no place here. He was convinced of this, without pausing to ask himself why.

She never! he thought. She never came here with a fellow. Not then. Not when she thought of that poem. She was young. She hadn't a clue. She was wondering when her life would start, and when she'd get away from here. She was thinking of all the marvellous things she meant to do. And then . . . those dismal birds . . . *Never! Never!* . . . But she didn't believe it. Not then. She was too young to believe it, poor kid! And that's why she was able to go home and put it into a poem.

He walked on reflecting in parentheses that Kitty would raise the roof if her big emotional scene had to be played among all these cow pats. If any of it was to be shot here, Farmer Giles must do something about his cows, which meant more on production costs. Adelaide had a mania for exteriors. Released from her one-piece indoor set she ranged the country-side and sent everybody out of doors whenever she possibly could. It would be his business, later, to bring them all in again.

But that poor girl, he thought, returning to Dorothea, never did get away from this dog's island. She spent her whole life at Bramstock, took to writing prissy books, and ended up as a revolting old woman in a cap. Why had she stayed? What kept her? She had money. The prissy books had earned a fortune. Why had she done so little with it?

As he spied and crossed the footbridge over the river he reviewed the other characters in the story, searching for some explanation. None of them flashed into vivid life, as she had done. They were still shadows, populating Adelaide's script. Grant Forrester, the mystery man of the poems, the G: of the diary, had never been very substantial, even in the play. He had little to say and nothing to do save gallop about on a horse, since Dorothea had written a poem about him called *The Night Rider*. Mary, the rival sister, was easier to picture. She was one of those competent brunettes who always played as a foil to Kitty Fletcher—beautiful, but insipid enough to ensure audience identification with Kitty, however shady the games that Kitty might be up to. The dear old parson, Mr. Winthorpe (pronounced Winthrop), would be played by Hugh Farren, who would always play holy old men in B.B.B. pictures until confined for good in an inebriates' home. And, for a B.B.B. starlet, a small part in the play had to be written up—little Effie Creighton, a cousin, a dainty tomboy, whose innocent tumblings about in lace pantaloons were to provide a contrast to the dark doings going on around her.

They were none of them valid enough to provide a background for this girl on whose behalf he had begun to feel a kind of wondering sympathy. It was easier to think with indignation of the contemporary Hardings. To them she was obviously no more than a source of revenue. She lay now buried in Bramstock churchyard, while her sins and her sorrows were travestied to line the pockets of a great nephew.

The sun finally vanished, as he came to a rickety gate into the woods. The river here, taking a wide curve, flowed close under a grassy bank where an old cottage or cowhouse was falling to pieces. He untied the rope which fastened the gate and turned once more to look at the valley before he left it.

At that moment a profound and paralysing sadness

gripped him, as though he had passed into the precinct of some grief which hung over this spot like an undispelled mist. His senses received it first. He grew very cold, not from a chill striking upon his flesh, but within, from a lump of ice between his ribs. Then, by degrees, the living world drew away from him—rejected him, leaving him conscious but alone in darkness.

Never could he have imagined such helpless, hopeless despair, yet it was not completely alien or unrecognised. Part of him had reached out to meet it.

He was running through the wood, his footfalls muffled by a mat of last year's leaves. He was afraid of losing his way, but he dared not turn back, for he knew that the wretchedness from which he fled was close at his heels. It was with extreme relief that he emerged into a weedy drive, turned a corner, and beheld the house.

To his surprise it was very ugly, ill proportioned and clumsy, built of the local brownish stone, with a meagre conservatory protruding from one of its wings like a large blister. A drive ran round a space of rough grass in the middle of which was a half-dead monkey puzzle. A shabby little car stood by the open front door. He inspected it briefly before he rang the bell and decided what he would not give for it. The Hardings must keep a dog. A filthy old rug on the back seat was covered with white hairs. Perhaps, when they had cashed in on Auntie, they would run to a new dog rug.

The bell trilled through the house, but nobody came. He could see into an untidy hall whence a double staircase ran up to a gallery. Some faint scufflings were going on somewhere. He was sure that his presence had been perceived.

As he waited, a clock among the trees struck six. Another clock, inside the house, whirred and struck three, with hoarse defiance. The scufflings became more agitated. A piercing whisper filled the upper hall: "Cecilia! *He's come!*"

The hair rose on the back of his neck; the line was so sinister. But then all sounds ceased. A door shut. Losing patience he rang again, whereat the whisper started once more, as though there had been no pause: "You go! You go!"

Light footsteps were coming down the stairs. He felt no surprise when he saw the girl, for he had half expected some such apparition. Her black hair hung in curls on her shoulders and she wore a dark red dress. She came slowly, because she did not want to come, and as she approached the light he saw that she was frightened. Her grey eyes were full of loathing and alarm.

"You," she said accusingly, "are Mr. Shattock."

Her voice was high and clear. It reminded him of the Queen's voice.

"No," he said, "I'm not. I'm Roy Collins. From B.B.B."

"Oh?"

She gave a little gasp of relief. The fear melted from her eyes and a faint colour stole into her cheeks.

"Blech Bernstein British," he explained, seeing that the initials conveyed nothing to her.

"Oh!" she said again.

Perplexity gave way to a glance of disgust as though he was something that the cat had brought in. When he had delivered his message she said icily, "I'll ask my mother. Come in, please."

He followed her down the hall to a long dim room

where she left him to cool his heels for a considerable time.

The place was cold and smelt musty as though the fire was never lighted, the windows seldom opened. He stood uneasily, half way down the room, amid a haphazard collection of chairs and sofas, all covered in a chintz which had been washed to a whitish grey. Three windows gave onto a garden, disconsolate in the fading light. At the end of the room, above the fireplace, was a huge tarnished mirror in which he saw his own face, glimmering, a long way off. And then that terrible feeling shut down on him again, completely freezing him.

With a tremendous effort he managed to move and walked over to one of the windows. Nearer to that fireplace he could not have gone for a thousand pounds. He turned his back on the room and peered into the withered, untidy garden.

Concentrate! he told himself sharply. Think of something . . . work . . . *The Bramstock Story* . . . I'm here on a script . . . this is an exterior. . . . how could I use it?

Bringing a cold professional eye to bear upon the scene outside, he decided that everything would have to be tarted up before any use could be made of it. There must be well kept lawns and flower beds; the Hardings had been rich in those days, whatever might have happened to them since. That monkey puzzle in front of the house would be a headache. Perhaps synthetic branches could be fastened onto the dead ones.

Gradually the horror wore off. He grew warmer. He was able to turn round. Nothing dire was to be seen, only a large neglected room fast vanishing into night. He began to hope that he was psychic because this explanation of his panic would be reassuring. Anything was better than the possibility that he had been upon the point of making some discovery about himself—that, proceeding down the slopes of normal melancholy, he had come suddenly on an ordained abyss. He preferred to believe that he had encountered something quite outside his own life.

At last he went up boldly to the fireplace and stared at his face in the blueish glass. It looked unfamiliar; scared and young. He could not believe that he generally looked as young as this, put on the face which he hoped was normally his, and thought it seemed constipated rather than tough.

There was some agitation amongst all the pallid furniture behind him. A greyness detached itself and moved. He whipped round and saw that a lady was advancing; the carpet had muffled the sound of her approach. She wore a grey knitted suit and had a mass of untidy white hair which looked dampish and smelt of shampoo. She must have been washing it when he arrived. That explained all the scufflings and the long delay. She gave him a predatory smile and extended a hand upon which he observed a couple of valuable but dirty rings. His apologies for so late a call were waved away. They were, she told him, thrilled. She hoped that he would have a drink. Her daughter was bringing it. She sat down upon one of the forlorn chairs, gesturing him to another.

"Do sit down, Mr. Simpson!"

Again he had to explain who he was. The fact that he was not Elmer did not appear to disconcert her; she hardly seemed to grasp the difference in their status. She repeated that they were thrilled. Miss Lassiter could, of course, come and drink in atmosphere whenever she liked.

"Tell her to go anywhere, all over the house, if she cares to. A most inconvenient house, in these servantless days. I can't think what my daughter . . . the sherry is only in the dining room . . . I told her . . . poison to me, unfortunately. But I hope you'll . . . the room where Dorothea Harding wrote her novels! I expect Miss Lassiter would like to see that. I'm afraid it's unfurnished now, but that won't . . . such a cold room . . . facing North. . . . Ah! Sherry!"

The scornful girl was approaching Roy with a tray upon which stood a bottle with a very little sherry in it and one small wine glass. At her mother's suggestion that she get a glass for herself she shook her head and put the tray down beside him. Then she retired to a window seat where she sat looking out at the garden. Her attitude proclaimed that she would rather die than drink sherry with this visitor. It tasted very nasty. Roy wondered if she could have laced it with arsenic.

"We're so out of things," quavered Mrs. Harding, with a glance of apology for her daughter's rudeness. "I very seldom see a film I'm afraid. But Cecilia does. She's very fond of them. She tells us how good they are nowadays. So much better than they used to be, when we used to laugh at them. The foreign films . . . what was that one you were talking about yesterday, dear?"

"*Voi Che Intrate*," said Cecilia in her high, sweet implacable voice. But she did not turn round.

The room was, by now, almost quite dark, but neither lady attempted to switch on a light.

"Ah yes. Italian. Did you think that good, Mr. Collins?"

Roy was aware of a stiffened attention in the girl by

30

the window. This picture had been, to his mind, greatly overpraised. Much of it was admirable but he detested the dead monotony of its pace; from beginning to end each uniform minute had been ticked through as though in bond to a metronome. To Roy, who doted on variety in pace, it was a fatal blot. But he could not hope to explain such a point to anybody outside the Industry. He said briefly that he did not care for it, and knew that he had branded himself as a hack studio writer, without culture, taste or sensibility.

A wan light stole into the room from a low watt bulb in the central chandelier.

"Ah," sighed Mrs. Harding, "the electricity! We can't have any light till a man comes from the village to work the machine. Very often he is late. So tiresome!"

The mournful inefficiency of this conveyed, more than anything else had done, a picture of their poverty. He began to blame them less for taking that £500. Ed Miller, who always managed to know everything, had said that they would get nothing unless the picture was actually made; in such circumstances it was not surprising that Mrs. Harding should be civil and co-operative. She could scarcely have made more fuss of Roy had he been the producer. When he rose to go, and she discovered that he had no car, she insisted that Cecilia should run him back to Beremouth in theirs.

"You can't go by bus," she told him. "There isn't another from Upcott till nine o'clock. It will be no trouble. Cecilia has to go to Lower Upcott, in any case, to collect some tea urns. The run on into Beremouth is nothing, is it, dear?"

Cecilia allowed it to be understood that she would

transport this piece of human garbage if there was no other way of getting him out of the house.

Just as he was taking his leave the master of Bramstock appeared, followed by a wheezing white bull-dog. May's description of him had been just; he was a thorough gentleman, but Roy doubted if he was much of a hand at reading the lessons in church. A distinct spark of resentment flickered in his faded blue eyes when the visitor was introduced. He made it clear that Miss Lassiter would get little welcome from him. She had not, he complained, troubled about accuracy when she wrote her play, had not asked anybody's leave. His objections were soon disposed of by his wife and at last he growled his assent, with such a look of shame and bewilderment that Roy blushed. It was plain that he regarded the whole transaction as humiliating and disgraceful. It was also plain that the lady, who ruled the roost, was determined to get that £500.

Roy murmured his thanks and followed Cecilia out of the room. Pausing for a moment in the hall he heard Mr. Harding say, "But what is that fellow exactly? A *writer?* Good Lord! I should have thought he was the plumber's mate."

3

The engine was running when he reached the little car by the porch, and the rear door had been left open for him. He was however by no means inclined to sit on that dog rug and he took the front seat beside the driver. In a hostile silence they bucketed off down the drive; it lasted until they had passed a lodge and turned into a road. Roy then thought it time to give Miss Nose-in-the-Air a mild comeuppance, and blandly observed that *The Bramstock Story* might, in his opinion, be dropped any day, since Miss Fletcher was so fond of changing her mind. Heaps of scripts, he added, were written for her and then shelved. The news appeared to startle Cecilia, who swerved across the road. She was not a good driver.

"Wouldn't it be made without Miss Fletcher?" she asked.

"Oh no. It was only bought as a vehicle for her. Nobody is keen. Mr. Simpson hates it. You mustn't imagine that we are all up in the air over it, Miss Harding. We work on it because we're told to. We'd much rather be doing something more worth our while. I've an idea you'll be glad if it's dropped. Well, we'll all be."

She took a little time to digest this. They turned onto a high road. A light mist, clouding the windows of the car, blew into Roy's face and tasted salt. The sea could not be far away. The headlights swept over bare, glistening hedges, some farm buildings, and a milk can standing on a board by the road side.

"Mr. Collins . . . I'm afraid I've been very rude. I apologise."

"Not at all, Miss Harding. I'd be sore myself if B.B.B. made a picture about my relations."

"We couldn't stop it," she murmured.

So why not cash in on it? he thought. Money was terribly short. The whole look, the smell, of the house told him that.

"But it's so revolting! That we . . . our family . . . should seem to countenance it. I can't bear it. Ever since Mr. Mundy published his horrible book . . ."

She broke off and shuddered.

"How did he ever get hold of that diary?" asked Roy. "Couldn't your family have stopped that?"

"Oh, they'd have done anything to stop it. But, you see, she left everything to her favourite niece, Katy."

On this she paused, and gave him half a glance. He nodded. He had heard a good deal about Katy.

"Katy lived, you know, to be very, very old. Ninety-five. She only died in '48. She lived with us at Bramstock."

"Did she? Then you must remember her quite well."

"I do," said Cecilia gloomily. "Well, she had all the copyrights. She could do what she liked with them, and nobody could interfere. She allowed the poems to be published in 1902 and that started a lot of gossip and speculation. They were so unexpected; Aunt Dorothea had only been thought of as a novelist till then. And they were so unlike her: I mean poems like *If Thine the Guilt* and *I Never Feared the Dawn Till Now* and *The Night Rider,* and all the sonnets to G:. People wondered who G: could be. And then, about twenty years ago, Mr. Mundy got wind of the diary and came here and persuaded Aunt Katy to let him have it. My father didn't even know, till the book came out."

"But why did Mundy want to write it?" asked Roy. "He doesn't seem to think so much of Dorothea; he talks about her in a very sneering sort of way."

"Oh does he? I expect he's sorry he did, now: his book's out of print. It would all have been forgotten if Miss Lassiter hadn't written that play. But you see, in the thirties, there was a sort of vogue for her; a pose, really, I imagine, started by a certain little clique. It was the thing to say that she had hidden depths. That's what I gather. So I expect he had a public then, for his horrid book."

Nobody, thought Roy, had ever really wanted to know the truth about Dorothea. He himself had felt no curiosity until that dire panic seized him by the gate into the wood.

"Did she ever," he asked, "have some great tragedy happen to her?"

"Why yes!" said Cecilia, in surprise. "Grant!"

Galloping about on a horse? Grant? No!

"Never anything worse? Did it hang over her all her life? Weigh her down, I mean?"

"I shouldn't think so. She must have got over it or she wouldn't have written all those books. They're unutterable rubbish, but full of vitality."

Unutterable rubbish, he thought, could proceed from misery.

"Perhaps she wrote them," he suggested, "because, for the rest of her life, she couldn't care less what she did."

"He's only free to choose his path who cares not
    Which way he goes . . ."

"Come again?"

"Don't you recognise it? Her poem: *Harsh Liberty*. You know her poems, don't you?"

"Never read a line of them."

He could feel that her opinion of him, which had risen slightly, was now sinking.

"Don't you feel you have to?" she asked.

"Not my job. Miss Lassiter writes the script. Mundy puts in all the culture and the poetry. I put in the cinema."

They were driving into a village. Cecilia slowed down and drew up outside a long, low building. Chattering groups of women were coming out of the lighted doorway.

"This is the Institute," she said. "I see the Whist Drive is over. If you don't mind I'll go and collect the tea urns now. I want to catch some people to discuss a Book Tea."

He went with her into the hall and carried out the tea urns for her, which he stowed into the back of the car. As a townsman he found the setting and atmosphere a little unfamiliar. His quick eye took in many details, as he observed these rosy efficient women, stacking chairs and packing up the buffet. They were not quite like townswomen. They knew more about one another than neighbours in a city might, were able to conceal less. They seemed to be at ease, yet on their guard.

Cecilia's pretty voice stood out among the others like a solo instrument in an orchestra. A good deal was being heard from her. Discuss, he thought with a grin, was one way of putting it. She was telling them, and he wondered that they should take it from a kid of that age.

When he had finished with the urns he waited for her by the car, listening to fragments of gossip which drifted past him as the assembly dispersed.

"I must say," murmured a voice, "I don't think it's very nice."

"Oh, but I expect they're getting thousands. Carrie! Did it say how much they're getting?"

"Not in the paper. It was mostly about Kitty Fletcher really. Only a little bit about Bramstock."

"Thousands! My word, they could do with it. Their gates! All tied up with rope."

"Oh that's not what it's wanted for. Mrs. Harding herself told Mrs. Wallace . . ."

A sudden silence fell upon the group. Cecilia was coming out, distributing gracious good nights.

"Have you been to college?" asked Roy, when they were driving out of the village.

"No. I'm going to Oxford in the autumn." She looked round at him and asked sharply, "Why?"

"You seem to know a lot about books."

"I'm going to read English literature."

Which meant, he supposed, knowing all about William Shakespeare.

"Is Mr. Mundy," he asked, "a good poetry critic?"

"He? No! He doesn't know the first thing about poetry."

"Why does anybody pay any attention to him, then?"

"Oh, most people can't make head or tail of poetry, so I suppose they like a critic who explains it all away for them."

"Is that what he does?"

"Why yes. If he reads a line like: *My heart leaps up when I behold A rainbow in the sky,* he thinks it's evidence of some remarkable abnormality. *His* heart doesn't leap up in that maladjusted way. So he ferrets around and finds out that Dorothy went twice into Keswick to get digitalis for William. Ha! Cardiac trouble! And this line must mean that William suffered from some obscure heart disease which was especially troublesome in wet weather. That's his idea of criticism."

So who was Dorothy? wondered Roy. Not his wife. She was called Anne Hathaway, and lived in a little china cottage. On Mum's mantelpiece.

"We know absolutely nothing about the private lives of some of the greatest poets," Cecilia was declaring. "What about Homer? Can't we appreciate him?"

"To tell you the truth," said Roy gravely, "I've always been a bit worried about Homer. I lie awake at night, sometimes, wondering if I'd appreciate him better if I knew what brand tooth paste he used."

There was a long pause. She was probably wondering whether the plumber's mate could be laughing at her. They were getting into Beremouth and the mist was thicker. On the Esplanade it rolled in from the sea, surrounding the arc lamps with a diffused burnished cloud.

She drew up at the Queen's Hotel. Roy got out and thanked her for the drive.

"Shall you," she asked, a little timidly, "be coming with Miss Lassiter?"

He had not meant to do so, but now he thought that he might. Cecilia amused him; he wanted to find out if she was really so very different from most of the girls that he knew.

"May I?" he asked.

"Of course."

"Thanks. Then I will. Bye-bye, Miss Harding."

"Good-bye."

She drove off, and he stood for a moment in the clammy mist reviewing his impressions of her. That first tragic appearance on the stairs had been misleading. She had looked at him as though . . . he remembered, with a start, that she had then supposed him to be somebody else. *You are Mr. . . . Mr. . . .* an unusual name. But he could not recall it.

4

"And who," said May to Alice Budden, "do you think was here this afternoon? I bet you sixpence you'll never guess."

"Roy."

Alice laughed at May's astonishment and added, "But I won't take sixpence off you. It wouldn't be fair, because I knew. He came with Cecilia Harding into the Institute just as I was going out. I couldn't believe my eyes."

"With Cecilia! What were they doing? Did you speak to him?"

"No. I don't think he saw me. They came for the urns. But do tell me all, for I'm bursting with curiosity."

The news about *The Bramstock Story* was also stale. The whole Institute, said Alice, seemed to be discussing it. The money was going to be used to send Cecilia to college. Roy's connection with it provoked some astonishment, but not much approval. Alice merely said that she supposed it was a job, like any other. May, up in arms, disclosed his other success.

"Since then," she said, "I've been thinking. When you

were in London, just after Christmas, didn't you say you'd seen a picture about a Punch and Judy that you thought very funny?"

"Why yes. Yes I did."

"Was it called *Every Wednesday?*"

"Now you mention it, I believe it was."

"But didn't it have Roy's name on it?"

"It might. I didn't notice. I never bother to read all those names."

"But what was it like? Do tell me. Try to remember."

"It was quite good," remembered Alice. "Short, you know. Like a Disney, only not a cartoon. It was original. I remember thinking that."

May looked so wistful that she wished she could recall more than that. She cudgelled her brains, and later, after supper, she said, "Quite a lot of that picture Roy did comes back to me really, when I think it over. It was a Punch and Judy, in a poor little street. You know, a working people's street. And all these children. I think they must have taken a picture of real children, they were so natural. You know, May. The way little children look at a Punch. So fascinated, it makes them look all alike. Fair, dark, fat, skinny, they've all got the same face. Blissful!"

"I know," agreed May. "It gets hold of them more than Mickey Mouse. I've often wondered why. Mickey is much cleverer. It's got a lot more."

"It's too clever. It's got too much. Punch only says one thing. I thought that after I'd seen this picture. Little children . . . well . . . we're always teaching them to adjust. We have to. And they know it. By the time they're seven they know this world is a place they've got to fit into. And sometimes you catch yourself feeling it's a pity."

"Yes," agreed May. "As if they lose more than they gain. But it must be so."

"Well, Punch . . . he's not adjusted. He does what he likes. He's quite lawless. The person they've just left off being. You see them getting more and more to be him again. And there comes a moment when it's just too much. They suddenly all turn round and cuff each other, just as he cuffs everybody."

"Don't I know it! That's why I never liked a Punch at school parties. It always started a riot."

"Well, this little boy the picture was about, when it was over, he drifted off, and he still was Punch. And the street . . . you remember that sort of street scene they sometimes have at the back of a Punch?"

"Oh yes! Oh Alice! When I was a child I always wanted to get into that street and run down it."

"This child *did*. I mean, the real street had turned into *that street,* a mile long, with a milk bottle on every door-step, and he tore along it like lightning, kicking over all the milk bottles. Oh he was naughty! Oh they did have a time with him! Of course they couldn't imagine what had got into him. And all the time there was this sort of music, you know . . . the little drum and pipes . . . root-i-toot . . . you didn't see him so much. You saw things as he saw them. A kind of fog, with things suddenly appearing and people's faces saying things. So you knew why he was in fits of laughter. Of course he didn't mind being punished. They sent him to bed . . . that was another thing, some-times it went very fast, and then it would be almost slow motion. They sent him to bed and he ripped all the feath-ers out of his pillow and eiderdown. And these gorgeous feathers, they go slowly sailing up, in slow motion, and

42

stay up, circling round, for ages . . . weeks . . . and oh!
He's enjoying himself the way nobody ever does, any
more."

This must be Roy, thought May, nodding. This was
exactly the sort of thing that he would do.

"Go on," she urged. "So what?"

Alice propped up her feet on the fender and sighed.

"Gradually it all wears off. The fog melts and everything gets settled back into normal. After a week, you
know it's a week somehow, it's got very ordinary; the poor
little street and a quiet little boy, sent out to play. And
then: Root-i-toot! All the children running. It's the Punch.
It comes there every Wednesday."

"Let's hope his mother eventually spotted it. But you
liked it, Alice? You thought it was good?"

"Oh, I did. Yes. It was queer, but you could see what
they meant, and it was very funny. There wasn't much
talking. I mean conversations. Oh! One thing I forgot. At
school . . . of course he'd got the baby class turned up-
side down . . . out of this sort of cloud . . . comes a
face. . . . Do you remember Price?"

They both laughed. Price had been a young teacher,
bursting with diplomas, who had invaded their school two
years before their retirement. In her opinion May and
Alice knew nothing whatever about child psychology; she
made no secret of that fact.

"Price's face to the life. Asking all the damn silly questions Price would have asked. You knew at once the sort
of person she was and how *she* could manage him. Everybody roared. Really, if Roy made that up, May, I think he's
very clever. I can't think how he knows so much."

"He is clever," stated May. "I've often told you so,

only you wouldn't believe it. I wish he would make friends with some nice educated people, and take more trouble about the way he talks. He must make a terrible impression."

"He seemed to be getting along quite well with Cecilia Harding," observed Alice. "And she's educated up to the nines. Almost as brilliant as she thinks she is."

"She's not quite the type I mean. Too conceited."

At this Alice had to depart to the kitchen for fear she should burst out laughing. Doting mothers, she had often noticed, are reasonable compared with doting aunts. Poor May evidently considered that Miss Harding, of Bramstock, was not quite good enough for Roy.

5

The dining room was so warm that Miss Lassiter did not need her mink coat. She slipped it off her shoulders and hung it over the back of her chair. To leave it upstairs in her suite was not very safe; it might get stolen. Besides, she always liked to have this symbol of success within tangible reach, as a shield against depression.

Success had come late to Adelaide Lassiter and it was not as satisfying as she had expected it to be. For forty years she had been writing plays and sending them to managers, agents, publishers, actors, actresses and other playwrights. Back they always came. Sustained by an innocent conceit she wrote on, convinced that her work was good, and that any play of hers, if produced, would run for years. When *The Wild Swan* ran for years she was not in the least surprised, although nobody else could account for it. She bought herself the coat in which to meet all the clever, celebrated people who would now be her friends. She joined a number of literary associations and attended all their gatherings, coming up from Berkshire in the coat and standing in a corner, wistfully waiting for the fun to begin.

She looked like a retired Nannie—plump, pink, grey haired and comfortable. Her cordial, shortsighted smile was disarming. People who thought her play beneath contempt, and its success a disgrace to the theatre, found themselves smiling, when they were introduced to her. They often managed to say something pleasant about it, before escaping; they could always agree that the leading actress was wonderful. Adelaide took all this civility in good faith. She believed that the world admired her lovely play as much as she did herself, and that her two year run must be a source of unmixed satisfaction to playwrights whose runs did not last for two months. Of the envy, hatred and malice which can flourish among celebrated people she had no notion at all.

Mr. Mundy was the first to be unkind to her. His surliness and bad manners had so taken her aback that she was now glad not to be sitting with him at meals. She and Roy shared a window table. Mundy sat with his secretary, Basil Cope, at the other end of the dining room. This arrangement had, at first, affronted her. She had looked forward to Mundy's acquaintance and had thought Roy a very common young man, whose business it might be to break the material down into shots, but who could never appreciate the beautiful and subtle script which she intended to create—a script which should convince all those film people that they did not really know their own business. But, after a day or two, she had come to like him better. He never disagreed with her, did not attempt to interfere, and was a great deal more genial than the other two.

46

She smiled at him quite warmly, when he joined her, and accepted his apologies for being so late. He had, he said, been talking on the telephone to Mamie.

"That railway station is going to be a headache," he warned her. "Elmer's ordered designs for a colossal set."

"But Doda," she wailed, "never went in a train."

She always referred to Dorothea as Doda, insisting, upon no evidence at all, that this had been her family nickname.

"Mr. Mundy might know if she did," said Roy. "We must all go into a huddle after dinner."

"Oh dear! I hate conferences."

Up till now she had not confided her opinion of the others to Roy. But she craved for sympathy and she now confessed, "Mr. Cope makes me so nervous. I suppose it's because he's young. He makes me feel I'm . . . just an old thing. I feel he's . . . what I always call the younger generation knocking at the door."

"He's been knocking long enough," said Roy sourly. "He must be all of forty."

"No! Surely not."

"He was at college with Mr. Mundy. And he was around when they had that Spanish War. He has a thing about it. He fought in it, or didn't fight in it. I forget which."

The first decade of his own life was unexplored history to Roy. He added, "So then he went to America in Our War."

"But he looks years younger than Mr. Mundy."

This was true. Alec Mundy, who had fought in North Africa, achieved a tolerable reputation as a man of letters, and paid income tax, looked almost elderly. Basil

Cope, a haggard alcoholic with no known history, had managed to retain a blatant boyishness. He suggested, perhaps, juvenile delinquency, but was not one upon whom time had, as yet, taken toll. Lacking a past, he could still stake a claim in the future and imply the capacity to wipe the eye of such as Mundy, should he ever choose to get over some cosmic grievance which had hitherto forbidden him to exert himself.

He had a talent for formidable silence, which shattered the nerves of the diffident. They became aware that, to him, they were little victims, unconscious of a doom which he had long foreseen. Adelaide found this most alarming. She had never heard him speak. Roy, who had met him in several Beremouth bars, knew that, in his cups, he was a talker.

"Do you think he's very unhappy about something?" ventured the charitable Adelaide.

They looked at each other. Roy decided that the moment had come when he and she might safely do a little ganging up.

"Yes," he said. "You see, he caught his mother telling a lie, when he was three. He cries a lot about that, round about closing time. What he is . . . he's one of these haunted boys."

"Which haunted boys?"

"There's quite a few of them about. We had one, once, in B.B.B. His family had pull and got him a job in Direction, and he lasted quite three weeks. Just the same type. A continuity girl fell for him in a big way and used to stand up for him. Oh, she used to say, can't you see he's just a torn, haunted boy? He belongs to a doomed generation. So we said: For Pete's sake what haunts him? Oh he was born on August 4th 1914. People born that day have to be that way."

"Can that be true?" cried Adelaide, who was interested in horoscopes.

"Of course not. It was just a line. But it's quite smart. Everybody seemed to feel apologetic for letting him get born at the wrong date. Instead of calling him a bum, they kept bailing him out and finding him jobs."

"I sometimes wonder . . . he never seems to do anything for Mr. Mundy. Do you think he's really his secretary?"

Roy did not think so, but hesitated to mention his guess, which was that Mundy had summoned Cope in order to escape Adelaide's company at meals. The two did not seem to be very good friends, but people who actually relished Mundy's conversation might be in short supply. He had sent for Cope, who seemed to be mysteriously at his beck and call, for want of a more agreeable bodyguard. And just what Mundy had on Cope was something that Roy had yet to discover. None of the more obvious guilty secrets seemed to fill the bill.

"I wouldn't know," he said cautiously. "Maybe I'll find out. All I know is, he's writing a book."

"Oh is he? What about?"

"His sad, sad, torn, haunted boyhood, of course, and how it was worse for him because his family was rich and had a lot of class. So he lost all his illusions, one by one, till he got to think he didn't owe anything to anyone, except the Comrades. And then he read a book by Professor Joad, after he'd come back from Russia, and that put paid to everything. No. . . . Wait a minute . . . not Joad. Jeed. Some name like that. And he's putting all the other haunted boys in. He goes round the bars, after dinner, telling everybody about it. Perhaps sometime he'll come clean about Mundy."

"Put him in his book?"

"I don't think so. Mundy hasn't so much class. All Cope's friends were terribly aristocratic. And what makes him sore is that they've all been writing books about themselves and each other, and never said a word about him. They'll be sorry, if he ever gets to finish that book. He remembers them all right. Very nasty things he says about them in the bars. I'm always hoping Mundy's name will come up."

"I wish he didn't come to all our conferences."

"Then say you don't want him. You're the big noise here."

"I wouldn't dare."

Adelaide hesitated, and then yielded to her need for consolation and support.

"I can't bear Mr. Mundy," she exclaimed. "He is so rude. I gave him all the scenes . . . sequences . . . I've done so far. All he did was to correct my English! Like a schoolmaster, marking home work. I can't tell you! Words underlined and sarcastic remarks in the margin. Half of them I can't make head or tail of. What's wrong with the line: *I've been lying prone in the hayfield all afternoon, gazing up into the clouds and dreaming wonderful dreams?* He's underlined prone, and written in the margin: 'This must have given Miss Harding a severe pain in the neck!' What does he mean?"

"I haven't a clue," said Roy truthfully. "But don't worry. He couldn't write a play for toffee. I expect he tried and couldn't make it. So that's why he has to be a critic."

At this she looked happier and was able to enjoy the rest of her dinner.

Since Roy was insistent she paused by Mundy's table, on her way out of the dining room, and summoned a conference to discuss the railway station.

"Just us three," she said meaningly.

The hint was not taken. When Mundy joined them, in her sitting room, the haunted boy came too, flung himself into the most comfortable chair, stretched out his long legs and smiled bitterly at the ceiling.

"I don't see that this has anything to do with me," snapped Mundy, when the dilemma was explained to him.

"Mr. Simpson says," observed Roy, "that there's a wedding group in this old picture he's seen. Couple going off on their honeymoon. There's a wedding in our script. Could be a tie up there."

"But Mary and Grant never had a honeymoon," objected Adelaide. "Did they, Mr. Mundy?"

"I believe not. I believe they went straight to Elkington, only ten miles away. But surely such a very slight departure from fact need not trouble you, Miss Lassiter? Send them off for a honeymoon by all means."

Sarcasm was lost on Adelaide. She explained carefully that, if Grant went off on a honeymoon in a train, he could not very well leave Mary on their wedding night and go to Doda. This he had done, if Mundy's reading of the diary was correct. It provided the greatest scene in her play and would be even stronger in the picture, since Doda's struggles and final surrender could be punctuated by cuts to Elkington, where Mary lay, forlornly awaiting her truant bridegroom.

"We just can't sacrifice it," she wailed. "We can't."

"We don't have to worry very much," said Roy. "Just put in a station, that's all. I'm sure it'll have to come out again. It'll be too expensive. So we don't want to have to knock a big hole in the story taking it out. Couldn't somebody arrive by train?"

There was a short silence. In spite of herself, Adelaide began to glance nervously at the silent Cope. Then an idea came to her, and she clapped her hands.

"Little Effie Creighton!" she cried. "The bridesmaid. Arrives by train at Beremouth."

"Dorbridge," said Mr. Mundy promptly. "The line didn't come to Beremouth till 1868. But Frith's picture is a great London terminus. Dorbridge would have been a quiet little country station."

"Mr. Simpson wants crowds," said Roy. "Couldn't she be starting from London?"

"Oh but I see her arriving," declared Adelaide. "A charming shot. Those high old-fashioned railway carriages. And Effie jumping out."

Cope was too much for her. She turned to him and added timidly, "Don't you think so?"

Without removing his eyes from the ceiling he murmured, "Ooagh! Showing her drawers."

Adelaide gasped and burst into tears.

The conference broke up. Mundy and Cope rose, grinned at each other, and departed. Roy rang through to the office and ordered tea. Then he pursued Adelaide to her bedroom, whither she had rushed with her handkerchief to her eyes. She was lying on her bed, hugging her mink coat and sobbing bitterly.

"Do you have any aspirin?" he asked.

"Yes. In the bathroom. I can't . . . it's too much. I thought Mr. Mundy was a gentleman . . . write to my agent . . . throw up the script. . . ."

He found the aspirin and tried to console her while she took it.

"You write your script your own way and don't worry with him unless you want to know a date or something. Look! Here's some nice tea. Drink up and you'll feel better. Don't spill it over your lovely coat. I'll hang it up for you, shall I?"

He hung it in the large wardrobe, where her few, neat, middle-aged possessions looked forlorn and humble. They reminded him of his aunt May. Poor old trout, he thought. What a shame.

"They don't understand," gulped Adelaide. "Effie . . . little girls . . . wore these long lace trousers down to the ankles. Mr. Mundy says she was twenty, at the wedding. But I see her as a little girl, don't you?"

"We'd better," said Roy, "if the part is to be written up for Susie Graham. Don't cry any more. Go to bye-byes."

He patted her shoulder and went off in search of drink, because this sort of thing was getting him down.

6

An hour later he was still cold sober, although he had been drinking steadily. In desperation he attached himself to a party of sailors who were looking for a friend called Hawkie. Nobody seemed to know exactly why Hawkie was wanted so urgently, but they all migrated from one tap-room to another in search of him. The party grew like a snowball with each transit. Between The Plymouth Packet and The Lord Nelson it collected a seedy-looking little fellow who said that he was staying at The Old Ship. His home was in Thames Ditton and he had a boat, a lovely little boat—*The Brenda.* Named after his wife. Brenda.

This name, repeated a score of times, attracted the attention of a sailor, who shouted, "She never seen Hawkie. Not tonight. I ast her."

"She couldn't. She's in Thames Ditton."

"Na! In the Plymouth Packet, Brenda was. She said she never seen Hawkie. That red-haired tart in The Plymouth Packet."

"If you wish t'insult m'wife . . ."

Roy pushed Brenda's husband into a quiet corner. "He insulted m'boat. Called m'boat after m'wife, see?"

"I knew a sod who called his wife after his boat."

This came from the haunted boy, who was now part of the snowball, and it puzzled the little man. For a moment all three sat in their corner in a thoughtful stupor. Drunk as owls, thought Roy looking at the other two. What's the matter with me?

Upon the screen of his inward eye flashed a shot of Ed Miller, in a tap-room near Wardour Street, drinking off a disappointment. The distributors had just condemned, as too subtle for the public, a beautiful and evocative sequence, the fruit of some superb cutting on Ed's part. It had had an eventful history; its fate had been in the balance a dozen times. So many dangers had been skirted that Ed's friends had begun to count on success. Now the world was never to see it. Ed, resigned by long experience to such catastrophes, made a wry face over Roy's indignation.

"Trouble with you," he said, "you're a bloody artist."

This was not intended as a compliment and Roy told him that he was another.

"No. There's nothing I can't drink off. You! You drink because it's your birthday. But if you need to get drunk, you can't. That's bad. That's very bad. . . ."

And then Ed said something which Roy did not want to remember. . . .

"He couldn't do that, ole man," said Brenda's husband mildly.

"I say he bloody well could."

"When he got married . . . she hadda name already."

"Which he chose. He was her godfather."

"He was . . . his own wife's godfather?"

The little man looked deeply shocked. Cope, leaning over, bellowed into his ear, "So he called her after his boat."

(*. . . man who can't drink it off, he finally does one of three things. He puts his head in a gas oven, like poor Henderson . . .*)

"He hadda boat when she was a baby then?"

"She wasn't a baby. She was a Baptist."

Cope turned a slightly unfocussed eye on Roy and added, "My bloody brother-in-law was a Baptist once. Keeps it dark, doesn't he?"

"Don't know him," began Roy.

But then an implication struck him. *Brothers-in-law?* Was this the mysterious bond?

"Whaddy caller then? This wife?"

"Whizzo!" said Cope.

"He married your sister?" suggested Roy.

"Christ no!" Cope yelped with laughter. "He's not married."

"Whizzo? That's no name for a boat."

So Cope had married Mundy's sister?

A surging movement arose in the bar. The snowball was departing to look for Hawkie in The Four Alls. Roy hastily bought more drinks for his companions, in the hope of further details.

"Why did you marry her?" he murmured.

"Shot gun wedding," replied Cope, with a touch of complacency. "My last term, Coldingham. All over in three months. They went to Australia."

"She and the kid?"

56

Cope's eye focussed and he scowled. Roy was told what to do with himself and his questions.

"You going to put that in your book?" persisted Roy, unabashed. "How you got married when you were still at school?"

The reference to his book mollified Cope, who launched into derogatory reminiscences concerning a friend called Hervey, who had betrayed his generation by 'throwing in his hand', and was now frequently to be heard on the Third Programme.

(. . . *or he goes completely crackers, like Issy, down in the coal-hole* . . .)

Now that the snowball had rolled off, the bar was quiet. One customer was chatting to the barmaid. The lights were dim. Sea fog had blown in through the swing doors when the crowd was going out. The two drunken monologues continued simultaneously. Roy tried to listen —to drown the memory of Ed's voice.

"Man who'd caller boat *Whizz* . . . *Whizzo*, just couldn't 'preciate a boat. Musta been a motor boat."

"Hervey and I were staggering down the Turl——"

"You couldn't have been just walking?" interrupted Roy.

Cope looked startled. No haunted boy, in these riotous recollections, had ever been able to proceed at a walk. They had always been reeling or staggering.

"Whassat?"

"Oh, let it ride," said Roy wearily.

"Any time, if you're passing through Thames Ditton, drop in and I'll prove my words. Shattock's the name. Creighton Shattock."

Languidly Roy recognised the fact that he had heard

both names lately. To Cope also they meant something, for he immediately exclaimed, "Little Effie Creighton! Oh what a little bitch!"

Shattock bridled and exclaimed, "I'll thank you not t'insult m'godmother."

"You're wrong, comrade. She was your bridesmaid."

"Couldn't have been. I never had any bridesmaids."

"Same again?" asked Roy, and brought a fresh round from the bar. When he returned, Cope had apparently gone to sleep.

"Why didn't you go to Bramstock then?" asked Roy. "They were expecting you."

Shattock looked sly.

"Do them no harm to wait a bit," he said. "When I phoned she said come this afternoon. I don't take orders from them, see? I'll go when it suits me. That's no way t'speak to a relation. Which I am, all said and done. They're a snobbish lot, if you know what I mean. County family. Haw!"

"Treat you like dirt," agreed Roy. "Did you say godmother or grandmother?"

"They know perfectly well she was my grandmother. Trying to make out they don't know anything about us. Same when m'mother called there once. Not at home! Haw! But"—Shattock leant forward and tapped Roy on the knee—"*she* wasn't having any. Not cousin Thea. *She* was different. Very friendly. When she found out, she called. *Dear Effie's daughter*, she said. M'mother never would believe a word against her. All lies, she said."

"All lies," agreed Cope, suddenly opening one eye.

Roy was afraid that he might begin to cry, but he dropped off again.

"What's Brenda say?" asked Roy yawning.

"Oh she's very annoyed. She'd have come too, only leaving the dog. You'd better go, she said, if they can't answer letters. Well it was Brenda saw the bit in the paper, and she got very annoyed over that. So we wrote and got nothing but a line to say they weren't interested. Well, she said, this Brish Bleck . . . this Bern . . . Bern . . . British . . . they might be interested. Why should some people get thousands and others get nothing? What she wrote about it to Effie, isn't that worth anything? Thousands and thousands. Thousands and thousands. How'd they know it's true? *The Bramstock Story!* We laughed, really."

"All lies," repeated Cope sitting up. "Dorothea was a virgin. That sticks out a mile. But Mundy murders anyone who says so."

"Dirty crack to make about a girl," said Roy reprovingly.

"She was pathological. Why did she quote Sappho? Ooagh! She never had a man. She never——"

"Shut up," shouted Roy, interrupting an itemized list of the things Dorothea had never done. "Ladies present. Want to get us thrown out?"

The barmaid and the other customer were looking indignantly at Cope, who shouted, "They're barking up the wrong tree! G: wasn't a man . . ."

A muscular looking bar man appeared in a doorway. He looked at Cope too. Cope subsided and went to sleep again.

"He shouldn't talk like that," said Shattock. "I'm broad-minded, but I don't like it. You can say she was respectable without being vulgar."

"You have some letters she wrote to Effie?" asked Roy.

At this Shattock took fright. He stared fiercely at Roy and got to his feet muttering, "Godda go now. G'night."

He stumbled out. Fresh fog blew in as he passed the swing door. The bar, for a moment, was perfectly silent.

(. . . *a hundred per cent son of a bitch* . . .)

Roy, in a panic, pursued Shattock. The little creature's conversation offered a certain mild interest. He and his errand were now explained. He evidently hoped that the Hardings would part with a few of their thousands and thousands in exchange for some letters written to little Effie. That anything written to that phoney kid, whether she wore pantaloons or not, would be worth sixpence, was most unlikely. Roy detested Effie, and dreaded her arch incursions into the script; she was, for him, entirely identified with Susie Graham, so much so that he could not really believe her to be anybody's grandmother.

He plunged through the doors into vacancy and darkness. The fog blew in great swirls up the street. Shattock had vanished. Not even his footsteps were audible. The world was blanketed in silence, save for a foghorn which moaned intermittently away to the right.

Oooooooom. Ooooooooom.

Roy turned in that direction, walked a few yards, and found himself on the edge of a jetty. He all but fell into the water which he could hear clucking below, although he could not see it.

Oooooooooom. Ooooooooom.

That's what is happening to you. In fact, you're a sixty percent s.o.b. right now and everybody says so. Why! When Elroy had that combination safe put in his room somebody made the crack he needed it to keep his job in, in case Collins might want it. Nobody believes a word you

*say; they wonder what's behind it and why it suited you
to say that. I tell people it's merely because you can't get
drunk, and it's your way of keeping your mind off things.
But it's a pity, because nobody will be sorry when you die.*

Ooooooooooom. Oooooooooooooooom.

Next morning Ed had apologised. He had been drunk
and miserable. Roy, too fond of him to bear malice, had
avoided the memory as best he could. But tonight, in this
vacancy, this no-place, it had caught up with him.

*I am alone and I can't bear it. I've lost my way since I
got into Scripts. But how? How? Nobody but me can do
my work, my own work. I must do it alone. Needs a bigger
man than me to do it though. Needs more than I am. But
I never used to feel that. Am I getting smaller? Shrinking
. . . shrivelling . . . alone . . . all alone?*

Ooooooooooom. Oooooooooooom.

The water clucked and gurgled. He tried to retrace
his steps wondering how to find the esplanade and the
hotel.

An oblong of light appeared suddenly, just in front of
him. There was a scuffle and a thump. The light vanished.
He stepped forward and stumbled over something lying on
the pavement. It whimpered faintly, "Nannie!"

The haunted boy had been thrown out of the Lord
Nelson.

PART II

Gabriel

But I beneath a rougher sea
And whelmed in deeper gulfs than he.

Cowper

1

Effie Creighton snatched at her foundering patience. She
bent over her embroidery, forcing herself to push the nee-
dle through the material with measured calm. It would
not do to sit idle, waiting an answer. If she knew her
mother, they would be at it all the morning. Dorothea's
letter had arrived at breakfast and there was no reason
why they should not be discussing it for the rest of the
day. They had nothing else to do save attend occasionally
to her little brother Tom, who had fallen out of a tree and
was being nursed, by seven women, with solemn pomp.

The morning was very hot. The parlour windows stood
open upon sunlight and heavy, motionless foliage. But the
two women sat with their backs to the summer scene, on
either side of the fireplace. Effie, soft and pliant in her
light muslins, stitched industriously. Mrs. Creighton sat
like a statue, plunged into one of her long meditations.
Her crepe flounces fell about her like a black, frozen cas-
cade, topped by a pink marble face in a widow's cap.
Effie, without looking up, knew the expression on that face,

saw the determined set of the mouth, the two deep lines running from nose to chin, the lowered lids. It was not propitious.

The dazzled world outside was stirred by a faint sound, the trot of a horse in the lane. It grew louder. It might be the butcher's boy bringing sweetbreads for Tom. But it was not. It went past the house. And then it diminished, although it went on for a long time, the faintest tick-tick, like a watch, before melting into complete silence.

Her thoughts rushed to Dorothea who had once declared that the most thrilling sound in the world is that of an unknown horseman riding past the house at night. They had heard one once, lying in their beds in the nursery at Bramstock. Dorothea insisted that it was *Gabriel of Clone* and had written some verses in which he galloped, although the horse they heard only trotted. Nothing short of galloping would do for Dorothea.

> Till up the hill the hoof beats go,
> A whisper, on and on.
> And when I hear them not I know
> That all I am is gone.

Effie and Mary would have preferred that the horseman should be nameless; nobody should ever know where he went. Dorothea was always a little too peremptory in appropriating romantic material for Gabriel. She hardly left any over for Mary's Edward, or Effie's Bruno.

Just as silence shut down on them again there was a slight agitation among the crepe flounces. Mrs. Creighton opened her eyes, drew a long sigh, and spoke.

"I wish that poor Dorothea could learn to write a

lady-like note. This is so abrupt. It says no more than is necessary, which is not very civil."

She took the letter from her pocket and ran over it again with a disparaging eye.

"*I am writing for Mary, as she has gone into Exeter.* She might have told us why Mary has gone into Exeter. We should have liked to know. Wedding clothes, I dare-say. *We are so glad to know that Tom has got off with a broken collar bone.* No more concern, no more sympathy than that! She should have said a great deal more. *But, if you can't come to the wedding* . . . Can't! And later on she writes *won't*. Such very bad style. I should have been ashamed of you, Effie, had you written such a letter ten years ago. And Dorothea is twenty."

"Gentlemen sometimes write can't and won't," murmured Effie, who could not resist the impulse to defend Dorothea, however ill timed it might be. "Papa used to do so."

"They are no guide for us. One should not write as one speaks. Really, had I not known, I should have supposed this to have been written by a boy. Even the writing is not what I would call a lady's hand. And it is all very well to say that you have promised to be Mary's bridesmaid. Any promise of that sort must have been dependent on my permission. You cannot go without me. No servant from here can be spared just now. And a young woman, travelling alone, can have unpleasant experiences. Unless," added Mrs. Creighton, struck by a sudden idea, "old nurse could go with you."

"Oh Mama! No!"

Dismay at such an idea drove Effie into imprudent vehemence.

"I would rather give it up than go with Nursie. I'm sure she will do something to . . . to make me sink into the ground. You know what the Hardings are! My uncle, or one of the boys, or a man-servant, always helps one out of the railway carriage and whisks one off into the barouche, after that long journey, for a two hour drive. They never dream of giving one an *opportunity*. Oh those drives! They can be torture. And when one gets there it is not over. Mary and Thea are so high minded; I sometimes wonder if they are made like other people. They never offer to take one upstairs for ages. I'm sure I often envy gentlemen. They can just stroll off, as cool as anything, to that place behind the billiard room."

"I believe," said Mrs. Creighton mysteriously, "that it is more likely to kill them."

"Oh? Is it?" cried Effie, startled.

"I have heard so. That is a thing you should remember, Effie. Never make it difficult for a gentleman to *escape*."

With strong distaste Effie added this item to the list of repulsive things which she had been told to remember about men, against whom poor women must be perpetually on their guard. Men might be drunk after supper at a ball; a girl must remember this when accepting partners for the quadrille. Men said horrible things, amongst themselves, about any girl who gave them the slightest pretext for doing so. And there was a hint of worse things, to be revealed later, not fit for a maiden's ears—a secret known only to matrons.

"In any case," added Mrs. Creighton, "ladies must have self control."

"But Nursie is not a lady and she has none," asserted

Effie. "At the best she will make a fuss at Dorbridge station, nodding and winking and whispering. At the worst . . ."

She would not name the worst but her mother saw the point.

"Perhaps she is too old. We must think it over. . . ."

The *we* was a euphemism, and Effie knew better than to betray her extreme eagerness to go to Bramstock. Extreme eagerness about anything was likely to bring a prohibition down upon her. To feel more than calm, cousinly affection for Mary and Thea might be fanciful, and therefore suspect.

She had no sisters, and came between her two cousins in age. Ever since she could remember, her visits to Bramstock had been an escape into freedom, for she lived continually under her mother's eye, the object of incessant care. Mary and Thea were motherless; they had grown up in charge of a governess who took her duties very lightly. The world left them alone, as long as they made progress in their studies, were clean, neat and modest upon public appearances. Nobody enquired how they spent their play time. They did as they pleased, unharassed by warnings concerning all the prison bars awaiting them with womanhood.

Their reading was quite uncensored, and out of what they read they could create a world as thrilling as any story-book. They could determine its geography, history, population and climate; they could destroy, refashion and extend it, to include some continent recently discovered. As a child, Effie had been enchanted by this lordly command of cosmos, for at home she got very little food for fancy. She admired them for knowing so much. Not only could they read French, German and Italian; they knew Latin and Greek. Their father, who had been preparing to write a book on the Homeric Age, ever since he left the university, wished them to learn the classics, in order that they might be useful to him.

That romantic, childish admiration might have dwindled, and Effie might have begun to perceive faults in her cousins, but she still found an ease and freedom at Bramstock which she knew nowhere else. This, however, was not a circumstance likely to weigh favourably with her mother, who resumed the conversation an hour later, with some adverse comments.

"I am not at all sure that I like you to stay there by yourself, now that Miss Fothergill has left them. Mary seems to have grown very sensible and good, but she will be extremely busy. There will be no older woman to look after you and Dorothea."

"Selina, Mama? She is married."

"Selina has little sense and less breeding. Besides, she is entirely taken up with her children, and nursing poor Philip, while Dorothea runs wild and gets into scrapes."

"Oh no, Mama. Dorothea does not get into scrapes. She is very high principled and religious. I'm sure she would burn at the stake rather than do anything she thought to be wrong."

"Burn at the stake?" Mrs. Creighton pursed her lips. "It is not at all likely that Dorothea will ever be asked to burn at the stake. But that high flown way of talking is just like her, and it is a pity you should pick it up."

The rebuke was merited. Effie would never have

used the phrase unless she had been thinking of Dorothea.

"And, Effie, even if her principles are sound, her behaviour is often deplorable. She cares nothing for appearances; she is positively eccentric, and you know how bad that is. And she pays no attention to her duty. She does nothing in the house, nothing for her father, never takes the children off Selina's hands—leaves all to Mary. What she does with herself all day I cannot imagine."

"She reads a great deal."

"I know she does. She will sit with one for hours, reading a book in the rudest way, never speaking and never answering."

To be allowed to read in peace was one of the freedoms for which Effie envied the Bramstock girls. Neither Mary nor Dorothea had been obliged to acquire the accomplishment of chit-chat—the constant flow of polite little observations, meaningless as the coo of doves, which a well bred woman ought to keep up whenever she sat in company. Effie hated chit-chat and was often tempted to turn it into conversation by giving it point and sense. To say things which might invite discussion would bring upon her, she knew, the indictment of cleverness, a misfortune which all sensible girls must avoid, since men did not like it.

She sighed and then brightened, as a telling argument occurred to her.

"I think, Mama, that I can promise not to copy poor Thea. Her dress! It breaks my heart to see her take so little trouble. She would be so pretty if she were ever fit to be seen. But indeed she does attend to me a little about that.

I quite scold her sometimes, you know. How is she ever to improve if she has no friend to put her right? And I can't bear to think of her in her bridesmaid's dress, if I am not there to stand over her while she puts it on."

The thought that Effie might really exert a good influence over poor Dorothea did not displease Mrs. Creighton. It vindicated her own careful training and her success as the mother of a model daughter. She was secretly very proud of Effie; she knew of no other girl so docile, sensible and cheerful, or so impeccably well bred. She genuinely pitied her nieces for their deplorable upbringing and was astonished that Mary, in spite of it, should have made so good a match. Grant Forrester was, by all accounts, an excellent young man; his estate at Elkington was worth £6000 a year. But Mary had always been more sensible than Dorothea and had taken less kindly to the classics.

"We must think it over," she repeated, but this time with a hint of leniency. "In any case Dorothea will, in future, have no time for reading and nonsense. She will have to take Mary's place. When your uncle does not want her, she will be busy with the house or the children. She *must* improve."

Effie eagerly agreed, although a housewifely Dorothea was hard to imagine, and she had often been sorry for Mary, who could not call her soul her own.

"Perhaps," she said, "my uncle's book will soon be finished."

Mrs. Creighton sniffed. She had never believed in that book, which had been talked of now for thirty years. Her brother-in-law was, she considered, a silly, pompous, conceited, selfish old creature; his life work had been eleven babies, five of whom had died, inflicted upon her poor sister at barbarously short intervals. He was, in fact, rather worse than most men.

2

Effie had never travelled alone before and, although she kept up a valiant front, she had secret misgivings. It was with relief and triumph that she alighted at Dorbridge. No sinister strangers had tried to talk to her, no horrid men had stared rudely, and her new gloves were quite clean. Nor was she immediately dashed by finding nobody from Bramstock waiting on the platform to meet her. Rejoicing, she sailed into the ladies' waiting room. The two hours' drive need now have no terrors for her.

But as time went on, and nobody appeared, she began to grow anxious. At last she strolled down the platform, past the station buildings, to peer over a white railing which fenced off the station yard. One glance showed her the Bramstock trap. Dorothea was perched upon the driver's seat looking less fit to be seen than ever. Her sprigged cotton gown was crushed, she wore no gloves, and her dark curls were hidden under a huge, shabby old garden hat tied down with a striped roman ribbon.

At Effie's squeak of amazement she turned and said coolly, "Oh there you are! I was wondering what could have become of you."

"Why did you not come upon the platform?"

"Is the porter there? Tell him to get your things."

Effie did so and joined Dorothea in the yard, reproaching her for not coming onto the platform.

"I wasn't able," said Dorothea, glancing at the porter with a slight blush. "I can't get out of the trap just at present. I'll explain later."

Something which Dorothea could not mention before the porter must, thought Effie, be very indelicate indeed. She climbed into the trap. Her trunk and bandbox were put in behind. They set off through the sleepy little town by a road which ran southwards, pleasantly shaded by poplars planted fifty years earlier. This had been done by French prisoners, and gave Dorbridge a faintly continental atmosphere.

"I hope you are not offended that it's just me and the trap," said Dorothea. "Selina wanted the carriage."

"But why can't you get out of it?"

Dorothea gave a kick and displayed, for an instant, five rosy toes, before her little foot vanished again beneath her skirts.

"Thea! Why . . . you . . . you haven't——"

"My boots," declared Dorothea, with great energy, "pinch me so, there's no enduring them. Half way here I could bear it no more. Oh the relief when they were off! You've no idea how delightful it is to feel the cool air round one's poor dear feet."

"But you started in them?" cried Effie anxiously.

"Oh yes. But I never shall again. Only the worst part is, I have no button hook and I can't put them on again. So when I got to the station I was obliged to sit tight."

Effie, remembering her promise to be a good influ-

75

ence, declared that she would never drive again with a barefoot cousin and scolded Dorothea for wearing such a hat.

"I don't care to get sunstroke. Our bonnets, nowadays, are all made to fall off the backs of our heads. I can't carry a sunshade and drive, you know."

The good influence was not perceptible, but Effie persevered. She smoothed her crisp skirts, pulled out a minute crinkle in a glove, and asked all those questions proper in an arriving guest. How was her uncle? How was her cousin Philip? How were his wife Selina, and their children, Katy and Pip? How were her cousins Henry and Robert? Had any letter been recently received from her cousin Charles?

They were all, said Dorothea, as well as usual, except Philip, who was as ill as usual. To be an invalid was Philip's role, ever since he took a fever in the West Indies. Bob and Henry were coming to the wedding. Charles had sent Mary a Maltese cross.

"And Mary? Is she very happy?"

This question was important to Effie, so she had left it to the last.

"Yes," said Dorothea gloomily.

"And Grant? What is he like? What do you think of him? You have never really said much, in any letter. I thought . . . I feared . . . if you like him you would leave one in no doubt about it."

"Why . . . you must have met him when you were here before. At some ball or other."

"If I have, it made no impression on me."

"That's easy to believe."

"What do you mean?"

76

Dorothea's face gave Effie her answer. But after a moment she exclaimed, "I would rather not talk about him at all. I will *not* say anything about him which might hurt Mary's feelings if she could hear. Pray believe that he is all he ought to be. There's nothing in the world to be said against him. I'm sure he is very good and he is not at all bad looking. But of course if I could understand what Mary sees in him I should be in love with him myself, I suppose. And that would be a pretty kettle of fish."

Which was a vulgar expression, thought Effie. But she could not be for ever reproving Thea. She smiled and said, "Nobody could be quite good enough for Mary. I suspect that you find him a little dull?"

"Dull!" cried Dorothea, with so much emphasis that the horse pricked up his ears. "He's the dullest . . . Imagine! He has been to Naples and can tell one nothing about it. I was at him for an hour at least, and I could only get the barest crumbs of information. Is it not very hard, Effie, that the people who go to Naples are so seldom those who really need to go?"

"Why do you need to go to Naples?"

"I must go. I am determined to go."

Much as she would have liked to discuss a trip to Naples, Effie felt it her duty to dismiss the topic.

"I suppose," she suggested, "that you will take on all the housekeeping when Mary goes. You will be very busy."

"Oh that! It will be a great bore, but I can assure you that I don't mean to let it crush me as it has Mary. A great deal of it, you know, is pure humbug. Mary goes into the kitchen with an important look and is told by the cook what we shall eat. I think I can do that without dying of exhaustion."

77

"But the keys? You will have the keys?"

"Why should anybody make such work over those grand keys? I shall give out the stores on Monday mornings. The servants are not fools or knaves; I shall give them what they ask for a week. Oh I know one is supposed never to give them enough, so that they are always having to pester one, at every minute, for soap or sugar or candles. Such humbug. Women do it just so as to feel busy and important. So many of them have nothing to do at all; they run mad with boredom. And so——"

"Thea! The horse is having a very nice meal off the hedge. Had we not better go on?"

"Oh! Has he stopped? I never noticed," said Dorothea, whipping up the horse. "But it's all nonsense, you know, and I don't think Mary should have given in to it. If I had thought any of it necessary, I should have helped her more. Why should she slave her life out? Selina should engage a reliable nursemaid. And why cannot Papa engage a secretary?"

At such heresy Effie felt bound to protest. A daughter living at home, she said, must expect these duties. It would be very shocking for a man with a daughter to be driven to hired labour. But Dorothea was unconvinced, and when Effie murmured something about expense she revealed her own intention to do without a horse. She liked riding, but she much preferred her liberty. She would give up her horse, halve her dress allowance, do without a fire in her bedroom; out of such economies the cost of a secretary might surely be squeezed.

"I'd willingly sell my pearls. Why should I be loaded with luxuries I don't care for and be denied the one thing for which I crave—my leisure?"

They were now out of the shady avenue. A long upland road led to the rampart of hills which lay between Dorbridge and the coast. Under a fierce sun they crawled along, between dusty white hedges. Effie put up her parasol and tried to think out an answer.

Thea's debating powers were formidable and she could always manage to sound persuasive. The most cogent argument against her could not be stated crudely; it was implicit in all the training which Effie had received from her mother, but had never exactly been put into words. Such behaviour was eccentric, and men, the unpleasant all-powerful creatures, disliked eccentric women. Should Dorothea persist in her refusal to behave like other girls, no man would ever want to marry her. Far from getting to Naples, she might never escape from Bramstock. Effie tried to put this point in a roundabout way.

"I expect Grant loves Mary for her unselfishness. I daresay that is what attracted him."

"I'm sure I hope not. I should like to think better of him than that. To tell the truth I don't know what he does admire in Mary. He stands by the piano when she is playing, and says, Capital! at intervals. But he never knows the names of her pieces. Oh, he is a dreary—But no more of that!"

"It's very mysterious," mused Effie. "Love . . . what makes people . . . why they . . ."

"I know. I look at Grant and think: How can she? And I remember Edward. And I think of Mary then, Edward's Mary, and Mary now. That Edward could once mean so much to her. And now . . . Grant!"

"Edward?" cried Effie, bewildered and doubtful.

"Oh Effie! Edward of Clone!"

79

Clone.

The word was like a wave breaking on some distant shore, a bell tolling in some hidden tower. Effie sighed assent.

How it had been minted neither of them could remember. Perhaps it had once been Cologne, mentioned in the hearing of a five-year-old Dorothea as a superlatively beautiful place. And she, emerging from the vegetable coma of infancy, awakened by one of those dramatic flashes in which children behold the world, had seized upon it as the home of all magic. Clone! A place where kittens could talk, where one might walk across a rainbow, where people might be made very small and shut up in bottles. In Clone, she told Effie and Mary, they did all this. Until Clone became so real to them that they told her about it.

Clone stories took so much hold on them that, when they were parted, their letters contained little else. Effie still had all those Clone chronicles, mostly written by Dorothea; she kept them because she could not bear to part with anything appertaining to Bramstock. They had been hidden under a floorboard in her bedroom ever since Mrs. Creighton found and read one of them. Her lecture upon the dangers of overexcited fancy had been so impressive that Effie, on her next visit to Bramstock, had timidly suggested the abandonment of Clone, only to find herself signing a document in which all three children swore never to do so.

The Clone heroes included many of their favourite characters, in romance and history. The purely magic modulated into the romantic. Solid rainbows and talking rabbits were discarded in favour of Gothic architecture. Some fields were tacitly excluded as unsuitable. No Bible scenes or characters figured in Clone; religion was respectfully ignored, although there were some picturesque monks, nuns and hermits, and an Inquisition into which the heroes sometimes disappeared. All three chroniclers were stout protestants. Certain historical characters were also banned, after a fierce argument over Leonidas, who was, maintained Dorothea, too great to be altered in any way so as to fit into Clone; to invent new things for him to do or to say was a kind of blasphemy. Mary laid the same interdict upon Montrose. We should not need Clone, said Dorothea, if there were more men like them. We must always allow that they were superior to Bruno and Edward and Gabriel.

These three tremendous fellows had dominated Clone in its final phase: Mary's Edward, amazingly good, Dorothea's Gabriel, amazingly wicked, and Effie's Bruno, of lesser stature than the other two but endowed with amazing charm. Their earlier prototypes had perhaps been Sir Philip Sydney, Lord Byron and Henry Tilney. Three young ladies, Christabel, Laura and Alice, partnered them through many harrowing scenes: Bruno and Alice were the only couple who ever got to the altar, for Effie, in the face of her cousins' disapproval, still preferred a happy ending.

The dissolution of Clone took place silently, at some time during their mid teens. A day came when they spoke of it no more. Effie could remember no overt decision; the fantasy was abandoned just as, at an earlier date, her dolls had been discarded, without formal farewell, to lie forlorn in whatever drawer or cupboard had been their final home. She had always supposed it must have been the same with Mary and Dorothea.

"But that was when we were children," she protested. "You can't compare Mary's Edward to a real man."

"I believe she once loved him more than she loves Grant now. Have you ever seen a real man you thought better than your Bruno?"

Effie never had. Her mother's counsels had not encouraged her to suppose that there could be any real men as nice as Bruno. Yet she cherished an idea that somebody might turn up, someday, capable of bridging the gap.

"Not yet," she murmured.

"But you mean to wait till you do? Mary has not done that. I'm positive that she has not. Don't you remember how she used to look when she told us about Edward? How rapt! How transported! Oh, she worshipped him, and she will never worship Grant. Don't you remember that night when she came in and told us that Edward had sold all he had and given it to the poor? Her look, standing there in the moonlight and telling us?"

Ah, could I ever forget it? thought Effie.

The summer after her confirmation Mary had been promoted to a room of her own, while Effie and Dorothea still shared the old night nursery. One night she had burst in upon them with this electrifying news of Edward. Her look, as she stood before them in the moonlight, had astounded them so much that they both sat up, open mouthed, in their beds. Her gentle, ardent voice, her long hair falling on her shoulders, her white night-gown, her blazing eyes, were like things perceived in a vision.

"Oh he has done it! Edward has done it! He has renounced all, and gone to live the life of a poor shepherd in a little cottage. All that he has is sold and given to the poor."

"Even Fountainhall?" cried Effie, anguished at the loss of this beautiful house, so many times altered and embellished by Mary.

"Even Fountainhall. It was a temptation. When he saw the people dying . . ."

"Why did they die?"

"Of a fever. It broke out because his steward did not repair their cottages and they were unhealthy. Edward knew nothing of it: he was in Rome, buying Raphaels for Fountainhall. And when he knew, he swore that he would never sleep under that accursed roof again. He nursed them with his own hands . . . all the surgeons had fled . . . many a scene of horror did he witness. . . . Oh, but it makes me so happy that he has been able to renounce all."

"But where was Christabel?"

"Oh she was there, but he did not recognise her because she was disguised in a black veil. He only knew that a silent figure was beside him, aiding him in the work of mercy."

For some irritating reason Christabel had not been able to remove the black veil and marry Edward. Effie had forgotten what it was. But she could remember her own astonishment at Mary's aspect, her unearthly beauty, with its hint of promise, a pledge of something wonderful in store for Mary.

"But Thea . . . she made Edward up. He was never real."

"What of that? If she can imagine a man she loves better than Grant, she has no business to marry Grant."

"She may have changed her ideas. She may now think it wrong and foolish of a man to give away all his money."

"Perhaps. But she does not worship Grant as she once worshipped Edward. She has accepted a lesser good. Edward's ghost will haunt her. Her soul is Edward's grave."

"Oh no, Thea, nonsense! All children make up those kind of stories. I know Tom and Frank have a Clone; they call it Jezreel, I believe. I heard them talking about it once. Their great hero is Gustavus Adolphus. When Tom grows up you won't say his soul is the grave of Gustavus?"

"It might be true," said Dorothea sadly.

They had now reached the summit of the hilly range. After winding for a little way among gorse-covered hummocks they came out upon a spur called Westing Hill, which gave them a great view of Beremouth Bay. The road plunged down again steeply to the woods in which Bramstock was hidden. Beyond them were the river valley, fields, a long ridge of shingle called Hodden Beach, and the hazy sea. Dorothea drew up so that they might enjoy the view for a few minutes.

"Thea . . ." began Effie, "when did you and Mary give up Clone? I can't remember when I did. Can you?"

"I know when Mary did. It was when Aunt Belle offered to take her to Paris. Mary was wild to go and Papa consented, and then changed his mind, because he could not spare her. Oh, she was in despair. She cried and cried, until she grew quite thin. I said something about Edward, trying to comfort her, you know. And she said, Oh, he's of no use. Never speak of Edward to me again. We feared she might make herself ill. But then Mr. Winthorpe talked to her and persuaded her that it was wrong to be so very unhappy. It's ever since then that she has become so good—as I consider, unnecessarily good."

"But perhaps Mr. Winthorpe was right. It is our duty to be content with our lot. I daresay it was wrong and foolish of us to feast on fancy so much. When . . . when did you give it up?"

Dorothea made no answer. She took off her hat and let the cool breeze, which always blew on Westing, toss her curls about. Her eyes ranged the horizon, as if looking for something.

"How I love this spot," she murmured. "Always . . . always . . . whenever I come. Though it is best in the spring . . . when the curlews are crying. Some part of me seems to stay here always, and greets me when I come back. I wonder what will happen to it when——"

"Thea! I want an answer. When did you . . . ?"

"Why should you suppose that I have?"

"No! It's not possible! Not still!"

"In . . . a sort of way . . . yes."

"Telling those stories? About Gabriel? Telling them to yourself?"

"Not exactly."

"To whom then?"

This seemed to puzzle Dorothea. She considered and said, "I don't quite know. When one writes a story down, it's as though one told it to somebody. . . ."

"You write it down. You are writing a book? A novel?"

"Why yes. I suppose that's what it is."

"About Gabriel?"

"Not exactly. He has . . . he is a good deal altered."

"But he's still called Gabriel?"

"Yes. I never thought of calling him anything else."

"And Clone? Does it happen in Clone?"

"No. At present he's in Naples."

"Oh! So that's why you need to go to Naples?"

"Yes. In a novel I find that necessary. To have been to a place."

Dorothea put on her hat again, tied the striped ribbon under her chin and settled down happily to explain. Now that the secret was out she had a great deal to tell.

"It's not like poetry. Poets can write of places nobody has ever seen—Xanadu or the Inferno, because in some ways, you know, they have never lost Clone. You remember how, when we were children, we were quite certain about the Clone landscapes? It never troubled us that we had not visited the North Pole or the Great Wall of China. We were quite certain. We knew what they were like. And a poet never loses that assurance; he brings Clone with him into manhood and . . . and makes it the landscape for a man's thoughts. Think of Shelley's desert! *Boundless and bare, The lone and level sands stretch far away*. Effie, there's no such desert. Geography forbids it. Desert sand is dry and the wind blows it into ridges and hills. No desert is absolutely flat, like the sea-shore sand, which stays flat because it is wet. That's pure Clone, that perfectly flat sand stretching away to the horizon. But one believes it absolutely: one sees it. He forces one to do so. He had that power, that force, to exalt Clone into something mature. Poetry is much more difficult than a novel, because it needs that power. I used to think it easier, but it is not."

Effie gave but half an ear to all this. She was thinking about Dorothea's hair and how well a little wreath of dark red rosebuds would set off those silky curls. At the great dinner party, before the wedding, she thought, I will make her such a wreath, and lend her my crimson sash, and she will look so beautiful that He will certainly fall in love with her.

He was Gerald Grimshaw, the best man, of whom she had heard the most charming accounts, not from Bramstock, but from friends in Hertfordshire. He was Grant's cousin and he lived in Cumberland, but he came sometimes to stay with a family in St. Albans, quite near Effie's home. This family was not acquainted with Mrs. Creighton, and Effie had never met him; curiosity to do so had accounted for some of her eagerness over this visit. Girls who had danced with him at a St. Albans ball reported him to be so very kind, clever and amusing. Of his looks nobody could say much, for it appeared that he had carroty hair and a magenta complexion, but all agreed that this did not signify, after one had danced with him for five minutes. Effie herself thought red hair an unsurmountable obstacle, but believed that Dorothea would not mind it much. He was very rich and would probably take her to Naples for a honeymoon. The rosebud wreath might settle the matter if only Thea would keep it straight and not talk too much about Shelley.

When Dorothea fell silent, Effie dismissed these plans to ask if Gabriel was still so very wicked.

"He believes that he is. But then Vesuvius erupts. That's why it has to be in Naples. He saves the lives of all the villagers, and, among them, his worst enemy."

"And then he becomes good? Is that the end?"

"Oh no. That's only the beginning, although I have not got as far as that yet. He begins to doubt if he is wicked. But then, he acted without conscious resolution, when he did this heroic deed, and this does not, he thinks, justify him in calling himself a good man. So he goes back to Avonsford——"

"That was in Clone!"

"Yes. I use some Clone places. He was born there. And he lives over all his life again, step by step, in all the places he has been in. And he finds that it is all quite different, not what he supposed before. His own part in every episode is altered, and so are the people. Those whom he had thought of as wicked, he now sees to have been good. And the good become wicked."

"Is Laura in it?"

"Yes. There are two Lauras. One he had thought an angel; he now sees that she was a mean, base, paltry creature. The other, who is dead, he had believed to be entirely bad; he now perceives that she was a kind of saint. And at last he returns to Naples. The people of the village never realised that it was he who saved them. They thought it was a stranger, whose body they found. They have put up a monument to him: to *L'uomo ignoto* . . . the unknown man. And he discovers that this is himself."

"And then?"

"That is the end."

To Effie it was a most unsatisfactory end. She did not know what to make of it all, but it did not sound very sensible.

"Don't you think," she ventured, "that it is a little wrong and dangerous to mix up good and bad like that? There ought not, surely, to be any confusion? We know good from bad."

"But do we know good people from bad people? I believe that our idea of them must largely depend upon our idea of ourselves. That is really the theme of my novel."

Dorothea whipped up the horse and began to descend the hill, to the tune of a long, dragging scream from the brake.

"Will you let me read it?" begged Effie.

"Someday. When it's finished. Perhaps . . ."

"Oh you must. Promise! Does anybody else know?"

"Nobody. I show some of my verses to Bob sometimes. He's a good critic, and very hard upon me. But I could not show him this. I can't think why I told you; I suppose because it is so nice and comfortable to be with you again."

"Shall you try to get it printed?"

"Yes. I shall send it to some publishers, when it is finished. If I could get some money I could give it to Papa to pay a secretary; then I should feel perfectly easy. But I must write it, Effie. I must. Gabriel is more important to me than anything else upon earth. I can't resist. He quite takes possession of me."

"Oh dear! Are you sure it is right to feel so?"

They had reached the bottom of the hill, where a gate led through the woods. Dorothea turned the trap into a little triangle of greensward and pulled up again, asking if Effie had a button hook. Effie produced one from her travelling bag, and watched her cousin wrestling with stockings, garters and boot buttons. How, she wondered, could anyone ever hope to influence Dorothea? And what a scrape they would be in, should somebody come by.

"I think it is wrong and dangerous," she said firmly.

"Which? To write a novel or to take off my boots?"

"Both. You have too many ideas. They unsettle you."

"On the contrary. If allowed to think, I am perfectly calm. Tight boots I find unsettling."

"Oh Thea! Quick! Quick! Somebody is coming down the . . . a *man!* Oh it is Mr. Winthorpe! Oh what will he think?"

"Be calm. My skirt hides the top buttons."

The rector of Bramstock advanced, smiling, as Dorothea returned the button hook and pulled her skirt over the tops of her boots. He was not thirty years old and he had been their pastor for five. Everybody admired him very much. He had published a volume of religious verse and had contributed some powerful articles, in defence of ritualism, during a recent church controversy. He was unmarried, but only very romantic ladies believed that he had taken a vow of celibacy. Since he was reckoned very handsome, a good many girls were known to be on the catch for him. The Miss Hardings had never been of that company and for this reason, perhaps, he was more intimate with the family at Bramstock than with any other in the parish. He had prepared them both for confirmation and treated them as younger sisters, aware that no false construction would be put upon his frequent visits.

With Effie he was more cautious. For all he knew she might have an eye on Bramstock Rectory. She, instinctively, knew this, knew that the war between the sexes was active—a war in which she had been skilfully armed. Her face changed as he approached them; it lost a certain luminous candour which had brightened it while she talked to Dorothea. She became very demure and gave him exactly the smile which her mother would have wished to see, an impersonal, decorative grimace.

He removed his hat, and opened the gate for them,

glancing with obvious amusement at Dorothea's hat. When it turned out that he was going to the house she offered him a lift.

"I should crush your gowns," he objected. "There is really not room for three in front, and the luggage is behind."

"Oh no. We are very thin, and it is much too hot to walk. Jump up!"

This was not the language in which a lift should have been offered by a young lady to a clergyman. He jumped up, with commendable agility, but did not smile quite so much. By sitting so nearly on the edge of the seat that he was nearly off it, he avoided contact of any sort with Effie. Dorothea whipped up the horse and they set off down the drive very briskly.

"You must all be much interested by Henry's tidings," he said. "What do they think of it at Coldingham?"

"What?" cried Effie. "The new headmaster? Is he appointed?"

"A Dr. Cadbury, Miss Creighton. A very sound man and a fine scholar. I know something of him."

"Why Dorothea! You never told me."

"I forgot," said Dorothea.

"We must suppose that her head was in the clouds. Aha! Aha!" Mr. Winthorpe shook a waggish finger at Dorothea, thus putting her in her place for telling him to jump up. Turning to Effie he explained, "I know your cousin so well. I am allowed to tease her."

"I really asked so many questions I gave her no time to answer," explained Effie, distressed at having exposed Dorothea to this impertinence.

"Oh we will forgive her," he conceded. "Her days of

wool-gathering are nearly over, are they not? When she is mistress of Bramstock she must come down to earth. My dear Dorothea! Pray don't drive so recklessly! We shall all break our necks."

They were flying towards the house at a canter. Effie also gave a little moan of protest at which Dorothea slackened the pace.

"She looks very fierce," commented Mr. Winthorpe, "but we know her better. We know that she will do her best to fill dear Mary's place."

Men! raged Effie inwardly. Oh dear, how I do hate them! Why were they put to rule over us, the odious creatures? Fancy anybody wanting to marry Mr. Winthorpe! Fancy having to sleep in the same bed with him and see all his horrid toes! Oh dear! What an indelicate thing to think about a clergyman!

3

Bob Harding looked down the long table, studied its load of glass, silver, damask and white roses, and wondered, not for the first time, whether the old man might be outrunning the constable. They certainly did themselves very well down here, in a quiet way, but this had not struck him until he had lived for a while in London. As a boy he had taken the stable full of horses, the wine in the cellar, the costly additions continually made to the library, the glass-houses, the shooting, the three sons at public schools, the army commission bought for the fourth, as sure evidence that his father possessed ample means. It was not until he had begun to earn his own living that he realised what such things must cost, and began to speculate upon the exact extent of these means. It came to his notice that a man might have a large income and yet contrive to live beyond it, that a carriage and a good table are not always proof of money in the bank, and that extravagance does not always proclaim itself by ostentation.

This doubt had first been raised in his mind by the

abrupt withdrawal of his own allowance, as soon as his first little briefs had begun to come in. He had hinted that he still found things pretty tight and had been answered with unusual petulance. Did he think Mr. Harding was made of money? If so, he must think again. A younger son must fend for himself as soon as possible. Which was, in itself, fair enough. Bob never meant to ask for money again, nor did he expect to come in for much when the old boy popped off. The estate would go to Philip, and provision must be made for the girls out of the money brought into the family by their mother. One thing was certain: the original income must be, by now, considerably depleted. Prices had risen. Repeal had hit Bramstock as it had hit most landed estates. Yet there had been no cutting down of expenditure—not a servant turned off, not a pony the fewer in the stables, not a lump of coal the less on the fires.

What was the old fool doing? There he sat, at the end of the table, wagging his beard at Mr. Winthorpe's mother. Belief in Papa, his immense scholarship, his great book, might hold, down at Bramstock; Bob nowadays could feel sure of nothing save the beard. Was he running into debt? Was he raising money on future income? Had he got through all Mama's fortune? What about the West Indies property of which little had been heard since Philip went out to look after it and caught that fever? What if, one fine day, the wolf walked boldly in at the door? Who would then support Philip, Selina, Pip, Katy, and other children, probably, for Selina had an ominously fecund look. Who would support Dorothea, should she not marry, and the old boy himself, if he survived the exposure of his misdoings? Who but the younger sons? It was scarcely fair that such a fate could secretly be preparing for them. When the crash came they might be married themselves and have families of their own to support. They had a right to know.

Charlie would be willing enough, thought Bob, helping himself to ice pudding, but he never can keep sixpence in his pockets for five minutes. The Hen will wriggle out of it. Upon my word, if I don't look sharp, it may all fall upon me. But how can one find out? I wonder if Grant knows anything?

Grant, though a dull dog, was perfectly wide awake where money was concerned. He would scarcely have thought Mary a suitable wife had he suspected anything amiss; his courtship was, in itself, reassuring. But he would be most unlikely to put his hand in his pocket to help Mary's relations.

The betrothed pair were sitting just opposite, Grant hidden by a great epergne full of white roses. Mary, bridal in lace and pearls, with a wreath of mock orange flowers, was talking placidly to Winthorpe. Poor Mary! Dear Mary! She must have had a life of it lately, and it was lucky she liked the dull dog well enough to marry him. She had gone off sadly and looked nearer to thirty than twenty-two. All the bloom and glow had vanished. Her hair was still thick and golden but its lustre had departed; soon it would fade into greyness. The fair face was as yet unlined, yet settled into a mould which indicated where lines would be, lines of patience round the mouth and sorrow round the eyes. And a certain sweetness was gone, which had once hung round her like the fragrance of a rose.

As she smiled at Mr. Winthorpe, however, Bob

thought he saw an afterglow of it and remembered a surmise, once secretly entertained, that she might be sweet on the parson. Ever since Winthorpe talked her out of going into a decline she had turned him into a patron saint. She quoted him on all occasions as the best and wisest creature on earth, and was always scurrying off to consult him on the minutest details of conduct. Bob could almost believe that she had asked his leave before accepting Grant Forrester.

If she had, Winthorpe's advice had been sound. Provision was safe for Mary, whatever happened to the rest of them, and it only remained to hope that Dorothea would marry too, as soon as possible. That, for so pretty a girl, should be easy, if only she would take a little trouble over it; at present she seemed to care more for a brother's opinion of her verses than for any other man's opinion of her eyes.

Tonight she was looking very well indeed. He liked the fetching little wreath of red roses she sported, and she seemed to be in lively spirits. She was laughing, actually laughing, at something said by Gerald Grimshaw, who sat between her and Effie. That droll fellow must be surpassing himself to make both the girls laugh so much, in spite of a phizz which might put any woman off. He had a fine property in Cumberland, and was moreover a very good sort, a thorough gentleman. In fact he might be a highly desirable brother-in-law, far more liberal and open handed than Grant, should it ever come to a question of forking out. Dorothea liked him. She was talking to him so eagerly that she failed to notice Selina's signals.

Philip's wife, at the head of the table, was trying to collect eyes. Everybody else perceived it. Effie did so, in spite of her amusement. All the ladies were collecting their bouquets, their gloves and their handkerchiefs. Selina, wriggling and fidgeting, could not rise until she had secured Dorothea's attention. A gradual silence fell upon the table in which that eager young voice became audible to all:

". . . evidence of metempsychosis?"

The five dire syllables tripped out, to the embarrassment of some, to the malicious amusement of others. Thea was, as usual, making a fool of herself. Grimshaw, however, dealt with it.

"What a parting shot!" he exclaimed, glancing up the table so as to direct her attention to Selina. "You know I can't answer. You know that's a word upon which I dare not venture *after* the port!"

Everybody laughed. Dorothea, aware at last of the situation, started up in dismay before anybody else had time to rise.

When the last lady had rustled out, and the door was shut behind them, Bob moved round to sit beside Grimshaw, who was examining the silver filigree holder of Dorothea's bouquet. She had, in her confusion, left it behind her; Grimshaw was absorbed in the little legs, released by a spring, upon which the whole affair stood beside her plate.

"You must not make the bridesmaids laugh too much," said Bob, "or you will none of you be able to keep straight faces in church tomorrow."

"Oh I know what I am doing. I've been best man before. The real danger is that they will cry. I boast that *my* bridesmaids never do that."

"I can believe it. What were you telling them?"

"A tall story about my grandmother's cat. After her death it adopted many of her ways: sat in her chair at family prayers and squalled if we said anything of which she would have disapproved. We really began to think that the old lady must be still with us. Pure nonsense, but your sister, I believe, thought that there might be something in it."

"Thea likes nonsense very well," said Bob, who was anxious to erase the impression caused by metempsychosis. "But she hears too little of it, nowadays. She has nobody to talk it with, now that Charles and I are gone."

"Her cousin's visits must be very welcome. Miss Creighton seems to dote on nonsense. Does she come here often?"

"Not as often as we could wish. There are too few young people in the house, and it will be worse when Mary goes. My sister-in-law is so much taken up with poor Philip that I am afraid she will not be able to go out with Dorothea very much."

"She lives near St. Albans, I understand?"

Bob gaped and then realised that Grimshaw's *she* was Effie.

It was hardly surprising. What man wants a wife who talks in words of five syllables? Yet Effie, thought Bob, could not hold a candle to Thea, for looks or brains. It was a great shame. All that poor Thea needed was to be laughed into light-heartedness by somebody who loved her enough to undertake the task. She would fall quickly under the influence of a mind which she really respected, and her brains would, in that case, do her no harm. Effie had a considerable fortune and need never look far for a husband; it might be many a day before so good a match as Grimshaw came Dorothea's way.

The port was excellent. (What had it cost? Had it been paid for?) He sent it trundling over the mahogany in its little silver trolley and made up his mind. If Papa had got into the soup, he and Philip must break the entail; no younger son should be asked to fork out unless that was done.

Which reminded him that he had not yet seen poor old Philip, who was too unwell to dine downstairs. After the trolley had been round again he left the dining room and went upstairs to Philip's quarters, where he was greeted by a hideous squalling as soon as he opened the door. His niece Katy lay bellowing on the hearthrug, her great red face the colour of her plaid frock. Such lungs in a child of three were phenomenal. As she roared she drummed steadily on the floor with a pair of stout little boots.

Philip lay on a couch by the window, which was closed although the night was very warm. He appeared to be in a fainting fit. An untouched supper tray stood on a table beside him. The room, as usual, smelt of sickness.

Bob seized a bony hand, and heard his brother whisper, "For God's sake . . . take her . . . away!"

"Where?"

"Old . . . night . . . nurseries."

Reluctantly Bob went across to Katy and shouted, "Whoa! Stoppit!"

She roared on. When he picked her up she kicked him in the stomach. He got her under one arm, whereat she bit his hand. But he stuck to it and bore her up to a

room with two cots in it. Pip, a sickly looking child in a
dirty night-gown, already sat on one of them. Bob threw
Katy into the other and asked where the nursemaid was.

"Gone down for 'er beer," piped Pip. "Katy will stop
if you slap'er face wiv a wet towel."

He pointed to a stand with an ewer and basin on it.
Bob hated Katy so much that he followed this advice with
no compunction. Wetting a towel, he wrung it out and
slapped her face with it. She immediately broke off, in
the middle of a roar, and went to sleep. The silence was
wonderful.

"She's ninepence in the shilling," observed Pip.

"You ought not to say that about your sister."

"Nursie says so. Kin I have my supper? I did put myself to bed."

"Who usually puts you to bed?"

"Aunt Mary. I wa-ant Aunt Mary."

"She is busy. There's a party downstairs. I daresay
your nurse will bring you up some supper."

At this Pip began to howl. Katy awoke and joined
him. Bob fled from the unsavoury room. In the passage he
encountered a slatternly looking woman carrying a tray
with two basins of bread and milk.

"Miss Katy," he said severely, "had got into her
father's room. She was screaming the house down."

"Lor!" said the woman indifferently. "Is that where
she was?"

If she had been down for beer, she had certainly got
it. Bob was surprised at Mary for engaging such a servant, and then remembered that the nursemaid was Selina's affair, not under Mary's jurisdiction. He recollected
rumours of friction between Mrs. Philip's nursery and the

rest of the household. The unlucky Selina always seemed to get hold of the wrong 'uns. She would. She was not a lady, not even English. Her mother had been a Creole. Poor Philip, on that unlucky trip to the West Indies, had not only ruined his constitution but had picked up a disastrous wife.

He had recovered from his swoon when Bob got back to his sitting room, and was drinking a glass of wine from the tray.

"Try to peck on a little, old boy," urged Bob. "I'm sorry to find you like this. They said you had been better."

"Last week I was spry enough. But it never lasts."

"Shall you be able to get to church tomorrow?"

"No hope of that, I'm afraid," said Philip despondently. "At the best I'm never up to much."

Conversation languished. Bob wondered how long he could stand the airless room and remarked that Mary was looking happy.

"Glad to get away from us, no doubt," muttered Philip. "What we shall do without her I cannot imagine. Nobody else can manage Katy."

"I suppose Thea will take all that on."

"Dorothea has made it perfectly clear that she intends to do nothing of the sort. She refuses to have anything to do with Katy."

This was most unwomanly in Dorothea, but Bob, nursing his bitten hand, found it hard to blame her. He knew very little about small children but it seemed to him that there might be something very much amiss with Katy. She could not talk at all, and, when not yelling, had a disagreeably vacant expression.

That squalid nursery, the neglected children, had

been a disturbing discovery. He had imagined that Mary, even behind the scenes, was in some way contriving to maintain their mother's standards. In his own infancy those nurseries had been so snug, so clean, ruled over by old Miggie, in her great frilled cap. She lay now in Bramstock churchyard. A handsome headstone, praising her for faithful service, had been put up by the family. *How much had it cost?*)

"I say . . . Philip . . ."

"Eh?"

Was it fair to disturb an invalid with these forebodings? There might not be another opportunity, and the matter was, after all, of great importance to Philip himself. He might know something.

It seemed that he did not. Upon hearing of Bob's uneasiness he merely shook his head and said, "I know nothing and care less. Whatever there is will last my time, I daresay."

Selina returned just then, breathless and full of apologies for having stayed downstairs so long. She had not been able to get away from Mrs. Forrester, Grant's mother. The sight of the uneaten supper distressed her and she looked angrily at Bob as though he had, in some way, been to blame. Whatever her shortcomings she was clearly devoted to Philip. As she bent over him, insisting that he should eat a few grapes, her soft, lamenting voice took on a certain sweetness heard by nobody else in the house. She had been reputed a beauty when he married her, but had lost her looks by the time he brought her back to England. Her mop of greasy black curls sometimes aroused uneasy speculation in Bob as to that Creole ancestry; he hoped that it *had* been Creole. Her skin was pinched and sallow. When she stooped, the thickening of her waist was unmistakable. Philip might describe himself as up to very little, but there seemed to be one thing to which the reckless fellow was still up. Nobody had spoken of it, thought Bob; his father and Thea might not have noticed it, but Mary must have done so.

"Oh," she wailed, "I should not have left you. Oh dear! What shall we do without Mary?"

"Bob," said Philip, "commends us to Dorothea."

At this she drew herself up. Her eyes grew cold and venomous. That sudden turn, the green and yellow gleam of her dress, the small vicious eyes, reminded Bob unpleasantly of a snake. He thought suddenly that he might be sick if he stayed in this room an instant longer. With a muttered goodnight he fled, but Selina followed him, swept into the passage, shut the door, and faced him.

"All I ask," she said with something very like a hiss, "is that Dorothea will behave herself. I ask for no help with my children. I know that I have no authority. We are poor relations. . . ."

"Now! Now! Selina. . . ."

"But some things should not be inflicted on my innocent children and I, if we are to remain under this roof. I should have gone to your father, if I was not afraid of disturbing Philip. Perhaps she might attend to you, Robert. If you have any regard for her character, speak to her! Make her tell you who it is."

"Good heavens! What do you mean?"

"Who is it that she meets when she goes creeping out . . . creeping out at night? Where does she go?"

"Dorothea? You mean my sister?"

"I have watched her. When I have been awake on

103

one of Philip's bad nights. Creeping in and out like a thief. Sometimes it is daylight before she comes creeping back. I have spoken to Mary, and much good that did. Mary asks me to believe that she likes roaming alone in the woods!"

"Very possibly," cried Bob, remembering all that he had ever known of Dorothea. His moment of panic subsided.

"I'm sure Mary is right," he added. "Thea was always as wild as a hawk. But she must stop doing it. She might meet a tramp or a poacher. I will see that it stops."

"Oh? So you mean to take Mary's view of it?"

"To be sure I do. But I will settle it. I'm glad to know. Goodnight, Selina."

He ran down the passage, pursued by her mocking stare.

Downstairs the house was empty; they had all gone into the garden, where they were wandering about in groups, enjoying the sunset and the warm twilight. He took a great breath of pure air and looked about for companions. Above some bushes he spied a carroty head bent over a fair one, wreathed in cornflowers. Grimshaw had lost no time, on getting out of the dining room, and would not welcome a third on that promenade. Henry and Mr. Winthorpe, pacing the lawn, might do so, but Bob did not want to hear any more about the soundness of Doctor Cadbury, who was a true Christian, the good breeding of Mrs. Cadbury, also a true Christian, or the beauty of the Cadbury daughters who, with such parents, must inevitably be true Christians too.

He beat a retreat into the rose garden where he found Mary and Grant, sitting placidly side by side. He would have left them undisturbed had she not called to him, "No! Don't go Bob! I have scarcely spoken three words to you since you arrived this afternoon."

"Yes," said Grant, jumping up. "You have more right to her, this evening, than I have. Stay with her, while I go and find out when my mother wants the carriage."

Grant could always be trusted to do and say the correct thing. He strode off on his long legs with so complacent an air that Bob did not feel as grateful as he ought.

The stone seat where Mary sat was still warm from the sun which had shone on it all day. Bob took Grant's place beside her and tried to think of something to say, some suitable farewell to this sister who had done so much for them all. His recent glimpse behind the scenes had been disturbing; Botany Bay, he thought, could hardly be more disagreeable, and he no longer wondered at her for accepting Grant. But when I marry, he decided, I shall pick a lively girl who has led an amusing life. Then I can be sure that she does not marry me merely to get away from home.

"Look!" said Mary. "There is the evening star."

It shone, mild and solitary, just above the yew hedge. Mary's face, as she gazed at it, was so pure, so tranquil, that his uneasiness subsided. Some people, he remembered, like to be good.

She began to ask him questions about his London life and his little briefs. As a rule he would have welcomed these; he liked to talk about himself and Mary's qualities as a listener were outstanding. But tonight he answered absently. After a while he broke off to describe his encounter with Katy.

"That's a very strange child, Mary."

"I'm afraid she is rather backward."

"Only that? You think it will mend? I was wondering whether there might be . . . some serious deficiency?"

"Oh no!" cried Mary, much shocked. "Not in our family!"

"We know very little about Selina's family. But I don't pretend to know anything about children. And that nursemaid! I'm positive the woman drinks."

"I fear so. Selina swears by her and will not see it."

"Do you think Thea will be equal to it all?"

"She will have to learn. It will be hard for her at first. She had always had so much freedom, you know. She will not like it at all."

This was said so placidly that he was surprised.

"At least she will have you quite near," he said. "You will always be able to help and advise her."

"No," said Mary, still with the same tranquillity, "I don't mean to concern myself at all with Bramstock, when I am at Elkington. I should not be doing my duty to Grant, as his wife, if I did. Things here, you know, are never very agreeable. When here, it was my duty to think of them. When I am gone, it will no longer be my duty."

"But Mary! If poor Thea finds it very difficult . . . ?"

"She must put up with that, as I have done."

"Upon my word, I call that rather hard! You are fond of Thea, are you not? You would be sorry for her, if she is unhappy?"

"When Grant asked me to marry him," she said, "I could not immediately make up my mind. I thought perhaps I ought to refuse him and stay here, since I could not imagine how they would all get on without me. So I consulted Mr. Winthorpe."

(She did? I thought so. I should not relish the idea of that, were I Grant.)

"He made me understand that, by being overzealous, I might become a stumbling block to others. I might encourage Thea to neglect her duty. She has always, you know, been very spoilt and selfish. She does exactly what she likes, and to do what we like is bad for us. Now that God has called me to take up other duties, she will be obliged to attend to hers here, and will be all the better for it. If she finds it hard, that may, in the end, bring her to God. Mr. Winthorpe thinks that I have, in the past, erred in making life too easy for her. I shall not be tempted to make that mistake when I am at Elkington."

Bob found himself unable to reply to this. It frightened him a little, revealing as it did the abrupt frontiers of the domain of duty, and the uncharted deserts beyond, only to be explored by those who follow the heart. He asked himself whether Mary was as fond of them all as they had supposed, when comfortably accepting her unselfish service. Did she really love anybody, or had she been obeying Mr. Winthorpe? Even her conscientious enquiries after his little briefs might be suspect, if, behind all this gentle patience, had been concealed a slowly hardening heart.

So Mary, he thought, has got her heavenly warrant to wash her hands of us. Confound Winthorpe! I wish they would take him away and make him a bishop.

"But there is one thing," he said, "which you must help me to settle before you go."

107

He told her of Selina's suspicions, at which she displayed an unusual degree of anger.

"Oh how can she be so vulgar? And so sly! She ferrets everything out and makes mischief. She is past bearing."

"But does Thea really do this? Where does she go? What does she do? It is not very safe, even in our own woods."

"She goes to the old playhouse by the river. She has taken it over and has the key; she can keep all her papers and so on there, away from Selina's prying. It is quite warm and dry; she has some odds and ends of furniture."

"But why does she go at night?"

"When she's very much worked up over her writing, and can't sleep, she runs off down there. You know how it is with Thea when she gets a writing fit?"

He did know. He was almost reassured.

"You are certain that's all there is in it?"

Mary turned her clear eyes on him with a look of surprise.

"Of course! What else could there be?"

"But she must not do it any more. Not at night. I wish you would speak to her, Mary. Get her to promise . . . ask her tonight. She can scarcely refuse you anything tonight."

"Very well," agreed Mary. "I will. But in any case she will soon have very little time for writing. Mr. Winthorpe thinks that will be an excellent thing. He has never approved."

"Does he know, then? I thought you and I were the only people who knew about Thea's writing. And, possibly, Effie."

108

"I told him."

"Indeed? I doubt if you had any right to do that."

"He thinks that this poetry, more than anything, is likely to come between Thea and God."

Bob had never taken Dorothea's verses very seriously, but this remark irritated him so much that he exclaimed, "Oh he does, does he? I shall not be surprised if Thea, when she is older . . . why, already she writes better verse than he does."

"Bob! How can you compare them? His hymns have been printed."

"A great deal of rubbish gets printed. If Thea were a man . . . but women can't write poetry. They should never try."

"In that case Thea would have been born a man, had God intended her to write poetry."

"Has Winthorpe ever seen anything she has written?"

"Yes. I showed him some of her verses. He agreed that they were pretty, but he thought that it might be bad for Thea to be praised and encouraged."

"Hmph! He never objects to praise and encouragement where his own doggerel is in question. I daresay he's jealous."

"Jealous! No . . . no . . . it is not that. . . ."

There was a world of pain in the exclmation. She turned her face away, but he could see that she had coloured deeply. An extraordinary idea suggested itself to him.

"Mary! He doesn't . . . impossible . . . is he . . . *épris?*"

She did not answer. She would have done so, had there been nothing in the notion.

"She would never dream of taking him," he exclaimed.

"I'm sure he would never dream of asking her," cried Mary turning angrily. "Unless . . . until . . . she shows herself much more fit to be a clergyman's wife than she is now."

"Is that your guess, Mary? Or has he——"

"Oh I'm not in his confidence. I must go. I must find Grant."

Mary jumped up and ran out of the rose garden, leaving Bob to sit and fume.

So Winthorpe considered that a sentence to Botany Bay might render Thea more fit to be a clergyman's wife? That was the size of it. The fellow's impudence so enraged Bob that he began to consider plans for thwarting it, only to discover that none of them would do. That Thea should take Mary's place was no more than all the world expected. What other place in life had she?

4

Since all the guest rooms at Bramstock were full, Dorothea was sharing her bed with Effie. But they were in no hurry to get into it. Having taken off their gowns, and put on their dressing jackets, they settled down to hairbrushing and chatter.

"But where were you, all the evening?" demanded Effie.

"Oh I was in the drawing room with the old ladies. They went in quite soon, you know, for fear of the dew. I knew that Mary would never get off with Grant unless she knew somebody was doing the civil. But I believe it was a mistake. Had I not been there they could have told each other shocking stories. As it was, we were condemned to chit-chat. How awkward it is that one cannot buy red flannel in Beremouth! Yes indeed, it is very tiresome. Yawn! Yawn! It's their own fault. It's they who insist that a young lady must be some kind of idiot; they must suffer for it when they have got one on their hands. I sat and simpered. That's what I'm supposed to do, you know."

Dorothea did not ask where Effie had been, for she could guess. She added, "Are you not surprised that Grant should have such a lively cousin? I never met a more amusing man. What a pity he never came here before. Mary might have married him."

With this Effie could scarcely agree. She thought that Mr. Grimshaw did very well as a bachelor. She would not have spent quite so much time alone in his company if she had been in Hertfordshire. Her Mama would have called it flirting. But that kind of construction did not come naturally to the Hardings.

"Why are you fishing in your stays?" she asked.

"I am looking for the key of my diary."

"Oh dear, do you keep one? I never can do so beyond February fifteenth. The effort to describe my valentines exhausts me."

Dorothea had unpinned a small gilt key from her stays. She opened a drawer and took out a red leather book with gilt clasps and a lock.

"Papa gave me this on New Year's Day. It is to record my impressions. There is one page for each day in the year. How could impressions be measured like that, as if they were yards of calico? One day might fill up the whole book; or there might be nothing to remember in a month. But I have found a use for it as a kind of shorthand notebook, in which I can jot down anything which I wish to reflect upon, or to remember. It's useful to have something of that sort at hand, for all my letters and papers I keep locked up in the old playhouse."

"And you keep this locked too?"

"I prefer to do so." Dorothea flushed. "There are no great secrets in it. I doubt if anyone else could understand it. But, for all that, I would sooner that some eyes did not pry."

She began to make the day's entry, sitting at her little writing table. Effie knew that Selina's eyes were the implied danger. Only during the first few weeks of Selina's sojourn at Bramstock had Dorothea ever discussed her sister-in-law. Since then she had once told Effie that she preferred not to think of the woman more than was necessary. That she lived in a house with a creature capable of stealing into bedrooms, rummaging in drawers, and reading letters, was a fact upon which she did not care to dwell. An obstinate blankness was her way of protecting herself against certain evils; she would not recognise them. Effie thought it a mistake. Selina was so sly that her housemates should have their wits about them. Self preservation required that they should think about her a good deal, if they would guess what she would be up to next.

"There," said Dorothea, laying down her pen.

"May I see what you have written?"

Dorothea handed over the book. The day's entry ran as follows:

Mary's last day. A great party. Effie puts roses into the epergne and makes wreaths for us all. She takes rosebuds and throws them down; all the floor round her feet, scattered with flowers, her face intent on her great task, the scattered flowers part of it. *The Old Woman's Cat.* What if when alive she always walked, up and down, over one particular spot? Then, afterwards, the cat did so. Did the grass grow greener there? Mrs. W. does not allow Mr. W. to draw up bottles that have been left in the well to cool. 'The handle is stiff and heavy, I think it might strain the heart. The scullery maid does it.' Some such incident, recollected later, of importance to G:? He speaks of it with horror, although blind at the time.

"Why are you laughing?" asked Dorothea.

"At the Winthorpe's scullery maid."

"You think that amusing. I do not."

"Do you suppose he knows?"

"I daresay not."

"May I read some more of it?"

"Anything you like, if you can make it out. It is only jottings. I thought the cat might turn into a story sometime."

"And me making a wreath?"

"No. That is poetry."

"Merci, Mademoiselle!"

"Who is Mrs. H:?" she asked presently. "On January twenty-fifth you write: *Mrs. H: Her grim freedom. We regret recovery? This is extremely important.*"

"Oh that was Mrs. Holcroft. Her husband died, you know. And she said such a wonderful thing."

At the thought of it Dorothea jumped up and began to walk about the room, gesticulating with her hairbrush.

"I've thought about it so much since. I went to see her because there was something I thought I might do for her. She reads every week to the old women in the workhouse and I know that she hates it because they smell so. I thought I might offer to take her place. But she said that she did not mind the smell any more, because she did not care in the least what she did, or where she went. She said that to have a broken heart makes one very free. Can you see what she meant, Effie?"

"No," said Effie. "But I never had a broken heart. I hope I never shall."

114

"Nor have I. But one can imagine it. I think she meant that happiness is really a prison, and our gaolers are our preferences. We think that we like one person, or one place better than another. We regret the past, and we fear the future. But, to a broken heart, all places are the same, there is the same grief to be encountered everywhere. And time is not important. There will be the same grief tomorrow, and as for yesterday . . . *nessun maggior dolore!* And recovery must mean a certain loss of freedom, as preferences and hopes and fears come back. We might almost regret it, as though we had returned from some grand, bare, noble world where we had lived with the truth. But grim freedom is not the right name. Harsh liberty is better."

As often happened, Effie left off listening to this discourse long before it was over. Generalisations did not interest her. She began to put her curls up into rag rollers and said, "I don't understand you, Thea. You hate bad smells. You hate chit-chat. Yet you offer to read to these old women, and you spend a beautiful evening indoors discussing red flannel. Why? Because you feel that you ought. And yet you say——"

"Not because I ought. I longed to do something, some little thing, for poor Mrs. Holcroft. I wanted to set Mary free for a little time with Grant. I *wished* to do so."

"Our wishes have nothing to do with duty. Just because you dislike to work for your Papa you refuse to allow that it is your duty. But what, after all, is duty?"

"Stern-daughter-of-the-voice-of-God," rattled off Dorothea.

"And does not . . . *that Voice* . . . tell you to help your Papa?"

"Certainly not. It tells me that I could, and should, be better employed."

"But . . . is it for us to decide what it tells us?"

"Who can, if we do not?"

"Our duty . . . what it is . . . has been settled for us by older people . . . they teach it to us. Our spiritual pastors and masters."

"They can guide us," agreed Dorothea. "We should consult them, if we are in any doubt. But they cannot be The Voice of God to us. Here . . . and here"—she struck her forehead and her breast—"I feel a command telling me not to waste my life on useless labours. If Papa were very ill, I would nurse him. But to spend my days copying passages from books, at which he is never likely to look. . . . Do you know poor Mary has filled a whole shelf of these note-books, which will serve no purpose whatever——"

There was a tap at the door. Mary came in.

Effie sprang to her feet. The two girls stood gazing at Mary, with wonder, with enquiry, with a sharp sense of grief. This entry carried them back to an earlier Mary, standing before them as now, the long hair falling on her shoulders, but with a vanished ecstacy in her eyes. The same, and yet not the same. They were not losing her on the morrow; they had lost her long ago.

Together they ran to her, clasped her in their arms, kissed her, fondled her and cried over her.

"Now, now," she said at last, gently pushing them away. "That is enough. There is nothing to cry for, you know. Thea dearest, will you come with me to my room for a moment?"

Left alone, Effie burst into fresh sobs. These subsided

when she remembered that *his* bridesmaids were never allowed to cry. One should not, she reflected, cry over the past when the future is bound to be so much pleasanter.

She finished her curls and took up Dorothea's diary again. Very little of it was intelligible. G: continually cropped up, like an importunate visitor. Were Selina ever to get hold of this record she could scarcely discover Thea's secret. She might wonder who G: could be, but she would never guess that he was a book, although *escaped to the playhouse and to G:* might furnish a clue. To be writing so much at night could not be good for anybody. Even Thea allowed that her nights with G: were exhausting. *G.'s villa in Naples. Four great magnolias in the Cortile.* Was that a detail she had managed to get out of Grant?

Near the end came an entry describing her own arrival.

> Effie came. I met her in the trap. She does not know when Bruno died. I think she expects to meet him. No grave, then, in her soul. Bob came. I gave him 3 or 4 things to read. He says no woman can write poetry. . . .

Then came a line in Greek which annoyed Effie. She asked what it meant, when Dorothea came back.

"That? It means: *But I sleep alone. Ego de mona katheudo.*"

"Why have you written it there?"

"Because Bob says women can't write poetry."

"Who wrote it?"

"Sappho."

"She was a woman, surely?"

A large tear rolled down Dorothea's cheek and

splashed onto the page as she leaned over Effie's shoulder. She gave a squeak of dismay and then chuckled.

"Oh Effie! Look! A tear-stained page. One reads about them but I could never believe it; I could not see why people should not blow their noses. I think I shall draw a little ring round it and label it: *Tear!* Oh dear . . . I believe it won't show when it's dry. What lies people tell!"

"My dear, you are overexcited. We must stop talking and go to sleep. We shall want to be in looks tomorrow. Parting with Mary has distressed you."

"You are quite right. Only, the worst of it is . . . I have just given her a promise . . . I could not refuse . . . but it will be very hard to keep. Ah well! What's done cannot be undone. I must say my prayers and go to bed. Where is my Bible? Oh where is it? Why do things never stay where they are put. Effie! Where is my scoundrelly Bible? I believe it has legs. I believe it walks. Bible? Bible? . . ."

"Here it is, under your stocking basket."

5

Mid sunlit scenes, serenely fair,
Mid calm and blissful hours,
  Oh may they bless that Father's care
Which strews their path with flowers.

Two people in Bramstock church sang this verse with unmixed satisfaction: Mr. Winthorpe, who had written it, and Mr. Harding, who thought that five thousand pounds were pretty good evidence of a father's care, although he had meant to give Mary ten.

If on a bleak and barren strand
Their shivering bark is driven:
  Oh may they bless that guiding Hand
Which shows the path to Heaven.

The metaphor of the shivering sail clouded Mr. Harding's spirits a trifle, for it reminded him of something unpleasant said to him by his solicitor, not very long ago. *Complete shipwreck!* It had something to do with Mary's marriage settlement; for some reason the ten thousand apiece, which he had always meant to give the girls, was not there any more, because all the money from the sale of the West Indies property had been given to the Jews.

The road to Eternal Life. A-a-men!

Mary and Grant were already kneeling. Mr. Winthorpe raised a priestly hand. The congregation sank to its knees. Gerald Grimshaw looked ruefully about for a hassock, found none, and lowered himself onto the stone floor. Only Effie and Dorothea remained upright above a sea of bowed heads and flowery bonnets.

"The Lord bless you and keep you . . ."

A man kneeling, thought Effie, melts my heart. They are so much stronger and cleverer and wiser than we. To see them kneel and bow their red heads . . . I am sure that he is very good and religious. *May I call when next I come to Hertfordshire?* Will Mama like him? I hope he will not, at first, make too many jokes. She might not think him steady enough.

Bob is only down on one knee, thought Henry, who had got onto both. Barristers . . . loose thinking . . . worldly cares . . . fears for the future. Sufficient unto the day! Tomorrow we can safely leave to Him. In ten years' time, Dr. Cadbury might be offered a bishopric. And I might be called upon to undertake the heavy responsibility of a headmaster. I shall receive the necessary guidance when that time comes. And that is my attitude towards family cares, too.

The Hen, thought Bob, will be guided . . . to look after himself. Mary has been guided. I had better be guided myself. I never signed on in this shivering what d'ye call it. I was told to paddle my own . . . Oh Dammit! I should be praying. God . . . God help us all!

They were all struggling up again. Effie nudged the tranced Dorothea and they joined the general move into the vestry. There was much kissing and crying, which ended in laughter when Grant, to whom Mary was at last consigned, administered an abrupt peck on her cheek. Dorothea was startled out of her life at receiving a salute from Mr. Winthorpe. Effie's cheeks were as red as her roses. She had, for a moment, thought that the best man was going to . . . but he did not: he merely gave a queer grave little bow.

"Mary and Grant are going out now," she told him. "Listen! There is the wedding march. We must wait until they have got to the bottom of the church."

"And then we three will prance down, arm in arm."

"No indeed! Dorothea and I will follow them. You must slip round by the side aisle."

"Oh I say! I call that pretty hard lines. *Pum* pumpa-pum! When I get married I shall cry off Handel."

"How can you? One would not feel married without him. Come, Thea. We should go now, I think."

Effie twitched her cousin's bonnet strings and they set off. Young, demure, they rustled side by side between pews full of ladies and gentlemen and, nearer to the door, pews full of men and women, tenants, and the upper servants from Bramstock and Elkington.

The path from the church to the gate was strewn with rose petals, flung by Mary's Sunday School children. More men and women lined the way, people too humble and poor to be given a place in the church. There were bobbed curtseys, pulled forelocks and broad smiles on every side. They looked with unenvious pleasure at the lace on Miss Mary's bonnet, which had cost more than

121

many of them earned in a year. They raised a cheer when the pretty young ladies appeared.

"Did you notice a tall girl with very red cheeks?" asked Dorothea, as they drove off. "She was by the gate, staring at us as if we had been a vision. She is Molly Shaftoe. The scullery maid at the parsonage."

"Is she? Oh Thea! Was it not a pretty wedding?"

"I expect so. We could have judged better if we had not been in it. I still wish that we could have worn green ribbons."

"Oh no. Green is not the thing. No lady wears green."

"And why not pray? Nobody will tell me. I believe it once meant something improper, but everyone has forgotten what it was. Bob snapped my head off, once, for singing *My Lady Greensleeves*. It is not a drawing room song."

"What a mercy that Katy had to be taken out before it began."

"Was that so?"

"Oh yes. How my heart sank when I saw Mrs. Philip arriving with Katy in that horrid little pork pie affair. The very last hat for poor Katy. But what a sweet hymn! How clever Mr. Winthorpe must be. And oh Thea . . . how you jumped when he kissed you. As if he had bitten you."

"I was so much startled. He can't have known what he was doing, poor man. It was most unpleasant. Oh Effie, I wish you were not going tomorrow. We could talk it over so much better when I am less distracted. And here we are!"

As the carriage drew up in front of the house Mrs. Ames, the housekeeper, ran out with a face of woe. She and the other servants had taken the short cut through the woods and arrived before the carriages.

"Oh Miss, oh Miss! The buffitt! Mis Katy . . . that nurse let her in there, and she tugged at the cloth and had everything over. The cake! The cake! Oh what is to be done?"

"Good heavens! I can't think. Ask Miss Mary."

"Mrs. Forrester," said the housekeeper in reproving tones, "is in the drawing room. I said to Griggs, 'What's to be done?' He said, Better ask Miss Harding. That means *you* now, Miss."

6

Upon the day after the wedding Bob departed on a visit in Devonshire, returning to Bramstock for a night only, on his way back to London.

He found the house empty of its guests. Philip, enjoying a spry spell, sat out in the garden with Selina in attendance. Mr. Harding and Dorothea were shut up in the library and did not appear until dinner.

It was an uncomfortable meal. Mr. Harding was in so violent a rage that every remark provoked a rebuke, every incident an explosion. After growling over the fish he sent the veal back into the kitchen, and accused Dorothea of giving them nothing fit to eat. Bob saw nothing wrong with the veal, but did not venture to say so. He was glad to see that Dorothea did not take it much to heart. She opened her eyes very wide, looked shocked, and murmured in a deprecating way, but she did not change colour, which she would have done, had she been genuinely agitated. Selina, smugly silent, looked uncommonly like a cat with a saucer of cream.

When the ladies had departed, Bob settled himself to

hear what had gone amiss. His father had a strange habit when displeased: he would chew upon some imaginary morsel which tasted very nasty. Now, over his port, he was chewing away furiously and making faces of disgust. At last he said, "That girl's an idiot. She can't copy the simplest passage without making a dozen mistakes. She takes half a day to look up a reference."

Bob looked, and was, astonished to hear this.

"Not a patch on Mary. I used to think her the brighter of the two. Upon my soul, if I'd known what I was letting myself in for, I'd have shown Grant the door."

"Thea is new to it, sir. She will improve."

"She'd better."

"It is only a week . . ."

"I know. I know. If I thought she was making an effort I should try to have patience. But I believe she does it on purpose. No open insubordination, mind you. Perfectly docile. Perfectly civil. No sulky looks. Yes Papa! No Papa! But . . . I'll tell you what it is, Bob. If she won't do better than this I shall . . ."

The chewing beard undulated wildly. You will do such things, thought Bob watching it, you know not what they are. . . .

"I shall give the keys to Selina."

At this terrible threat Bob had some difficulty in keeping a straight face. Thea, he was sure, cared nothing for the keys.

"I don't think Miss Thea will relish that. She is at present mistress of my house, as Mary was. I never would put Mary under orders to that silly woman. She deserved better."

"But will Selina ever have time for it?" ventured Bob.

"She will give the orders. Thea will obey them. She likes her liberty y'know, Bob. I don't think she'll get much, with Selina in the saddle. No! I don't think so. Hang it, she's had plenty. Mary did it all. It is no odds to me which of 'em does it. But now that Mary is gone, Thea must buckle to or suffer for it. I shall give her another week's grace. Then, if she don't improve . . ."

Round and round went the beard. Bob could not believe that Thea's secretarial powers were really inferior to Mary's. She must be swinging the lead deliberately, hoping, perhaps, to annoy her father into making other arrangements. She must be warned of the horrible fate in store for her, should she fail to come to heel. Under Selina's orders she would have but a dog's life of it; the unusual liberty which she had hitherto enjoyed would only increase her sufferings.

Thea must be lectured for her good. After dinner Bob went in search of her. Since she was nowhere in the house he thought that she must have fled to her refuge by the river. She had promised Mary never to go there at night, but she might consider that the day lasted until sunset. He set off through the woods wondering how long it might be since he last set foot in the old playhouse, which had been originally built as a swanherd's cottage, on a bank between the river and the trees.

Twenty years ago he, Henry and Charles had regarded it as their private domain, a place for their toy boats and fishing rods. Later, when all the boys were at school, the little girls took it over; their brothers, affronted, called it the Dolls' House. But Mary and Dorothea were not fond of dolls; they too kept fishing rods there until Miss Fothergill declared that they were too old for splashing and wading. After that the cottage fell into disuse until Dorothea staked a claim in it.

Bob walked in without knocking, upon which Dorothea started up from a table where she was writing and asked if anything had happened.

"An't you glad to see me?" said Bob. "I thought I'd come and see what you are up to, down here."

He looked round curiously at a chair or two, a bare deal table, an old truckle bed, some book shelves, and a shabby collection of cupboards and boxes. It was a curiously workmanlike little place, furnished and arranged for a purpose. Had he not known better he would have supposed it a man's room.

"Your boudoir?" he said, laughing a little.

She stood in front of the table as though defending her property. He saw a sheet of paper lying there and picked it up.

"What's this? More verses?"

"Oh pray leave it, Bob! That is not to be shown to anybody."

"No, no! You must not run away from criticism."

He took it to the door so as to catch the last of the light. *First Love*. Aha! No wonder she was coy. This broke new ground. Mary's marriage must have struck a chord in the maiden bosom.

In the room behind, he could hear her hastily putting other papers away. One incomprehensible stanza followed another. He could make no sense of any of them save the two last. These shocked him considerably.

> A ghost stands o'er the bridal bed
> Of every wedded maid.

And, like a wail above the dead,
It cries: I was betrayed.

Her broken vows, her ravished truth,
Lie in the grave with me.
I was the first love of her youth,
And my creator she.

Bob's eyebrows nearly met his hair. What business had any sister of his to be writing so glibly about bridal beds? And *ravished!* She could not have known what the word meant.

"I say, old girl," he said, going back into the hut, "you are coming it a bit strong. If I were you I'd tear this up."

"It was not meant for anyone to see."

"I should hope not. And one line is lifted from Byron: *Like a wail above the dead.* You can't do that, you know."

"I shall change it when I have thought of a better line."

Despite his displeasure he could not help laughing. "Better than Byron's?"

"Better for my purpose."

"I should think twice about my purpose if I were you, Thea."

He tore up the poem and threw it into a wastepaper basket. Then, sitting down, he looked at her severely.

"I've come here," he said, "to read you a lecture."

She heard him in silence, but when he warned her of the threat in store she grew very pale, leaning at last against the table for support.

"So really now," he finished, "don't you think you'd better come to heel? I only say this for your good."

"Yes, Bob. I know that you do."

"Climb down. Try to please Papa."

The hut was growing dark. A wind had sprung up at sunset and the reeds at the door rattled drearily.

"I could," she said thoughtfully, "refuse to obey Selina."

"You will never be such a fool."

"I would rather die, I think, than live a slave all my life. I have often thought that I could never endure Effie's life—not a moment unsupervised, every thought dictated to her. But her Mama does love her. You know that Selina hates me. Would you bear such a thing, Bob? Could you bear it for a moment?"

"My dear girl, it's not the same for women as men. Consider! We keep you. We feed you and clothe you and fend for you. We shelter you. Is it not fair to expect your obedience?"

"No. We could support ourselves, if we were given the opportunity; if the professions were open to us. Cottage women, servants, do so. They have more freedom than we have, I think, and more self respect, even though their husbands beat them. It is only ladies . . . you keep us, yes! As you might keep animals. Should you like to be a woman, Bob?"

"No," admitted Bob, getting up. "But we can't change these things. That's all I've come to say. If you know what side your bread is buttered you'll keep in with Papa. Think it over, Thea. And don't stay down here too late."

"I'm coming now. I promised Mary not to stay after sunset."

She came with him to the door and then turned to

look back at her little house, as though saying farewell to it.

"This won't last long," said Bob. "You'll marry."

"No," she said, and added very low: "Never, never."

She locked the door and followed him, out of the rosy sunset into the dark wood. Pad, pad went their footsteps. She kept turning to look behind her and once she gave a low exclamation.

"What is it?" he asked.

"I thought somebody was coming behind us."

"There is nobody. I can see the whole length of the wood."

He took her hand. It was burning and her voice was feverish. Drawing her arm through his, he forced her back to the house, where he summoned Mrs. Ames, to whom he consigned the trembling girl.

"I think she has caught a feverish chill," he said. "Put her to bed. Give her something . . . you will know what."

Dusk, with night on its heels, was closing on Bramstock. The empty rooms daunted him by their silence, nor did he want to rejoin his father. He went out and stood for a while in the drive, watching the night fall, watching the flickering bats, hearing their faint squeaks.

A melancholy place, he thought. I don't care for it now.

Off tomorrow.

A soft-hearted man never gets anywhere in this world.

7

Mrs. Winthorpe met her son at the rectory gate, on his return from a visit to an upland cottage.

"Oh my dear boy! You must go at once to Bramstock. A message came . . . they are in frightful trouble. Mrs. Philip is dying."

"Good God!"

"A miscarriage last night. They have sent to Exeter for Dr. Nichols. I am afraid it is very bad."

"Poor thing! Poor thing! I will go at once."

He took a step or two and then turned, exclaiming, "If it is as bad as that, perhaps . . ."

"I have it ready in the hall. Betty! Betty!"

"Did she send the message? I mean . . . Dorothea?"

"I don't know. The knife boy brought it. He was very incoherent; you know how those people are. 'You must please to come!'"

A maid ran out of the house with the bag which accompanied Winthorpe in his visits to the dying.

"Thank you, Betty. Well, Mama, don't wait dinner for me. If I am not back you may take it that I am getting something there."

"If I can be of any use, mind you send for me."

He hurried off, taking the short cut through the woods.

The house bore a strange air of calamity. The front door stood wide open and there were wheel marks in the gravel of the drive, which would normally have been raked over.

Oh! It seemed to cry. Oh! Oh!

Nobody appeared to answer the bell until Pip came slowly down the stairs, planting both feet on each step and staring steadily at the visitor.

"What have you got in that bag?" he demanded.

"I hear that your poor Mama is ill," began Winthorpe.

"You never saw nothink like it," agreed Pip, nodding violently. "Nothink but a shambles, poor dear. Enough to turn a person's stummick. And now she's a dead corpse."

"Oh, my poor little man!"

"Aunt Thea did it."

"What?"

"Made Ma ill. Weren't she wicked? An' she locked Katy up in a cupboard."

"Where is your Grandpapa?"

"In the liberry. What have you got in that bag? Is it something for me?"

Winthorpe put his bag down, knelt, and took the child in his arms.

"Your dear Mama," he said gently, "has gone away to a beautiful place where she will be very happy."

"No she ain't then. She's in bed upstairs. I seen her."

"It seems so. She has . . . has gone to sleep. Presently they will take her away. We shall never see her again. But she will see us. She will know, when you are a good boy, and that will make her very happy."

Pip stared at him fascinated and asked, "Why'nt you got hair in your nose like Ganpa?"

"Where is your nurse?"

"Feeding Ma chicking broff wiv a spoon."

"What?"

"Chicking broff. Ma said she fancied chicking broff."

"Then your Mama is not . . ."

Winthorpe rose from his knees.

"What have you got in that bag?"

"Nothing for little boys. No! Pip! Put it down! Naughty boy. Give it back directly. Do you hear me, sir?"

The library door opened, and Mr. Harding emerged with two doctors. Winthorpe, chasing Pip, bumped into them, but managed to secure his property before Pip dashed out of the house yelling, "Garn!"

"Bless my soul!" exclaimed Mr. Harding.

He burst into a guffaw. The doctors looked at their boots until he could control himself enough to introduce them. It appeared that Selina was out of danger, although they had been much alarmed during the night. A trap was brought round for the local man, a carriage and pair for Dr. Nichols of Exeter.

"Has Mary been sent for?" asked Winthorpe, following Mr. Harding back into the library.

"We sent for her last night but she has not come yet," grumbled Mr. Harding. "I can't think what is keeping her."

"Can I be of any assistance?"

"Why yes, if you would go up to Philip. He has nobody to attend to him till Mary gets here; he refuses to see Dorothea. Try to get him to brace up a little. He's not the only person in this house who has had a disturbed night."

"Is . . . Pip said something . . . as though Dorothea . . ."

"Entirely her fault, the whole thing," said Mr. Harding cheerfully. "Can you find your way up, or shall I ring for . . . ?"

"Thank you. I know the way."

Winthorpe set off for Philip's room with the alert air of a hunter who sights his quarry from afar.

"My dear fellow," he cried, advancing upon the supine Philip, "what a shocking trial you have had! Words fail me. But we must thank God that things are no worse. When we think of what might have been, we may well lift up our hearts."

"They are bad enough," replied Philip despondently. "Selina has lost her child. And God knows what harm may not have been done to Katy."

"What happened? I have not heard."

"Selina went into Beremouth yesterday. She does not often go; she does not like to leave me, you know. She put Katy in Dorothea's charge. The nurse and Pip were going to Beremouth too. When they returned Katy was missing. Dorothea's story is that she thought Katy was playing in the conservatory, but she has admitted that for some time she forgot all about her. We searched the house. We searched the garden. My wife . . . you can imagine! She was beside herself. Personally I was convinced the child was in the river, and said so. But at last we heard one of the servants screaming on the attic floor. There is a cupboard in one of the large empty attics. It is easy to overlook, for the door is papered like the walls. By heaven's mercy this woman remembered it. Katy was there, lying on the floor. The whole household rushed up. The shock was too much for Selina. The screams. Katy's screams were frightful. An hour later we were in despair for Selina's life."

Philip sat up and his voice became quite lively. Illness was, for him, an animating topic. He proceeded to give a detailed account of Selina's alarming symptoms.

"Should you not like me to open the window," suggested Winthorpe, who began to feel slightly faint. "It is very close."

"Thank you, I always keep it shut. I am obliged to avoid draughts. We then applied ice; luckily there's a good supply in the ice-house."

"Ah! Who thought of doing that?"

"I don't know. But it proved to be the right thing. Might I trouble you to ring the bell? I think they must have forgotten my egg-nog. I always have it at this time. Dorothea sees to it. But I do not think that I can ever speak to her again, when I think of the harm she has done. My poor Selina! Our ruined hopes! And above all, her cruelty to helpless, innocent little Katy. To lock her up in that dark cupboard. Alone. For hours. It is enough to unsettle the child's reason."

"Locked? Was the door locked?"

"Ah . . . no. I believe that door does not lock. But it cannot be opened from inside, once it is pushed to."

"Might not Katy have done that herself . . . pulled it to?"

"Possibly. But how did she get up there alone? There must have been great neglect. I can never forgive . . . Ah! Come in."

It was Mrs. Ames with Philip's egg-nog. She curtsied to Winthorpe, who condoled with her upon the trials of the night.

"Dreadful, sir, it was," she agreed. "Such another night I never hope to pass again. Not one of us knew what to do. Helpless as new born babes. If Miss Dorothea had not brought the ice and showed us how to make packs, this would be a house of mourning today."

"We must thank God for His great mercy, Mrs. Ames."

"We must indeed, sir."

When she had curtsied herself out, Winthorpe turned upon Philip a smile for which he was well known in Bramstock. Some people thought it singularly sweet. Others did not. Philip had never much liked it until this morning; he now felt that it suggested some compromise whereby Dorothea might still attend to his egg-nog yet remain in disgrace. Nor was he disappointed.

"I think that you will forgive poor Dorothea. I think so."

"Never. I could not."

"It is very natural in you to feel so, at the moment. But God has been merciful to you. Out of gratitude to Him you will have mercy on her. If she is truly repentant——"

"Oh I daresay she is sorry. But that won't mend——"

"This may be a turning point in your sister's life. We have all been concerned over her lately, have we not? As her pastor I have been praying for her. There has been so much pride, such obstinate independence, resistance to God's will, defiance of authority, determination to ignore the duties to which she has been called. It has been griev-ous to all who know her. But now . . . she must face the truth. To what has it led?"

136

"It is far worse for us than for her."

"True. Yet if you take her by the hand, it may mean the dawning of better things—a humble and contrite heart. She can never atone, of course. Never make amends. There can be no question of that. But if she is willing to do everything in her power to prove her penitence, then, as a Christian and a brother, you should forgive her."

"If she were to promise, in future, to behave as she ought . . ."

"She will. She will. I will talk to her," said Winthorpe, with decided relish. "And if I bring her to you as a suppliant, you will not turn away? I'm sure you will not."

"I could try. But I can't answer for Selina."

"Oh your wife will be guided by you."

Philip agreed with this, but urged Winthorpe not to mince his words. Time alone would show what harm had been done to Katy.

"I shall not mince my words," promised Winthorpe. "I will see her before I leave the house. Good-bye and God bless you. He will bless you for this day's work."

Winthorpe left Philip in a softened mood, since the egg-nog was now in little danger, and returned to Mr. Harding who was taking a nap in the library. The offer to rebuke Dorothea was accepted with enthusiasm.

"By all means," said the Squire, tugging at the bell, "give it to her, Winthorpe. Somebody must put the fear of God into that girl. She is too much for me. As a secretary she is worse than useless. I am thinking of hiring some youngster . . . you don't know of one I suppose? He should have a thorough classical . . . Oh Griggs! Tell Miss Dorothea that Mr. Winthorpe wants to speak to her— Where will you do it, Winthorpe? The drawing room, eh?

So be it—Mr. Winthorpe wants to speak to her in the drawing room."

Griggs withdrew, sent a maid to summon Dorothea, and informed Mrs. Ames that Parson was about to give Miss Thea what Paddy gave the drum. Opinion, in the servants' hall, was strongly upon Dorothea's side; had she murdered Katy they would not have blamed her much.

"What should I pay the fellow?" asked Mr. Harding. "Have some port. The decanter is over there."

"Thank you," said Winthorpe, helping himself. "I hardly know. I suppose you would be thinking of an elderly man?"

"Lord no. I thought some youngster just down from College."

"Would that be quite the thing, in this household?"

"Eh? Why not?"

"Mrs. Philip Harding is so much occupied . . . and her health, for some time to come . . . she could scarcely act as chaperon . . . the two young people would inevitably be thrown together. At the best there might be unpleasant talk . . . a wrong construction. . . ."

"Oh I take your point. Sheeps' eyes at Thea, eh? That would never do. Better get some old fellow with no teeth, eh?"

They sipped their port and discussed the matter. Dorothea would be by now waiting in the drawing room. To wait for some time would do her no harm. The days were over when she could coolly command an ordained priest to jump up. They chatted until a note was brought in from Elkington.

"Mary!" cried Mr. Harding. "But why don't she come?" His face darkened as he scanned the few lines.

"Unable to leave home . . . friends expected . . . Home! Is not this her home? Upon my word, there's sympathy for you. Why! I expected her here last night, as soon as she had my message."

"She has other duties now," murmured Winthorpe. "With your permission, I think I will go to Dorothea."

"Oh, ay, I'd forgotten her. I'm sure we shall all be grateful if you can bring her to her senses. I remember you tackled Mary once when she had a fit of the whim-whams." Mr. Harding's face darkened as he glanced again at Mary's note. He muttered, "Daughters! I don't know what the world is coming to. If a man can't depend on his daughters . . ."

In the hall Winthorpe paused for a moment, endeavouring to master emotions which threatened to become too intense.

A great moment was at hand, and one for which he had long waited. No member of his flock had caused him more disturbance than Dorothea. He was always thinking of her. Since she was in danger of becoming a lost sheep, it was his duty to think of her. But she had a trick of invading his mind whenever he tried to think of anything else. Her youth, her beauty, her grace, distracted him, and his bitterest grievance arose from the knowledge that this was not by her own wish, that she was unconscious of it. She inspired sensations which he could not feel to be entirely pure, and affronted him by her innocence. The desire to crush her, subdue her, see her at his feet, filled him with guilt which would have been far less oppressive could he have believed her guilty too, a temptress, and conscious of her power over him. This untamed virginity which maddened him, was not, he felt, admirable or holy.

True virtue, in a woman, had nothing to do with such heathen wildness; it implied submission and acknowledged a master. Dorothea must submit or be lost.

If I am too harsh, he thought, that may harden her heart. She will feel it more if I am gentle. Yet she must suffer. I must see to it that she does.

The confusion of his feelings was so great as almost to deafen and blind him when, at last, he went into the drawing room. He did not see her at first, and knew only that the room, on this warm day, was fearfully cold. That chill he recognised; he had often felt it, in a lesser degree, when ushered into the presence of the dead.

No coffin was there. She stood by the fireplace, looking at him as the dead might look, no longer needing help and deaf to exhortation. He might have been a chair or a table in this unreal room, so icy, so full of sunshine. Everything that he had meant to say deserted him. Tears or defiance he might have met with words. Before that look he stood speechless, halfway down the room, unable to advance. It was she who spoke first.

"You wish to tell me something, Mr. Winthorpe?"

"I . . . I . . ." he muttered, "I am . . . I have a message. From Philip. You must not . . . he forgives you . . . he knows that you never . . ."

This was not how he had intended to open the interview. Philip's magnanimity should have been announced at the end, and only after many tears. Nor did she seem to understand it.

She broke in with, "But Selina? You have come to tell me that she is . . . dead?"

"Oh . . . no . . . no!"

Again he broke into unpremeditated reassurances.

"Oh thank God!" she exclaimed. "Nobody would tell me. Nobody seemed to know. Last night I thought that she must die."

Remembering how faint he felt at Philip's description of last night's commotion, Winthorpe could well believe it. For so inexperienced a girl it must have been terrifying, although she had kept her head enough to think of the ice. They might have told her that all danger was over, he thought, and had to remind himself that she did not deserve such consideration. It was probably better for her to be left in suspense.

"I never knew she was going to have a child."

In this could be detected some trace of self excuse and he revived a little, was more sure of his ground, could speak in a more normal voice.

"Ah Dorothea, would that trouble you now if you had a clear conscience? He who is faithful in little things may sometimes find that his charge has been greater than he supposed. You knew that you were betraying your trust and doing wrong. *How* wrong, *how* important a trust, you did not know. Doubtless, had you known, you would have acted differently. And now, when all the terrible consequences are before you, there is this bitter, bitter thought: If I had only known! That need not have been so, had you tried to do as you ought, and you must not regard it as an excuse."

"You misunderstand me. I meant . . . I am so ignorant . . . I know so little about these things . . . will she recover completely? Is that possible?"

"We must pray that she will. And that you may fully understand your fault."

"Oh I know that it was my fault. She told me to take

care of Katy and I did not refuse. I had grown so tired of refusing. I said nothing. That might have implied consent. Had I said: No! She would have made other arrangements. I must accept the blame."

The misery in her voice again shattered his resolution.

"God's mercy," he said, with a softened voice, "is infinite. He loves you, Thea, and He forgives you. He wants your soul. All this may have been His way of bringing you to Himself. He has taught you a terrible lesson, after which you can no longer be blind yourself to the hideousness of self will."

"I cannot believe that He killed poor Selina's little baby to save my soul. That would be so very unjust."

"Dorothea! What? Still resisting His will? Still questioning His ways?"

The reproof made no impression on her. She said anxiously, "I am so very ignorant. Would it already have a soul? Could it go to Heaven? Or is its soul still in the palace?"

"What palace?"

"In that Imperial palace whence we came."

She quoted the line so confidently that his ire rose again. To speak of such things was his province, not hers.

"It is wrong," he said sternly, "to speculate upon matters which are hidden from us. You would do better to consider your own conduct, to ask yourself how this terrible thing came about. I need not dwell upon the consequences. Their full gravity may not be clear for some time; it may be long before we can be sure that no lasting harm has come to poor little Katy. It might have been enough to destroy her reason. Think of it, Dorothea, left alone, in the dark, for hours, screaming with terror——"

142

"Oh, no, no! Indeed I hope it was not as bad as that. She may not have been so very much frightened. She was asleep, you know, when Ellen found her. She has a way of wandering off and going to sleep in some odd corner. . . ."

"I have been told that her screams were fearful."

"They always are, on any occasion. She did not begin, I gather, until she woke up and found everybody else screaming."

"We must hope for the best. Time will show. But how did it ever happen, Dorothea? This is not an isolated instance. Pride and self will were the cause. This determination to go your own way, to ignore your duty, has led you into wrong doing for which a life-time of repentance and humble submission can scarcely atone. If this had not happened you would have continued as before. Do you mean to change your ways or do you not?"

"Oh I see that I have been wrong. Ever since Mary's marriage I have been coming to see how selfish I was to her, as I understood better what she must have endured. I ought to have helped her more, and then perhaps she would not have married at all. And now . . . nothing that I valued could signify as compared to . . . to a child that should have been born . . . Katy's safety. . . ."

"You see that? If you do, it is the beginning of true repentance. My dear child, this makes me very happy."

Her puzzled look seemed to ask what his happiness had to do with it. There was a certain intransigence, even in her manner of acknowledging herself in the wrong. He pressed his point home.

"Nothing that you value?" he said softly. "And what is it that you value, even above God? I think I know."

That startled her. That got under her guard.

"Your writing, is it not? You have persuaded yourself that your verses are of great importance? Nothing must be allowed to take the place of them?"

"How did you know that?"

"Perhaps I know more about you than you think. Believe me, Dorothea, you will show true repentance by giving it up. That must be your sacrifice. You will never live as you ought, until you do."

She nodded and said after a while, "That is so. One cannot serve two masters."

"And what Master will you now serve?"

"Oh, I must try to do everything I can for poor Selina and little Katy. I must try. One can't do two things at once."

This was not quite the submission envisaged by Winthorpe. She was by no means completely subdued. She sought guidance from no man and was still governed by the dictates of her own lawless heart. But he found himself so much exhausted that he decided to leave it for the present. The contest could be resumed upon some other occasion. She had been driven from her fortress and was fighting a losing battle.

"That's a good girl," he began, but his voice was drowned by the sound of an enormous gong in the hall outside. He had to wait for silence before he could proceed. "Let me now take you to Philip. I should like to see my task of reconciliation completed before I leave the house. When you tell him what you have told me, I know that he will forgive you as a brother should."

"It would not do now," said Dorothea. "That was the

dressing gong and he likes to rest, completely undisturbed, for half an hour before meals."

There was a pause. Winthorpe would have liked to go
up to her, touch her, take her hand. But he did not know
how to manage it or to rebut the suggestion that he had
been dismissed.

8

A postal packet was delivered to Effie a few days later. It came upon a morning when she was full of happy agitation. Gerald Grimshaw had duly paid his call, in the course of his return journey to Cumberland, and now he was again in Hertfordshire. She knew that he had arrived, on the preceding night, to spend some weeks with his friends at St. Albans. She was sure, almost sure, that he had come back so soon on her account. Should he call that morning, seizing the very first opportunity, she might be quite sure.

He had managed, already, to make a most favourable impression on her mother; his air of steadiness had been almost tedious, although a look in his eye raised Effie's spirits, when he praised the cabbages in her Berlin work and had to be told that they were roses. His friends at St. Albans, a most respectable family, had subsequently called upon the Creightons. To Effie's surprise, her mother had accepted their acquaintance, in spite of a maxim that old friends are better than new ones, which had sadly constricted Effie's social circle. Although obliged to practise a certain amount of duplicity, Effie was, in some ways, unusually artless. She felt needless relief at her mother's readiness to hear more, from these people, about Mr. Grimshaw, his steadiness, his settled opinions, the respect in which his family was held, the value of his estate, and the satisfactory marriages made by both his sisters. It was, she thought, an inexplicable piece of luck.

When she got up that morning she put on her new poplin, took it off, and put it on again, resolved to risk enquiry and comment. None came. Mrs. Creighton herself showed signs of suspense and preoccupation. She did not immediately subside in her chair after breakfast, but walked about, straightening a picture that was not really crooked, and rearranging the books on the side table. It was some time before they were both settled with their needlework, waiting with unspoken anxiety, for a knock.

Rat-a-tat!

It was he! At the earliest possible moment. This must mean . . .

A maid brought in a parcel. It had merely been the postman. Tears started to Effie's eyes.

"For you," said Mrs. Creighton, handing the parcel to Effie, after she had examined it. "Dorothea's hand I think. Take it upstairs. Parcels lying about in the parlour look so . . ."

Effie disconsolately took it up to her room and then decided to stay there as long as she dared. To sit quite placidly under her mother's eye, concealing her feelings, was almost impossible. If he never came she might cry. If he did come she might blush. To wait upstairs would be simpler; she could be tripping down, as if by accident, as he came into the hall. Nobody save Hanson could then observe their greeting, and Hanson would look the other way. They could go into the parlour together.

In order to pass the time she unpacked the parcel. It contained a long letter and a manuscript, both in Dorothea's boyish handwriting. One glance at the latter told her what it was, even before she had turned a page or two. *Four magnolias in the cortile.* Thea's story. Finished? Surely not. A full three volume novel would make a much larger parcel.

She turned to the letter for enlightenment, half listening for sounds of arrival below, half enthralled by these dramatic events.

Selina . . . miscarriage! I thought as much. But one is not supposed to have eyes. *Katy . . . cupboard . . . entirely my fault. . . .* Oh I am sure it was not. *May affect Katy for life. . . .* Oh Thea! Thea! How simple you are! Anything affecting Katy for life must do her good, for she could not be worse. *Neglected my duty . . .* What? Is Thea becoming good? No, no! That would be disastrous. Thea is so . . . so absolute. She would be too good for words. *Send you my novel since I promised to do so. Read it or not, as you please, and then burn it. Never speak of it to me again. I shall never write again. I have renounced all thoughts, all longings in that direction. . . . Mr. Winthorpe . . . the only amends I can make . . . atone to Selina. . . .* Oh dear! Oh dear! It puts one out of patience with goodness. Can she not see that Selina will only take advantage? Now they will saddle her with all the care of that revolting child! Oh it must be stopped. When I am . . . when I . . . if I have a house of my own she shall come and stay with us . . . me . . . for ever so long

. . . and we will find a very, very nice. . . . Is that a carriage in the road?

Mrs. Creighton must not see these documents. If the morning turned out as Effie still hoped, the parcel might be forgotten in excitement over other matters. Both manuscript and letter went to join the Clone papers, under the floorboard beside the fireplace. Sometime or other Effie meant to read poor Thea's story, but there was no hurry, since comment was not expected. At the moment other things were more pressing. The loose board was replaced and covered by the carpet. She went to her glass to pin up a curl.

I will read it later, she thought. And never read it, although in due course all the treasures under the floorboard went with her to another home, in the box which held her discarded dolls, her sampler, and a china figure of Queen Adelaide. So much was to happen, so soon, to erase this moment from her memory.

Rat-a-tat!

She darted from her room and peeped over the bannisters. Hanson was going to open the door.

It was! It was!

Light-heartedly, as though by purest chance, she was tripping down the stairs as Gerald Grimshaw entered the house.

PART III

The Stranger

Far, oh very far behind,
So far she cannot call to him. . . .

Kipling

1

"Hullo? Is that Bramstock?"

"Bramstock speaking."

"Message from Miss Lassiter for Mrs. Harding."

"Oh? Is that Mr. Collins? Good morning. This is Cecilia Harding speaking."

"Oh? Hullo, Miss Harding! You got home all right last night in that fog?"

"Yes thank you."

"Miss Lassiter would like to come and drink in atmosphere Thursday afternoon, if that's quite convenient. About three?"

"Oh I think so. Yes."

"And . . . I hate to tell you . . . Mr. Mundy wants to come along."

"We can't stop him."

"Also . . . a favour . . . have you got any of Dorothea's novels?"

"All of them, naturally. Why?"

"Could we borrow one? Miss Lassiter wants to have me read it."

"Which one?"

"It couldn't matter less. Just one."

"Take care not to overwork."

"Come again? Oh I see. Well, she didn't start writing them till years after our fadeout."

"Still I think it strange you never read a word she wrote."

"I'm sorry."

"I'm coming into Beremouth this morning. I'll leave your homework for you at The Queen's. Good-bye."

"Bye-bye."

The Bramstock telephone clicked. Roy hung up. He was speaking from a booth downstairs, as the chambermaid was busy in his bedroom. On his way up again he looked in on Adelaide to tell her that the Bramstock appointment was fixed. She was already at her typewriter, tapping furiously.

"I'm doing the big scene between Doda and Mr. Winthorpe," she told him. "The renunciation scene."

"But that's nearly at the end."

"I always write my big scenes first, and then do the in between bits."

Roy could never have tackled a job in this fashion. The between bits, in his own compositions, were infused with a mounting excitement, the sense of a climax ahead with which he might not have the rapture of dealing until he lawfully came to it.

"I can't decide where it should happen," she said.

"In the drawing room," he said quickly.

"The drawing room at Bramstock? Oh no! Not very likely. Why?"

"I only . . . I saw it yesterday. I want a shot there, a long shot right down the room, in some big scene."

"I thought perhaps it might be in Mr. Winthorpe's study, at the rectory."

"That means another set."

"In a picture that wouldn't matter."

"That's what you think. We're trying to keep production costs down to £250,000."

"How can it cost so much?"

"Easily. Think what we all pay down here."

"But that wasn't really necessary."

"I couldn't agree with you more."

"Anyway I use the study another time; when the four brothers suspect something wrong, and go to consult Mr. Winthorpe."

"Four? I thought there were only three. The invalid, and the soldier, and the lawyer."

"There was another one. Henry. A clergyman. He wasn't in the play, but I put him back in the script. Of course Charles, the soldier, will remain the most important brother at the wedding. But I thought four, tall distinguished men would be more impressive than three."

"I hope that's the lot. I get mixed up; I can't keep track of the family. Did she have any more tall, distinguished brothers?"

"I think not. You'd better have a look at the family tree Mr. Mundy gave me. I didn't need it, but he seems to think I did."

She fished in a drawer in her desk, while Roy pondered on his shot in the drawing room. He was determined to have it in his own script, as soon as Adelaide was out of the way. Nothing else interested him in *The Bramstock Story*.

"Here's the pedigree," said Adelaide, handing him a paper.

He looked it over, without much interest.

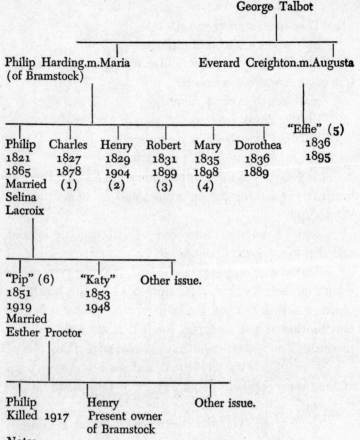

George Talbot

Philip Harding.m.Maria
(of Bramstock)

Everard Creighton.m.Augusta

Philip	Charles	Henry	Robert	Mary	Dorothea	"Effie" (5)
1821	1827	1829	1831	1835	1836	1836
1865	1878	1904	1899	1898	1889	1895
Married	(1)	(2)	(3)	(4)		
Selina						
Lacroix						

"Pip" (6)	"Katy"	Other issue.
1851	1853	
1919	1948	
Married		
Esther Proctor		

Philip	Henry	Other issue.
Killed 1917	Present owner	
	of Bramstock	

Notes

(1) Charles Harding became a Colonel in 1867. Died unmarried.
(2) Henry Harding became Headmaster of Coldingham in 1866 and ended up as a bishop. He married Sarah Cadbury, daughter of the great Bishop Cadbury. Had numerous issue.
(3) Robert Harding became a Lord of Appeal in 1881. He married Lady Julia Liston, daughter of Lord Crowne. Had issue.
(4) Mary Harding married (1) in 1856, Grant Forrester. No issue. He was killed in 1860. (2) Frederick Baines. Numerous issue.
(5) Effie Creighton married in 1856, Gerald Grimshaw. Had issue.
(6) "Pip" was the author of *D.H. A Memoir.* (1890.) Until my book appeared this was the only biography of Dorothea Harding.

156

The only date which interested Roy at all was that of Effie's birth, and this surprised him.

"Why," he said. "Effie wasn't such a kid at that. She was the same age as Dorothea. And . . . why . . . she got married the same year Mary did! . . . 1856."

"Oh, for pity's sake," said Adelaide, "don't you begin to make a fuss about dates. Mr. Mundy is bad enough. It isn't your job to worry. You're supposed to look after the shots."

"Too right," agreed Roy, giving the paper back.

This shot, upon which his heart was so much set, must have the girl at the end of the room, by the fireplace, and the man, his back to the camera, half way down the room. The great looking-glass, over the fireplace, should reflect his face during most of the dialogue: later shots would show the two of them—the girl with this face behind her, instead of in front of her. The effect of the reflection must be to make the audience know that they saw something which she did not. What secret was to be revealed upon Winthorpe's saintly old face, Roy had not yet considered. But he was more likely to get his way if he wrote this scene for Winthorpe rather than Grant.

He thought that he would ring up Issachar, who was designing the sets, and enlist his help. He would describe what he had seen in his mind's eye and get Issy to make a little sketch of it. Issy's sketches often provided visual arguments for a point which nobody would take if it was explained in words.

"What's Mundy's book say?" he asked suddenly. "About her and Winthorpe, I mean."

"I've forgotten. It's years since I read it; not since I used it as a basis for my play. I don't think it matters. Why?"

"I'd like to see what that diary says about it," he explained, searching round the room for the book.

Adelaide shrugged her shoulders and went on typing. He found the book but could not find the passage. After spelling his way helplessly through some of Mundy's views upon poetry he asked, "Where does it say about Winthorpe?"

"Oh what a bore you are," said Adelaide snatching the book. "You said you didn't hold with reading."

But she took a little time to find it herself, for she had long ago cut adrift from Mundy's facts and had only brought the book along with her in order to get his autograph in it.

"Here it is," she said at last. "It was the final entry in the diary. For more than a week she'd written nothing and then just this."

She handed it to him. He read:

I shall not need this diary any more. I have sent G: away. For ever. All that is over. Never again. Mr. Winthorpe is right. I have been very wicked. I have brought suffering upon others. To some I may atone. To Katy perhaps. But Mary—Never to Mary. God help me now to do what I ought.

Tappity-tappity-tap-tap . . . tap! went Adelaide's typewriter.

He put the book down and slipped out. He felt that his shot for Issy might be upset if he read any more.

Up in his room he switched on the fire and went across to look at the sands, of which he had a fine view from his window. The fog had cleared and the tide was out. Very few people were on the beach but already the sand was criss-crossed by many footprints. On the first morning after his arrival in Beremouth these tracks in the sand had started him off on an idea for a picture. He had looked out very early and seen a single track following the curve of the bay, as far as eye could see, in either direction. So you see this, he had thought, and what do you see next? Far away, coming, the *other one,* following . . . plodding round the bay. As he gets nearer you feel his terrible anxiety. He *must* catch the first one up.

Later, when this single track had been smudged by others, he could still detect it. But the pursuer, he decided, should be confused, and follow a wrong track, off into the sand dunes, although the beholder could see that the right one curved on by the sea.

Now, as he returned to the topic, he realised that these sands had got so strong a hold on him as to have invaded his dreams. All night he had been troubled by horrible dreams, a legacy, probably, of his fruitless drinking in the Lord Nelson. He could not recapture most of them, but he thought that Cecilia Harding had cropped up several times. There had been a kind of funeral. He sat with a lot of other people in chairs round the wall of a very dark room. In the centre was an open coffin on a bier. All sat rigid, unable to move hand or foot. A voice said: *Not yet!* But later he was looking into the coffin where she lay, dead, yet aware of him. Then he had been following the track on the sands which were now huge, the sea having withdrawn to an invisible horizon. Again it was very dark. He came to a great crack, a bottomless gulf, running right across this vast, darkling plain. Upon the far side an indistinct figure was wandering up and down. He called, Are you Cecilia? She would not answer, although he thought that she was weeping. The crack was too wide for a jump, but he knew that he must get across. That's why I've come, he told himself.

He was trying to shake off the memory of these nightmares when his telephone bell rang. A voice announced a personal call for Mr. Collins, from London, and then Mamie's greeting transported him to the bustling world of B.B.B.

"Mamie darling! How's tricks?"

"Harry Heemers," said Mamie, meaning, in their private argot, that tricks could scarcely be more bloody. "Just a minute. Mr. Fraser wants to speak to you."

There was a pause which alarmed Roy. The Script Supervisor was not a man to waste time on unnecessary conversation.

He liked and respected Hector Fraser as, indeed, did everybody in the Industry. The script department at B.B.B. was admirably run. No mercy was shown to fools, or to those who imagined that screen writing was easy money; they were out of the studios before they had time to warm the seats of their chairs. But, to those who deserved it, Fraser could be just, considerate and helpful.

At last his voice came through, asking how things went at Beremouth.

"Thought I better have a worrrd with you. Mr. Hobarrrt has read the play."

This was bad news. Mr. Hobart was the greatest man in B.B.B. He was full of enthusiasm over *The Bramstock Story* and had been responsible for signing up Mundy, sending the whole party down to Beremouth, and pledging Elmer to shoot exteriors on location. All good men hoped that this enthusiasm might soon abate.

"*Can* he read?" murmured Roy.

Fraser chose to ignore this.

"He's shocked."

"Well! Well!"

"He's worried about the censor. He was in airly this morning, and sent for me."

"The child is out, you know. Not mentioned."

"What child?"

"Her child, Katy."

"I never hairrd they had a child. That's not in the play."

"Mundy thinks so. Passed off as one of Selina's children."

"Deefficult to manage."

"Oh . . . crinolines. Mundy has it all cut and dried. She felt guilty about this kid and left it all her money."

"It's a mairrcy Mr. Hobart doesn't know. He's shocked enough as it is. He says there's to be no suggestion of anything wrong at all. The relations between Dorothea and Grant must be pairrfectly innocent. Mind, I'm only talking of the script."

"I get you. We can leave it to Miss Fletcher."

Fraser produced a series of dry hiccups which were his way of expressing mirth.

"Hck! Hck! Ye must watch the dialogue. Two sisters in love with the same man—yes! Two sisters sleeping with the same man—no! And there's to be no furniture at all in the hut where they meet."

"Sets aren't my job."

"No, but ye must have it in mind. They must speak all the dialogue standing up, puir things. No sprawling. Nothing to sit on, not even a wee campstool. Hck! Hck! I'm sorry, Roy. It's an awfu' nuisance, but Mr. Hobart's on the warpath. And I'm just not happy about the censor myself, not to mention a U Certificate."

"I know. It's too highbrow for a U Picture."

"I wouldn't just call it highbrow."

"No. But two sisters sleeping with the same man is more the sort of thing they pick on for a prestige picture. All right. I'll tell Adelaide to keep the dialogue clean, if she can."

"That's right. Good-bye."

"Bye-bye."

Roy sat down upon his bed and laughed until he choked.

He was beginning to feel rather sorry for the unfortunate actor playing Grant. According to Mundy, both the Miss Hardings had surrendered to this libertine, although Mary's seduction was not conclusively proved, since she wrote no poetry. In Adelaide's play the score was halved. Mary had merely fallen so desperately in love with him that her health and reason were threatened. Dorothea, fearing for her sister's life, had insisted on the marriage and then failed in her resolution to break with him herself. But in the picture the poor fellow would now have nothing at all to do save ride his horse. Through eight reels he must register sinister remorse over no crime in particular, and exhibit an overwhelming sex appeal by which no young woman had actually been overwhelmed.

This fit of laughter had a stimulating effect. Roy looked at his watch, saw that the morning was wearing on, and wondered when Cecilia would turn up with the promised book. If she came soon he would invite her to come out with him for a cup of coffee somewhere. Her

Book Tea conversation would soon drive those dreams out of his head.

He went again to the window to watch for the arrival of her tacky little car.

2

A storm was raging at Bramstock. Mr. Harding had received yet another letter from a kinsman, upbraiding him for lending countenance to this iniquitous picture. These had been pouring in ever since the first publicity paragraphs appeared in the newspapers. All Hardings had risen up in wrath, and so had many other people, claiming cousinship, who did not even call themselves Harding. Some merely abused him. Others demanded upon some flimsy pretext a share of the loot. Many offered to sell him letters, alleged to have been written by Dorothea to their forbears. Few appeared to understand that no such letters could be published without his permission, since he now owned all her copyrights, left to him by Katy.

Mrs. Harding merely scoffed at these expostulations. Having decided that £500 was extremely desirable, she was carrying off the situation with a high hand. She declared herself delighted and thrilled, would hear no arguments against the project, and scolded her husband and daughter for their lack of enterprise. In this attitude she had secured the support of her older children, the married daughter and the two sons. They were enthusiastic because Cecilia's career had been a little on their consciences. So much had been spent on them that nothing was left over for her, which was hard, since she had won a scholarship large enough to cover half the necessary expense. The size, on paper, of the Harding income disqualified her for a State Grant. It was the first time that Mr. Harding's overdraft, upon which they had all lived comfortably for years, proved insufficient for anything badly wanted. Everybody felt sorry for Cecilia, but nobody had been able to suggest a solution until the offer came from B.B.B.

"You promised not to take any notice of such things," complained Mrs. Harding. "Throw it in the fire."

"I can't ignore this one. It's from Edmund . . . Bob Harding's grandson. He's the most distinguished relation we've got. He says he blames himself. None of it would have happened if we had got together and done something when Mundy's book first came out. He says Mundy's book is nonsense."

"I could have told you that," murmured Cecilia, who was wondering which of her parents annoyed her more. "But what could you have done?"

"He says we should have set up some big fellow to make mince meat of Mundy. But it was in the summer, 1939, and we all had other things to think of. Nobody foresaw that it would matter so much: how could we guess that wretched woman would write a play? Edmund still thinks something might be done."

Cecilia sniffed. She knew that her father would, in the end, do nothing, although he might toy with the idea of renouncing his contract.

"But if you take no notice of people like this, they get tired of it and go away, like that horrid Mr. Shattock. . . ."

Mrs. Harding checked herself, flushed, and threw a scared glance at Cecilia who refused to catch her eye. Shattock's threatened visit had been concealed from Mr. Harding; he had been out when the telephone call came from The Old Ship. She had intended to deal with the fellow herself and send him packing, behind her husband's back. For a whole afternoon had she waited, and then Shattock never came, although she had been startled when, giving him up, she had gone up to wash her hair and the bell rang. Cecilia, determined not to connect herself with this disgusting business, had for some time refused to answer it.

These confused glances conveyed nothing to Mr. Harding, who was rereading Edmund's letter. He said, "Edmund talks of coming. He'll be in Dorbridge on Saturday and suggests coming over on Sunday afternoon."

"I don't see why he should. Our side of the family have never been on good terms with the Bob Hardings. They behaved very badly, didn't they, when the big crash came? Bob Harding wouldn't do a thing. Why should we take a lecture from his grandson?"

"I don't know that he wouldn't do a thing. But he thought they ought to break the entail and sell the property. My great grandfather wouldn't hear of it, and so they quarrelled."

"They've always been much richer than we are. Edmund Harding has no daughter wanting to go to College."

"Oh!" cried Cecilia, jumping up. "I shall be sick if you say that again!"

She rushed furiously out of the room. Never would she admit that this detestable picture had anything to do with her college fees. The money would be forthcoming, out of that overdraft, which in the past had provided many things at first declared to be impossible. That £500 might disappear into this overdraft, during the coming summer, was of no significance whatever. Had it gone to swell a credit balance she might have felt differently. It might have been difficult, in that case, to deny that the sum was ear-marked for a certain purpose. As it was, she felt that she could go to college in the autumn yet maintain uncompromising disapprobation of the picture and everything to do with it.

No girl, she thought, as she banged about the morning housework, had ever been cursed with a more inconvenient great grand aunt. Any advantages the Philip Hardings might have reaped from Dorothea's money had been offset by the legacy of Katy, to whom it had officially belonged. Bramstock had been preserved for them, with Katy permanently inside it. Nobody could turn her out, for if she went to live elsewhere she might take her money with her. Only so long as she stayed there would funds be forthcoming when the roof needed repair, or a bathroom had to be installed.

For more than ninety years, through two world wars, she had made life hell for everybody. Generations of children had grown up under the shadow of that bulky old crow, whose continual idiotic remarks must always be answered with patience and courtesy, lest she fly into one of her rages.

The telephone rang. It was the plumber's mate, with his message from Miss Lassiter. There was some malicious satisfaction in the prospect of Thursday afternoon. She informed her parents that Miss Lassiter, the plumber's mate, and the villain Mundy might be expected to appear at three o'clock.

"Mundy!" shouted Mr. Harding. "Then I shall be out. I won't meet that fellow."

"Tea," said Mrs. Harding. "We shall have to give them tea. Are you going into Beremouth, darling? Just stop in Upcott on the way and get some of Miss Budden's run honey."

"Honey! For Mundy!"

Cecilia laughed and went to get the car. She had been in half a mind to announce that she would be out too, but decided that, on the whole, this tea party might be amusing. She need do nothing, say nothing, to make it go: she could maintain her attitude of aloof disapproval. She could even, should they provoke her too far, disconcert them by coming out with the truth about Aunt Katy, concerning whom there had been a tribal conspiracy of silence. Although why, she thought, as she set off down the drive, we should hush that up, I cannot imagine, when we are ready to shriek so much from the housetops. Fornication and adultery in the family? Hurrah! Inform the whole world of it. A congenital idiot in the family . . . Ssh! Not very nice.

Miss Budden's hyacinths were, of course, remarkably fine. Their strong scent filled the little garden, as Cecilia went up the path and knocked at the door. She rather hoped that Miss Turner would answer it; of the two she was the less alarming. They were a difficult couple to place, strangers and townswomen. They might be useful members of the Institute, but they had not entirely taken on village ways. Bramstock did not mean as much to them, perhaps, as it did to the natives; in their manner to herself there was a detachment to which she was not accustomed.

Miss Budden appeared. There were, she thought, some jars of run honey in a shed at the end of the back garden. If Miss Harding would come in and wait, she would look for them. Cecilia had never before set foot inside the cottage, although she had often given messages at the door. The Vermeer over the fireplace immediately caught her eye and, for some reason, annoyed her.

Upon Miss Budden's return she said abruptly, "I was sorry you weren't at the Whist Drive last night. We were settling about the Book Tea."

"But I was," said Miss Budden. "I was coming out as you came in."

"Oh? I didn't see you. I thought all the Book Tea people would stay behind. We want you to read a short paper on Jane Austen."

"Don't you think they must be getting sick of Jane Austen?" objected Miss Budden. "I'd rather do Arnold Bennett."

This was typical of the woman. She would contradict and disagree in the coolest manner. Cecilia reddened and said, " I doubt if they'll have heard of him. I wish you'd mentioned it before. We've put Jane Austen in the notices now."

"I'm sorry. I didn't know there was to be a discussion. I thought you and Roy Collins had just come for the tea urns."

"Mr. Collins? Why . . . do you know him?"

"I should think so! He's Miss Turner's nephew."

"*Is* he?"

"We hear he's come to write that picture which is going to be made at Bramstock."

"Oh? How exciting for Miss Turner!"

"She's surprised," rejoined Alice.

Something in her tone stung Cecilia. Her own disapproval of *The Bramstock Story* was right and natural; that village people should share it was not a comfortable thought.

"It must be a great opportunity for him," she said.

"Well . . . no," said Alice. "A picture like this is rather a come-down for him. He'd sooner be making his own original screen plays, not adapting other people's rubbish."

Cecilia failed to conceal her surprise that Roy should be capable of writing original plays. She asked if any had been taken. Alice, in her eagerness to take this chit down a peg or two, gave details which May, as she very well knew, would not have wished her to pass on.

"But the Brickhill Shorts are getting to be famous!" exclaimed Cecilia. "*Every Wednesday?* What was it about? I've seen several, but I don't remember that one."

"It was about a Punch and Judy."

"Oh then I've heard of it. A friend of mine saw it and she . . . But did Roy really write that one? The existentialist one?"

May at this moment returned from the village and was warmly congratulated on her nephew's achievement. She looked pleased, but was angry with Alice for letting the cat out of the bag.

"He only told me in confidence. He'll be furious if he thinks I've gossiped. Please, Miss Harding, don't mention it to him, or he may never tell me anything again."

"Very well, I won't," said Cecilia. "But it will be very

self denying of me, for I'm longing to discuss it with him. I know some people who admire it very much."

"Miss Harding," said Alice, with a deadpan face, "has heard that it's existentialist."

"Oh?" said May, doubtfully.

When Cecilia had paid for the honey, and departed, the two friends had a tiff. May threatened never to mention Roy again to Alice. Alice replied that she could live quite well without hearing about Roy for a day or two.

"And what's existentialist, when it's at home?" she asked, as soon as the tiff had blown over.

"How should I know," snapped May. "Something silly. I'm sure poor Roy never even heard of it."

3

The alacrity with which Cecilia accepted an invitation to coffee, a hint of deference in her manner, puzzled Roy a little. For at least twenty minutes she did not lay down the law about anything. He took her to Badger's, at the other end of the Esplanade, where they got a window table.

She also was a little surprised, and flattered, by certain covert glances which he gave her from time to time. They were not mere light-hearted looks of admiration; they were searching and almost tender, as though he had guessed something important about her. Each was conscious of a quickened interest in the other.

This tensity did not last for long. He gave all the wrong answers to her questions about the cinema. Distinction, if he had any, was most effectually concealed. She was driven to think that the Brickhill people must be responsible for all the merit in *Every Wednesday*. Her deference ebbed and she began to patronise him, which put an end to searching looks. She could not, he decided, have been the girl who had haunted his dreams. The impulse to jump across that great crack, and do something for her,

172

must be explained in some other way. Miss Book Tea could never want anything from anybody save respectful attention.

She had brought two books for him to read. They lay beside her on the table and presently he picked up the topmost, which was called *The Survivor*.

"That's the last one she ever wrote," said Cecilia. "And I think it's typical."

He opened it at a frontispiece, ill drawn and messy. The heads of the figures were too large for their bodies. The scene was a narrow path between a cliff and the sea. Muscular young men, with very straight noses scantily but modestly draped, were combing their hair and crowning themselves with garlands. Spears, shields and crested helmets lay about. Upon the opposite page were two lines of verse:

> Go tell the Spartans, thou that passest by,
> That here, obedient to their laws, we lie.

"Is that some of her poetry?" he asked.

"No. It's the epitaph of the defenders of Thermopylae."

Roy thought that this sounded unpromising.

"Some of it is very good," she said. "One can't deny that she was gifted, in a way. She could write of the past, and of places that she had never seen, so vividly, she almost takes you there. I think myself it was because she never really grew up. She wrote like a child, with the same brash confidence in her own creation. Her Sparta is completely convincing as far as landscape goes. And the battle! It's terrific. You hear the shouts echoing from the cliffs. You smell it. You see the sort of steam from sweating bodies hanging in the air above it. You . . . you know about Thermopylae?"

"No. I only know somebody held a pass. Go on. I expect I ought to know."

She thought that he certainly ought to know.

"Here," she said, putting one slender finger to the right of the path in the picture, "along here, were all the great Persian armies—millions of them. And here, this side, was everything men fight for, their homes and their families and their farms and their cities and their laws and their gods. And these are three hundred men, told to hold the Persians up till Sparta's allies had time to gather. And they did. They held that pass for three days. They might have held it forever if they had not been outflanked. The Persians got round by a high path behind the cliffs. When they came up to attack on both sides, that was the end. But still the Spartans fought for time. They combed their hair and pulled creepers from the cliff to make garlands, and held a banquet with the last of their food and wine. And then they fought till they were all dead. They were found lying in a great heap, with Leonidas, their captain. They were buried there and those lines were carved on the rock above. The delay saved Sparta."

Her look and tone moved Roy. She would make a very good teacher, he thought. She would get the kids to listen. He sighed and said, "So what's wrong with that story? She didn't make it up. But nobody could, could they?"

"Oh the people. They're all impossible. Leonidas talks like a Victorian archdeacon. And the hero, he's a horrid little prig called Deinon, he has a healthy sort of Tom Brown's School Days hero worship for Leonidas. Not a bit Greek."

174

"Umhm," said Roy, who had heard a thing or two about the ancient Greeks.

"He's in the battle, but he manages to escape, and gets home and marries a tiresome maiden who is so pious and obedient that, although she loved Deinon, she allowed herself to be betrothed to the bad boy, who showed the Persians the way over the cliffs. But it all came right in the end, and in the last chapter Deinon, a bearded old bore, brings all his grandchildren to look at the epitaph."

"I see. Well . . . I'd rather hear you tell it than read it. What's the other one?"

"That's not a novel. It's the *Memoir*, written by her nephew, Pip. You ought to read it because it's so full of atmosphere. It starts, of course, where Mr. Mundy's book leaves off, and says nothing about the poetry, which nobody knew about till long after. At that time, just after her death, she was only thought to become interesting when her father suddenly went bankrupt, and Mr. Winthorpe made her write novels so as to retrieve the family fortunes."

"What?" exclaimed Roy, sitting up. "Is that why she wrote all those stories?"

"Oh yes. She saved Bramstock, just as Scott saved Abbotsford. Mr. Winthorpe was wonderful, and helped her to make a lot of money. Most authors in those days were cheated by their publishers. But he supervised her contracts and advised her about investments."

"You mean to say he went on interfering?"

"All her life. He practically stood over her while she wrote her books. That's why they're so terribly moral. Look . . ."

She began to search through the *Memoir* for a passage.

Roy caught sight of a pallid face pressed against the glass of the window, looking in at them. It was Cope, who did not generally get out so early. Roy, resenting his lascivious scrutiny of Cecilia, made a face at him. After a while he drifted away.

"Here," she said, handing over the book. "Read this!"

Roy read:

It was at this crisis that a lifelong friend came forward with a suggestion which was to prove a turning point in Dorothea's destiny. The Rev. Arthur Winthorpe, rector of the parish, was well aware of her childhood's proclivity for 'scribbling.' Latterly this hobby had been given up, as household duties became more onerous. But he had been secretly impressed by the promise of these early efforts and he now ventured upon the momentous proposal: Why should she not turn her talents to good and practical use? He was convinced that, with a little help and experience, she might achieve striking success as a professional writer. Her strong imagination, her lively fancy, her interest in the past, her classical education, might all be utilised. Historical novels were then very popular. It is a field in which the Titan 'Sir Walter' must always reign supreme; but there were many nooks and corners untouched by the great master, which might furnish material for humbler pens.

Much persuasion was needed, but our good friend was persistent. My aunt's diffidence, her distrust of her own powers, were not easily overcome. She showed at first a decided aversion from the idea, declaring that she would never find the time, occupied as she was with secretarial tasks for my grandfather and with tender care for my invalid sister Katherine. That these scruples were eventually overcome may have been due, in part, to the exhortations of the whole family. At last she consented. A room was set apart for her use and certain hours were, in future, to be kept sacred, during which she might not be disturbed. I remember well, as a lad, being told by my mother not to play noisily upon the stairs since something of great importance to all of us was afoot. And I can remember too all the little bustle of mystery and excitement, Mr. Winthorpe's frequent visits to enquire after her progress, often with some book of reference in his hand which he thought might be of use to her. I believe, although I am not quite sure, that the first subject, the Princes in the Tower, was suggested by him. And it was thus that *Two Red Roses* first saw the light.

Having read as far as this, Roy looked up and saw that Cecilia was smiling.

"What's funny about it?" he demanded fiercely. "She didn't want to write those books. And they made her."

"I can't help laughing. It's all so very, very Victorian. They indulged in such orgies of priggishness, she and Mr. Winthorpe. Do you know, he advised her never to read her reviews, in case they might make her vain. So she never did. He used to pass on any adverse criticism which he thought might be good for her."

"The old bas . . . old so-and-so!"

"It says that he even scolded her sometimes for wanting to take too much trouble over her work, and not being satisfied with it. He said if her books were written in good English, and had a moral, and were marketable, they had justified their purpose. It was wrong to spend

177

more time and thought and labour on them than was needed for that. They must never be an end in themselves, or they might tempt her to vanity and self indulgence. Don't look so horrified. They were like that, in those days."

"I thought she was unhappy. I thought so."

"Oh no. I expect she enjoyed it in a morbid sort of way."

"Forbidding her to take trouble!"

"It wouldn't have made very much difference if she had. She would never have been more than a second rate writer."

The stern look she got from him almost alarmed her.

"You despise her then?" he asked. "I thought you felt this picture is a sort of injury to her."

"I think it's an injury to our family. As for her . . . I'm afraid I've always thought her slightly ridiculous. I've no patience with her silly love affair. She was only a very minor poet, and her novels were tosh. But our family . . . we've been at Bramstock for two hundred and fifty years. I think it's a pity we should make ourselves so cheap."

"It's thanks to her you're still sitting pretty at Bramstock, isn't it? I suppose it's a comfort to think she couldn't ever have done better than tosh, even without her family to keep."

Cecilia's indignation held her silent for a moment.

"Considering," she said cuttingly, "that you've never bothered to read a word she wrote, I don't know where you get this high opinion of her capacities."

"Oh perhaps she hadn't any. I wouldn't know. If she'd taken all the trouble in the world, she mightn't have done better. But she shouldn't have listened to him, if he told her not to."

"I suppose you're trying to say that she sacrificed her integrity?"

This tremendous watch word was unfamiliar to Roy. Anybody using it in B.B.B. would promptly have been told where to put it. He thought it over and gave Cecilia credit for hitting on it, unaware of the frequency with which it was invoked in her set.

"Yes," he said. "That's what I do mean, I suppose."

"Perhaps she did. But I can't pretend to care much. So far as I'm concerned, the first rate is the only thing that matters."

She was fond of saying this and had found that it had an intimidating effect.

"And who says what that is?" demanded Roy. "*You?* Mean to say the only people who need take trouble are the ones who get top marks from you? All the rest can go boil the pot, so their great nieces can get to college?"

"What do you mean?"

She started to her feet, pale with fury.

"I've told you," she said, "that I would do anything to stop this picture being made."

Roy was taken aback, unable to understand her wrath. He quite believed her; it had never occurred to him to connect her College career with the B.B.B. contract. He had merely intended a general taunt against the Hardings for their exploitation of Dorothea.

"I know, I know," he said. "And you think a lot of yourself, I daresay, for taking such a high and mighty line about it. But I'd think more of you if you felt a little bit sorry for her. I daresay she'd have liked to go to college. But she seems to have spent her life doing chores, poor girl. She never got a chance to grow up. And you laugh at her!"

Perceiving that he had not intended the worst insult, she grew calmer.

"I'm sorry," she said. "Perhaps, all things considered, I oughtn't to."

She sat down again and added, "About being first rate . . . I only meant . . . well . . . you, in your work, you must feel that, surely? That it's the only thing that matters?"

Roy shook his head in bewilderment.

"I've never thought about it," he said. "Do the work I want to do . . . that's all I'm out for. I don't worry how it rates."

Here's Fraser, and Hobart, and the salesmen, and the distributors, all telling me what to put, he thought. Some day I get free of them all? Do I then have to be buggered about by a lot of professors, and critics, and kids going to college, asking how I rate? I'd be crackers if I worried about that.

When they left the café he took her back to her car and then went for a stroll on the sands, musing over what she had told him. His great shot in the drawing room was now much clearer. The man was more formidable, the girl in greater danger. A life-time turned on it, a story in which these two were the principal figures. For it must have been her poetry, her own work, which she had given up, during that interview. Grant scarcely came into it at all. She might have given him up, but she had also yielded much more to this fearful old tyrant who had, for some unexplained reason, gained so much power over her that he could, in the end, 'tell her what to put' for the rest of her life.

But it's not Cecilia's fault that she doesn't understand,

thought Roy. None of them do. They all think it's their job to tell us what to put. And we have to laugh it off.

They, to him, were the entire human race. *We* were Dorothea Harding, himself, and a myriad nameless others, swimming, sinking, fighting for life, in the same inclement ocean.

He lifted his head, smiled, and went back to the hotel in better spirits than he had known for many a day, sensible that he had, after all, got company.

4

The weather, which had been bright and fresh, changed during Wednesday night. Thursday was unnaturally warm for the time of year, enervating and airless. Bramstock lay inert under a roof of low grey cloud. Mrs. Harding, depressed by an attack of her spring rheumatism, found herself dreading the inevitable tea party.

To her relief, Cecilia was in a sunny mood and quite prepared to entertain these weird guests. She dusted the drawing room and put a vase of pussy willows on the piano. She cleaned the silver tea-pot. She cut cress sandwiches and put them into a cellophane bag, to keep them fresh for tea-time. She even took a little trouble over her own appearance; immediately after lunch she changed into her new coral twin set. Nor did she scowl when told that she looked nice. Peering into the glass over the drawing room fireplace, she smiled complacently and said that she needed a new hair-do.

"I always think your hair is so pretty," said Mrs. Harding.

"Down on the shoulders is little-girlish."

182

Quite in a fuss about her looks, thought the mother. Very odd, when nobody is coming. Nobody to come, in this part of the world, not a single young man! Nobody at all for Cecilia. She *must* get away. At college she will meet girls with brothers. . . .

Cecilia went to the window and stood there, listening for the car. She was extremely eager to see Roy again for she had been uneasy, almost unhappy, ever since their parting on Tuesday morning. They had not exactly quarrelled but they were not as good friends as they could have been; that stupid little misunderstanding over Dorothea had spoilt something very pleasant. She blamed herself for it and was anxious to set it right. It had been a mistake to laugh at the *Memoir*. Roy had read nothing. He was quite uncultivated. Having no acquaintance with Victorian manners and morals he had judged the whole case by contemporary standards. Only those belonging to the class which ruled the roost a hundred years ago could enter into that mood of affectionate nostalgic amusement with which Bramstock remembered the past. Roy had never, probably, met the kind of old lady (there were still a few of them about) who boasted that she had had *no* education, had been brought up on *dear* Dorothea Harding, and refused to read Mundy's book because she did not expect to like it.

Nor could Cecilia feel that she had explained herself clearly in the matter of the first rate. She had never meant to suggest that human integrity was superfluous save in the very small group of people to whom she gave top rating. She had been confused and bewildered by the fear that he suspected her of double dealing in the matter of the picture. He did not. She was quite safe in that quarter. But she had been too much agitated to set the misunderstanding perfectly right.

She wanted him to like her better and to renew those warm questioning looks which he had given her before they fell out. But she did not admit that to herself: she believed that she was in search of grounds for liking him better. He could not be so inferior as he looked or sounded. He must possess distinction, although she could not locate it and felt as though they were playing some game of hide and seek. A voice continually cried: Cuckoo! from some hidden thicket.

That she was strongly attracted to him was an idea which she would not have admitted for a moment. There were a dozen other reasons for wanting to see him again, and she had put on the coral twin set to please her mother.

"I hear a car coming!" she exclaimed, and ran to the door to welcome it.

A large hired Daimler was drawing up. A chauffeur got out. They were all getting out. Roy appeared, looking less distinguished than ever, for he had put on his pin stripe suit. A plump pink old thing in a gorgeous mink was creeping out, chattering and thanking Roy for helping her. The pear-faced man coming round from the other side of the car must be the villain Mundy. But it seemed as though there were four of them. Somebody else was getting out. Cecilia stared. She had never seen anybody who looked more interesting—so handsome, so sad and so romantic. Who was he? Who? Who?

Roy was greeting her and introducing Miss Lassiter with unexpected aplomb. Both her hands were grasped.

Miss Lassiter, her head a little on one side, exclaimed, "Yes! Yes! I see a likeness. Don't you, Mr. Mundy?"

"To the photograph?" said Mundy. "Perhaps."

That forbidding portrait of an ageing Dorothea, in cap and bustle, was the only photograph, and they all knew it. In the short pause, which followed this piece of malice, Cecilia's eyes turned to the interesting stranger. Nobody made any move to introduce him. They were all furious with him for having come, but could not help it, since he was sitting in the Daimler when it drove round to the hotel.

He now came up with an ease which made the other three look churlish, and said, "I must introduce myself. I'm Basil. Basil Cope. I really had no right to come along but I did. I hope you'll forgive me. I couldn't resist the chance to see . . . Bramstock."

His eyes assured her, quite respectfully, that nothing at Bramstock was better worth seeing than herself. His voice set him leagues apart from his companions. Warmly assuring him of her forgiveness, she took them all into the house to meet her mother.

Into Mrs. Harding's heart also fell a ray of astonished reassurance when she heard Basil speak. Amidst these alien hordes, here was one of her own kind. She gave him a cordial welcome and took notice of his tie, a detail missed by her heedless daughter.

Adelaide was fluttering round the dreary room, determined to find it full of atmosphere, although, actually, it daunted her considerably. The piano, she discovered, was just where she had imagined it would be.

"At the great party, you know, the night before the

wedding, Doda and Grant sing a duet. We've found such a charming period song for them, Mrs. Harding: *Through Life Unblest We Rove . . .*"

"Who is Mr. Cope?" murmured Cecilia to Roy.

"Friend of Mundy's," mumbled Roy, who was resentful and bewildered at the warm reception given to that bum.

"Oh? Does . . . does he write?"

"Says he does."

". . . through one verse we have a close up of Mr. Winthorpe listening. His wise old face . . ."

"Who is Mr. Cope?" murmured Mrs. Harding to Mr. Mundy. "What is he doing in the film?"

"Nothing whatever," snapped Mundy. "He happens to be staying at the Queen's and insisted on coming with us."

". . . the dining room. The set for the wedding breakfast . . ."

There was a general move to the dining room. Cope stayed behind and made himself agreeable to Mrs. Harding.

"You won't remember me, but I think I remember you. I believe you used to stay at Ayton Priors when I was a little boy. My uncle . . ."

So much Roy heard, as he followed Adelaide out of the room. But it must have gone down, for Mrs. Harding and Cope were well away when the party crossed the hall to the library, a few minutes later. Cope was saying, "Not for a good many years. I've been abroad. . . ."

Would you believe it? marvelled Roy, enlightened upon a point which had puzzled him. Cope, in his reminiscent moments, was fond of dwelling upon his success with gently nurtured girls. No debutante had been able to resist him, as he reeled and staggered through their lives, with all the other haunted boys. Roy had been sceptical because he could not imagine where Cope might have met these tender creatures or how their Mums could have allowed him within a mile of them. The answer was now plain; they had met him at Ayton Priors, a name of power before which Mums went down. As he bounded upstairs after the others, who were going to look at the bedrooms, Roy murmured it aloud.

"Ayton Priors. Ayton Priors. My . . . ah . . . uncle's place. . . ."

He had a notion that he did not say it quite as Cope did. In his mouth it sounded more like Aet'n Prahs.

Having taken a peep at a room in which Dorothea might have slept, the party proceeded to that in which she certainly wrote her novels. This played no part in *The Bramstock Story* but Adelaide felt obliged, in civility, to ask for it.

They climbed some uncarpeted back stairs and came to a damp dark room facing north. It was unfurnished save for a derelict basket chair in one corner. The stained wall-paper was peeling off in several places. The window looked out upon stable roofs.

"I suppose she chose this room because it's quiet and out of the way," faltered Adelaide.

"I bet Winthorpe chose it," muttered Roy.

Mundy, who had been following the party in silent gloom, gave Roy a queer look and said, "Perhaps *he* thought it quiet and out of the way."

"Of course! You've been here before, Mr. Mundy," said Adelaide, turning to him. "When you came to see

Katy. You must remember her quite well, Miss Harding. Tell us about her. Was she a very wonderful old lady?"

Cecilia looked at Mundy and saw that he was confidently relying upon the tribal taboo. She decided to let them have it.

"Aunt Katy," she told them, "was mentally deficient."

Adelaide and Roy both jumped. Mundy exclaimed, a little too hastily, "She didn't strike me as being so, when I saw her."

"Didn't she? I'm surprised. She was, you know. Quite, quite feeble-minded. She never really learnt to read or write. But . . . unfortunately . . . she could just sign her name."

No comment was forthcoming from any of the party. They stood busy with their own reflections.

The dirty dog! thought Roy. Taking advantage of an old loony. But then . . . couldn't the Hardings have stopped it? Got her put away? I suppose, if they had, all the money would have been tied up too. That didn't suit them.

"Outdoors!" cried Adelaide, in desperation. "Let's all go outdoors. I want to see the little house by the river where she met Grant. And then, a peep at the graveyard. . . . I've brought a wreath, Miss Harding . . . a little tribute."

When she and Cecilia had gone out, Roy turned on Mundy.

"You kept that very dark."

"I don't accept it," said Mundy, sulkily. "I daresay she got pretty senile at the end. But she wasn't so very old when I saw her. Nobody else in the family has ever suggested such a thing."

188

"M'yes. So now for the little love nest by the river. You coming?"

"No. I've seen it before. There are some books I want to look at in the library. First editions. I was wondering if Harding might think of selling."

"Say the right word and you might get 'em for nothing."

"The right word?" asked Mundy with raised eyebrows.

"Ayton Priors. Say that and all they have is yours."

"Eyton Pryers?"

"No. That won't do. It all depends on how you say it."

Mundy shrugged his shoulders and walked off. The word obviously conveyed nothing to him: Ayton Priors did not appear in the past which he shared with Cope.

So why should it, thought Roy, if he can't say it properly? That shows he's no class. Shotgun wedding. Sounds like a very respectable family. Perhaps old man Mundy was a fishmonger. So one day Cope staggers in to buy a pound of shrimps. And, behind the counter is lovely . . . lovely Peggy, the fishmonger's daughter. Wrong! We can't see Cope buying shrimps. What would he buy? A chemist! Lots of possibilities there. . . .

He turned to take a last look at this repulsive room where all the novels had been written, all the money made, and where so much had gone on of which he could not think without a shiver. If there had been grief and desolation here, nothing of it was left. The room was empty. Its very vacancy was sinister, as though no life, of any kind, had ever existed between these mildewed walls. There was no faint essence of humanity left by beings who had moved, breathed, suffered, slept, prayed or loved here. Yet it reminded him of some other room that he had known. He shut his eyes and traced the memory. In his father's establishment there was one room as empty as this although it often had an occupant. With his eyes shut he could almost smell the lilies.

All was silent downstairs. Mrs. Harding was pottering about alone, setting a tea table. She said that everybody had gone out. He hastened after them and came up with Adelaide waddling through the wood. Her high heels hampered her and she was much too hot in the mink coat.

"Where's Cecilia?" he asked. "Where's Cope?"

"I don't know. Oh Roy! What a horrid thing to say about poor Katy! Do you think it's true?"

"Cecilia ought to know."

"But do you think Mr. Mundy knew?"

"I rather think he guessed it."

"Then, in that case, he has no right to say that Katy was Doda's daughter. She obviously couldn't have been."

"Why not?"

"They were aunt and niece, obviously. It often happens, in that sort of case."

"I don't get you. What sort of case?"

"Where the poor child is . . . is mentally under-privileged. His aunt is often the one who feels for him most. I . . . I've known it."

Adelaide's voice shook a little. Roy wondered if she might not herself have been such an aunt.

"It makes me ask myself," she muttered angrily, "how much one can trust Mr. Mundy about anything. Look, Roy . . . will they have arc lamps in these trees when they take shots of Doda, stealing down at night to the cottage? They'll have to, won't they?"

"Oh they'll do that on the set."

"You always say that. What's the use of taking this house for exteriors when everything, in the end, will be done on the set?"

"Exteriors are a nuisance. It rains. Or, just when Sound's O. K., a dog barks or a plane comes over. Terribly noisy, the country."

"Why take them at all then?"

"Just another way of wasting money."

They went on through the wood. He was worried about Cope and Cecilia. However much of a fool her Mum might be, that heel had been brought into the house on false pretences, accepted as one of their party, and therefore furnished with credentials of a sort. Nobody had said to Mrs. Harding: This is an unscrupulous womanizer who saw your daughter through the window of Badger's Café, found out who she is, and has come here to make a pass at her. Somebody perhaps ought to have done so, for the fact was plain to Roy, plain to Mundy, although Adelaide was so scatty that she might not have tumbled to it.

For all Roy knew, Ayton Priors might be full of types like Cope, and Cecilia might be used to dealing with them. But he doubted it. She did not strike him as knowing much about wolves. Cope, by his own account, was a fast worker, expert in shock tactics. She would have, at some time or other, to go through that sort of thing with somebody, but Roy could not find it in his heart to leave her to her fate this afternoon. She was really taking pains to entertain them all, poor kid.

They went through the gate to the river-bank where stood the walls of the ruined playhouse. Cope and Cecilia were sitting on one of them, conversing amicably. The shock tactics had not yet begun; they were getting along very well indeed.

Roy listened absently to Adelaide's comments, agreed with her whenever she paused, and wondered what went on. Cecilia, he could see, was not entirely unaware of a wolf in the offing. She was more self conscious, less simple in her smiles and gestures; she was enjoying herself. As for Cope, his cosmic grievance had taken the form of a tender melancholy, half lifted by the pleasure of her company.

Just boy and girl, raged Roy to himself. Just a sad, sad boy of forty giving the works to a kid young enough to be his daughter. Yes she is! If he spoke the truth about that wedding, his kid might be her age by now. All right! I know young girls like older men. But older men ought to look like older men.

To his surprise he discovered that he was jealous of Cope, who would soon, by the looks of it, be taking liberties. If he still had his hands off her, it was probably only because Roy and Adelaide had butted in. Cecilia was very pretty, but her Book Tea manners had hitherto diverted Roy's thoughts into other channels. Beholding her for a moment through Cope's eyes he admitted angrily that she was quite a dish, broke away from Adelaide, and went to join the party on the wall.

"You two," he told them, "look as if you were having a Peter and Wendy conversation about what you did when you were kids."

Cope gave him a scowl but Cecilia laughed.

"How did you guess that?" she asked.

"Just all this . . . the old house and the river and the swans and the old nurseries and the rocking horse and everything. I had a hunch they might do something to Cope—carry him back to childhood memories, ever so long ago. Way . . . way . . . back. . . ."

From Cecilia's startled face it was apparent that this had been, in fact, the gist of their conversation.

"We'd got as far as our tenth birthdays," she said. "I got a pony. Basil was allowed to drive a train: on the little branch line from Ayton Priors. What did you do, Roy?"

"I had a cake with ten candles," remembered Roy.

He paused, allowed them to reflect how dull that was, and added, "Just when I was cutting it, a bomb came down and we got under the table. A minute later the ceiling was all over the birthday cake."

"What a shame!" she said. "I never heard a near bomb. Only a couple of distant thumps in Beremouth."

Cope said nothing. Roy was pretty sure that he had never heard a bomb in his life. A few dates, he thought, would make a mess of Cope's nostalgic line. It was a corny line but might be effective with a very inexperienced girl. This wily old wolf would treat her like a kid, and talk to her about her dolls, until she just had to convince him that she was out of the nursery.

"I wonder," he said, "what Mundy did on his tenth birthday. Let's ask him. I daresay he ate up all the pills."

"What pills?" asked Cecilia.

"The pills in his old man's shop."

At Cope's start of surprise Roy mentally patted himself on the back. It *had* been a chemist's shop. He rose and went to join Adelaide, who was calling impatiently. She wanted to go along to the foot-bridge and observe the swans. For a time the tall reeds hid the couple by the cottage.

"How hot it is," sighed Adelaide. "I'm worn out already. I rather wish I hadn't come. It's not as inspiring as I'd hoped. This valley . . . don't you think it's very dreary?"

"I think it's the bottom," said Roy. "I never knew a place that got me down more. Let's go and make whoopee in the graveyard."

He hurried Adelaide towards the cottage again. Cope, it seemed, had got a new line. He was talking with animation and what he said received delighted attention. As soon as Roy was within earshot Cecilia called out, "Mr. Cope has got such a wonderful theory about Aunt Dorothea."

No! thought Roy, remembering Cope's dissertation in the Lord Nelson. He can't be telling her that; she wouldn't stand for it.

"He says G: wasn't a man!"

Roy reeled. Cope tried to interrupt, "Now I never meant——"

"G: was the hero of the first novel she ever wrote."

"No—no—really," pleaded Cope. "Not in front of them! It's only my bit of fun."

"But you make it sound so plausible. Do go on!"

"I won't while they're here."

"Then you go away," said Cecilia to Roy and Adelaide. "It's a perfectly wonderful version of *The Bramstock Story*. Ever so much better than yours. I can't wait to hear the end."

Roy and Adelaide obeyed her, and set off through the wood.

"Sounds an improvement on Cope's other version,"

said Roy. "It seems to be Cope's homework, inventing new versions."

"I think he does it to annoy Mr. Mundy," said Adelaide. "I went to Mr. Mundy's room yesterday and they seemed to be having a terrible quarrel; they didn't hear me when I knocked. Mr. Mundy was shouting so I could hear through the door: 'I don't believe a word of it, not a word, unless you bring me proof.' And then something about Dorothea. And, when I went in, Mr. Cope was laughing. I'd never seen him laugh before."

"Laugh?" repeated Roy indignantly. "Laugh?"

He toiled on through the stuffy wood, fuming.

"It's beginning to get in my hair," he exclaimed, after a while. "What right have people to laugh at her, and get all these theories about her?"

"You laugh at her yourself," observed Adelaide.

"I don't now. Not since I realised how unhappy she must have been, that girl! It doesn't seem as if she had a single friend, or anybody to stand up for her. If I'd been around here, a hundred years ago, I'd have told those Hardings a thing or two. Too late now."

"This path seems much longer going back than coming," said Adelaide.

It did. He was surprised to find it so long. And he remembered that last time he had run all the way, in flight from panic. Despair, he thought. But was it hers or mine? I don't want to know. Oh I don't want to know any more.

5

If Mundy had hoped to escape the pilgrimage to the graveyard he was mistaken. Adelaide hauled him out of the library and took him there, announcing that she might, at any time, want some of the information which he was paid to furnish. She was losing her awe of him since the discovery about Katy. They drove round in the Daimler, since they did not want to carry the enormous wreath that she had brought. Roy took the short cut through the woods.

The heavy airless day was exhausting and he was sorry that he had come. Had he foreseen that Cecilia would desert him for Cope he would never have done so, for he disliked Bramstock intensely. In some respects this second visit had affected him even more disagreeably than the first. He knew more, now, about what had gone on there. He was continually getting clearer glimpses of the people who had surrounded the unfortunate Dorothea and he welcomed none of them. It was as though he were wandering languidly in some maze into which he had got by accident, but from which he could not escape until he had discovered the centre. He did not want to find out any more: what he knew was beginning to get in his way when he considered his script.

A wicket gate led into the graveyard. Bramstock Church, with its stumpy tower, stood in one corner of the enclosure. The place seemed to be full of Hardings and upper servants from Bramstock whose virtues had been commemorated by the Hardings. He looked about him but made no great effort to discover where she lay, half minded to slip away again before the others came. A heavy inertia held him there until they appeared round the corner of the church, lugging between them a mammoth wreath upon which Adelaide must have spent a good portion of her royalties. Mundy knew where to go. He steered his panting partner towards an ill-designed cross in white marble, on the south side of the church. Roy moved forward to join them and arrived just as they were lowering their burden. For a few seconds all three stood in silence, reading the inscription on the cross.

In Memory
of
Dorothea Harding

Born April 23, 1836
Died January 17, 1889

Truly my hope is even in Thee

Down below there, in her shroud, in her coffin, for more than sixty years, thought Roy. She only lived for fifty-three. Her death is already longer than her life. Why was I afraid of coming?

Mundy left them and walked off to look at another grave not very far away.

"Poor thing," quavered Adelaide. "It's sad. I . . . I almost wish I hadn't written that play, I don't know why."

"It can't hurt her now. Nothing can hurt her now."

"But the dead are so . . . so helpless. Only I never thought of her as dead, Roy."

"No. Your Doda, when the curtain went down, she just took off her make-up and went home."

"Exactly. How well you understand! But then . . . any life . . . when it's over, when you think about it, it seems sad, somehow. As if there's something unfinished."

"Don't cry old dear. It's too late. That's what I've been telling myself. It's too late for anybody to start feeling bad about her, because it's too late for anybody to help her. If we want to feel sorry for people, it's not the dead."

But he felt as if something was flowing out of him all the time, drawing out of him, and retreating to a distance, to wait . . . to pile up . . . to return. He shivered.

"Come along," he said taking her arm, "let's go."

They joined Mundy, who was scrutinising a more tasteful cross in rough granite. It said:

Here lies
In the confident hope of a glorious resurrection

Arthur James Winthorpe
For thirty seven years Rector of this Parish

Born March 12, 1827
Died January 24, 1889
Lord now lettest Thou Thy servant depart in peace

"Why," discovered Adelaide, for once attentive to a date, "he died only a week after she did!"

"He must have been very old . . ." began Roy, who still saw Hugh Farren in the part.

Then he too studied dates, started, and almost shouted, "But he wasn't! He wasn't old at all. Not old when she was young, I mean. There was only nine years between them."

"That is so," agreed Mundy. "He got the living very young. At the time of Mary's marriage he wasn't thirty."

"And when he made her write those books . . . they were both still young!"

"She was twenty-five. He was thirty-four."

A whole section of *The Bramstock Story* was crumbling and collapsing like the undermined bank of a stream. It had not been an interfering old bastard who came stumping up those stairs to that dreadful little room, laden with books of reference and bubbling with advice. It had been . . . had been . . .

"I always thought of him as old," said Adelaide. "And I am making him old in the script. I think Hugh Farren is to play him."

"Much wiser," said Mundy blandly. "I think a young parson would complicate the story; it might put ideas into people's heads, especially if he is playing with Miss Fletcher. It doesn't do to put ideas into people's heads about the clergy. I think it's a pardonable alteration if that scene of theirs is played by an old man and a young girl. Two young people——"

"Oh I agree," said Adelaide. "People would wonder why he wasn't in love with her himself. Why wasn't he? He never married, did he?"

So that, thought Roy, is what Mundy meant about Winthorpe thinking the room quiet and out of the way. I might have guessed. I would have, if I hadn't thought of Winthorpe as almost drooling with old age. Trust Mundy! If he makes a crack, it's dirty.

In a flash, he saw the face in the glass—the face which had never been clear when he considered that shot. He saw its smile. Something began to roar inside his head.

Adelaide was strolling off, making a comment which he could not hear. He only heard his own voice, speaking faintly behind this roaring wave which was rushing back.

"He was in love with her," it stated. "He wanted her."

"I shouldn't wonder," said Mundy. "She was said to be a pretty girl. But I don't think he meant a thing to her until after Grant's death. What went on between 'em later is anybody's guess."

"When they were writing the books in that room?"

"A woman with that temperament! Think of the poems. She could no more have lived without a man than she could live without air. But she was finished as an artist by then. What she was up to afterwards has no literary interest. She was just a common or garden bitch in—Christ!"

Roy thought that he had taken some big jump, leapt an immense distance. To his great surprise he was still standing in the same place. Mundy was lying on his back across Mr. Winthorpe's grave. There was a sensation in Roy's fist: he gradually realised that it had been in collision with Mundy's face.

"I'm sorry," he said, in a soft, bewildered voice. "But just because a girl is dead you can't talk like that about her."

Mundy sat up and his nose began to bleed.

"Pinch it," advised Roy, almost with concern.

"Have you god bad?" asked Mundy, pinching his nose.

"No," said Roy. "I only . . ."

The wave lifted him and carried him away. Riding on its crest, he listened, with a curious detachment, to his own voice. He appeared to have a good deal to say and it was being said without much effort or volition on his own part.

"Can't you see? There never was anybody. It was her writing. She gave it up. They were too much for her. He had all of them behind him, and it was too much for her.

"He couldn't stand knowing that it meant more to her than any man could ever mean. If it had been another man, he could have stood it. To know it wasn't anybody—that drove him crazy.

"There never was anybody. Grant! You just dreamt that up. It was because there never was anybody that all this happened, this fight between her and him, that lasted all their lives.

"Because he wasn't satisfied, even when he'd made

her give it up. He wanted her and he couldn't get her. So he kept on, and he kept on, till he'd got at it and smashed it all up. He won. She went beaten into her grave."

Mundy had risen cautiously to his feet. His nose had stopped bleeding. He looked round the churchyard and then back at Roy.

"Cope," he said, "has been having you on."

"Cope? No! What's Cope got to do with it?"

"Who then? If you've any evidence, any shadow of proof for all this, you'd better come across with it unless you want to run into trouble."

Roy shook his head.

"I've no proof. Not what you'd call proof."

"Where did you get all this? From whom?"

"I . . . I . . . Not from anybody."

"Oh I see. Like our excellent Miss Lassiter, you *know!* And how long have you been harbouring this revelation?"

"It was just now, looking at the graves."

"Really? It just popped into your head like that? Well, think it over. If any other explanation should occur to you, I'd be glad to hear it. At present I've an open mind. I might have you up for assault. I might not. You know best how to explain this business to your employers, if it ends in court."

Mundy blew his nose experimentally, examined his handkerchief, and walked off to the wicket gate into the shrubbery. Roy had the impression that he was not quite so angry as might have been expected. He had looked almost cheerful, as he turned away.

Evidence? Not any. So how do I know? I jumped. But I didn't. I'm still here. Where I was.

The great wave had now gone roaring on. It left him suspended in calm water but considerably out of his depth. He started off to tell Adelaide all about it, and then asked himself what he had to tell. How could he explain that this was not merely a guess?

It was not. He had only to compare it with any normal guess to be aware of the difference. Mundy and the chemist's shop had been a guess which hit the mark. This time he felt as though he had himself been the mark at which truth had been hurled. Projectiles had been coming his way for some days, ever since he first took notice of those swans. But he would have continued to dodge them, had it not been for his preoccupation with that shot for Issy, a purely professional effort, a fraction of 'his own work' which he hoped to smuggle into the script. It had, however, kept him in the line of fire.

Not that he believed anybody in particular to have been aiming at him. His reluctance to tell Adelaide was in part due to the fear that she might bring out her planchette. There was nothing phoney about it, he thought, starting forwards again towards the church. Only the truth is always there, zooming around, quite different to anything we make up, and when we knock into it we know the difference. It isn't looking for us and we're scared of it, like I was, that first day I came here. So if we do hit it we feel it's somebody else's doing. No. I'd better not tell anybody. I'm sorry I told Mundy.

Adelaide was coming from the church.

"Thank goodness the wedding scenes are to be shot

on the set," she said. "It's the nastiest little—Roy! What's happened?"

"Nothing."

"Where's Mr. Mundy? Have you quarrelled?"

"Er . . . no. I jumped. I mean, I didn't. I thought I did. And I sort of . . . hit him."

"Gracious! Is he cross? Where is he?"

"Gone back to the house. He says he might be going to have me up for assault."

"Oh Roy! I do hope you aren't going to get into trouble."

"I couldn't," he declared, from the vast liberty in which he floated, "care less."

"Anyway, let's get back to the house too. Let's have tea and go. We must stay to tea as they've got it ready for us, but let's get away as soon as we can. It's too awful, this place."

She seized his arm and hurried him back to the car, which was waiting on the village side of the church. As soon as they were driving off she said, "But why did you hit him really?"

"I'm not sure. He said something about Dorothea and Winthorpe, when they were writing those books."

"He didn't! He would. A poor old clergyman?"

"No Adelaide. Not old. That's the point."

"No more he was. I forgot. But a clergyman anyway. It just shows the sort of mind Mr. Mundy has. After saying what he did about Katy, he'd say anything. Oh Roy, it gets worse the more I think of it. Poor Doda, staying in this dismal place all her life, just because she felt she must look after Katy. It's too sad for words."

"How do you make that out? Did he tell her to?"

"Who?"

"Winthorpe."

"Mercy no, I shouldn't think so." Adelaide laughed crossly. "So she couldn't feel she must look after Katy unless some *man* told her to? That's as stupid as saying Katy was her daughter. Can't you see that Katy was the key to it all?"

"You make too much of Katy."

"And you, being a man, make too much of Winthorpe. Nobody but another woman would understand. That poor little creature . . . very ugly and unattractive probably . . . nobody caring for it and the parents ashamed of it. She must have felt Katy had nobody but her. She'd have stuck to Katy, even if a million Mr. Winthorpes had told her not to."

The car drew up at the house. They went into the drawing room where they found Mundy consuming tea, cress sandwiches, brown bread and honey, nervously watched by Mrs. Harding. She welcomed them with a gasp of relief, almost as though they had been old friends; Mundy must have managed to disconcert her badly.

"I can't think," she said, "what's happened to Cecilia."

A load off her mind if she can't, thought Roy, carrying tea to Adelaide.

The discovery that Cope had not been a graveyard pilgrim seemed to reassure the mother who commented cheerfully, "Then they're together somewhere. I hope they won't be very late, or the tea will be stewed."

"I hope they won't," said Adelaide, "for we really ought to be getting back. We . . . we . . ."

She paused and blushed, unable to invent a plausible reason for flying from Bramstock as soon as possible. Roy came to her rescue and said that they only had the car till five o'clock; they had promised the garage to return it by then. The smooth lie made him feel much more like himself, as though he had at last drifted to a point within his depth. He began to devour bread and honey with the hunger which sometimes succeeds intense emotion.

"Oh what a pity," said Mrs. Harding, visibly brightening. "Well, if Mr. Cope doesn't turn up soon that needn't matter. Cecilia could drive him back any time. I hope you've seen everything you want, Miss Lassiter?"

Adelaide, with a shudder, declared that she had.

"I forgot to mention, when first you came, that the water colours in this room were done by Mary Harding, the sister, you know, who married Grant Forrester."

Carrying their tea cups, Roy and Adelaide rose to make a tour of these pictures, glad to be able to turn their backs upon Mundy. Of Mary's work there was little to say. Bramstock House, which appeared several times, looked no nicer, but was blue instead of brown, since Mary had doted on blue, and managed to get it into everything.

"Here is the old playhouse by the river, before it fell down."

A couple of hours earlier this little blue love nest might have enchanted Adelaide. She now inspected it glumly and said that it did not look very safe for children so close to the water.

Katy falling in and Doda pulling her out, Roy thought. It's fierce, this thing Adelaide has about Katy.

"But here's a marvellous house," he exclaimed. "Where's this?"

Romantic gorges, rocks and mountain tops surrounded a vast azure pile of battlements, cupolas and towers.

"We don't know," said Mrs. Harding. "There's a name at the back: Fountainhall. But we've never been able to find out anything about it. This one is Elkington. Grant Forrester's house. It was burnt down sometime in the eighties."

Elkington was a small cobalt rectangle in a singularly bare park.

"And this one here shows another thing that is gone. The view, you see, of the hills from the river. This little column on Westing was here till 1942; they had to take it away when they had a radar station there. We've got used, now, to the skyline without it, but we missed it very much at first."

"Some kind of monument?" asked Roy.

"Nobody knew, I think. It had a slab at the bottom with R.A. 1751 carved on it. I never heard who he was, or why it was there."

"Can you tell us?" asked Adelaide, turning to Mundy.

Rather to the annoyance of Roy and Adelaide their research expert came up promptly with an answer.

"Man called Robert Aschcombe. Mentioned in *Local Worthies*. He lived in Upcott and he's buried in the churchyard there. One of those eighteenth century eccentrics; a bit of an antiquary, a bit of a poet. Dug up some Roman pottery in his garden: it's in the Beremouth museum. He put up the column on Westing because he liked walking up there. People could do that sort of thing then: stuck up monuments wherever the fancy took them."

"Poet?" said Roy, with a glint in his eye. "So what was the matter with him?"

"Matter?" queried Mundy.

"People only write poetry because something's eating them, surely, that they have to get out of their system? Did he have a floating kidney? Was he sleeping——"

"Alas! Alas!" interrupted Adelaide feverishly. "The time! The time! We must go."

The chatter and fidgetting of departure now set in and lasted for some minutes. Adelaide longed to be off. Mrs. Harding longed to see the last of them. But neither woman was able, thought Roy, to break it up without a lot of yap-yap. Mundy simply walked off and got into the seat beside the chauffeur in the waiting car. Roy hovered in the hall until a voice softly hailed them from above. He looked up and saw Cecilia leaning over the gallery railing.

"Hullo?" he said.

"Are they going? Will you tell them to wait for Mr. Cope? And then come up here? Please! I want your help badly."

He put his head into the drawing room and said, "Don't go without Cope. He's been located. He's coming."

Then he ran up the stairs to join Cecilia. She was, as he could now see, looking white and miserable.

"Oh Roy," she said. "He . . . he's locked up in a cupboard in one of the attics. And . . . and I don't want to have to let him out."

"Lead on," said Roy grimly.

She led him up some derelict, dusty back stairs towards the attics. And if she was daft enough to come up here all alone with the haunted boy, he thought, she ought to be locked up herself.

As though reading his thoughts she turned and explained, "We came to look for this cupboard. He had an idea . . . an extraordinary idea . . . part of his version of *The Bramstock Story.* I thought it so inspired . . . when he'd never been in this house before . . . I'd like to explain sometime. Could I . . . could we meet?"

"Sure. Tomorrow?"

"There's a bus gets to Upcott at ten. I could meet you there, at Upcott post office. I can't bring the car. My father wants it. We might take a walk on the hills."

"I'll be there. Did you lock Cope in this cupboard?"

"Yes. I . . . I had to."

They had come to a long, airless attic corridor, so low ceilinged that Roy had to stoop. She pointed to a door at the end.

"In there. The cupboard door is papered over. Not very easy to see. But there are some air-holes."

"That's a good thing. He been there long?"

"More than an hour. I was waiting till I could catch you. Oh Roy! I am so grateful. I think . . . I'll go now, if you'll let him out."

"Cut along then. I'll see him off the set."

She ran back along the corridor. Roy advanced to the room at the end, whistling *The Mistletoe Bough.* He was enjoying himself. Cecilia, he thought, did not seem to be very much the worse for the afternoon's adventure. That she should have found it unpleasant was just as well: she would know better another time.

The attic was empty save for a few trunks and a dressmaker's dummy. He spied the door, papered over, with air-holes. All was very quiet behind it.

"Cope?" he murmured, through one of the holes. "Cope*e*?"

"Is that Collins?" said a voice within.

"Having yourself a good time in there?"

"Let me out, can't you?"

Roy opened the door. Cope emerged, swaggering a little.

"Did Cecilia send you?" he asked.

"Yes," said Roy. "We nearly went home without you. But then we seemed to be one short, and Cecilia remembered. Oh, she said, I believe I left somebody in a cupboard."

Cope started, stared at him, and obviously decided that this need not be believed.

"I was afraid she didn't realise she'd banged the door," he said. "She was . . . well . . . you know, a little upset, and she ran off, and the door banged to. I didn't like to shout."

"Madly chivalrous," said Roy, leading the way down the corridor. "But nobody would have heard you. They mightn't have come up here for months. Then, I suppose they'd have smelt something."

"All's well that ends well," murmured Cope, with a satisfaction that suggested he had had the time of his life in that cupboard. "She was upset. They are . . . the first time."

"Oh you great big story!" retorted Roy blithely. "Oh what a whopper! Where do you expect to go when you die?"

They came to the door which led to the main stairs and he added, "You go on down this way, and out the back door, and come round the house to the car. You've been lost in the woods, see? And rub off a cobweb that's on the top of your nob, just south of the bald patch."

"If she wants to save her face she's going the wrong way about it," retorted Cope, who was growing very angry. "I'm going down the front stairs and anybody who wants to know where I've been can hear where I've been."

Roy looked at him and said sharply, "G'long! Get a move on, Grampa!"

This taunt had an astonishing effect. Cope blanched and bolted down the back stairs without another word. Roy sailed down the front, in gales of laughter, which had scarcely subsided when he jumped into the car beside Adelaide.

"So what's the matter now?" she asked in astonishment.

"Oh Adelaide! I'm not certain, but I believe I've discovered the heel of . . . er . . . Ulysses."

6

Above Upcott an unfenced track ran round all the line of hills encircling Bramstock valley. It was a wild bare downland, with a fine view of the winding river in its reed beds, fields, Hodden Beach, and, beyond, the sea.

The weather below was still unseasonably warm, but a cool breeze blew up there. Roy and Cecilia had to walk half round the circle before they could find a sheltered spot in which to sit. On Westing they found an angle of stone wall, just where the track joined the road to Dorbridge. Settling themselves to the lee of it they could look down over Bramstock woods to the Channel. The wind whistled in the dead thistles on the top of the wall, and faint wailing cries filled the air from birds, running about in the tussocky grass.

"So when I told him there was a cupboard, exactly like the one he imagined," said Cecilia, "we . . . we went up to look at it."

"Don't make such heavy weather over it," advised Roy, with a glance at her white face. "Forget it."

"I shall never forget it. I wish I could kill him."

The note of hysteria in her voice did not escape him.

She must not, he thought, be allowed to make a thing about it.

"You know," he said, "a lot of girls would be quite disappointed if they took a fellow into a cupboard and he only talked about their mad great aunt. They'd feel insulted. They'd think he must have something wrong with him."

"Is that," she cried furiously, "what *you'd* have thought?"

"Depends on the girl. Of course, if it was you took me into a little tiny cupboard, miles from anywhere, I'd know it was to discuss Elizabethian architecture or hunt for spiders."

This sounded as though it might be a kind of compliment. She was mollified and diverted by 'Elizabethian,' until he added, "But then, a lot of men just don't appreciate all the good it will do them to hunt for spiders with a nice educated girl. I'm sure Cope doesn't."

"So then they behave as he does?"

"I don't know how he did behave, do I?" said Roy, who was still not quite easy on this point.

"I couldn't tell anybody. It was . . . I couldn't——"

"Let it ride. I expect he didn't stick to the Queensberry rules."

"What are they?"

It was awkward having to explain jungle law to somebody who had never, apparently, emerged from a well kept shrubbery. Also Roy found this conversation disturbing. He could not help it. The image of Cope's behaviour to this pretty creature was a powerful aphrodisiac.

"A decent boy," he said reluctantly, "would . . . well . . . he'd say something, or pinch her behind."

"Oh? That's what a decent boy would do?"

"Yes. If she didn't like it she could go out of the cupboard. If she stopped in the cupboard and merely said: How dare you? he'd take it he had the green light."

"He'd know what kind of girl she was?"

"He wouldn't at that," said Roy ruefully. "Even then she mightn't be a nice girl."

"A *nice* girl?" cried Cecilia, in bewilderment.

"She might be a . . . she might have brought him there to make a monkey of him. Get him all excited and then rush out and slam the door. Some girls think that's funny."

"Oh! So that's what . . ."

She was blushing now and looked less strained.

"You think I treated him badly?" she asked.

"Oh no. If he didn't stick to Queensberry rules, why should you? He can look after himself."

If he had not thought that she might now be let down lightly, he would have told her just how well Cope could look after himself.

"So how do they find out if she's a nice girl?"

"Oh there are ways," he said vaguely. "But you don't want to know about that. It's not your line."

And if it had been her line, he thought, he would certainly have seized this opportunity for applying the Queensberry rules. Cope had frightened her by ruffianly behaviour, but a more sensitive technique might have gone down quite well. She could vow that she had gone up to that cupboard in a spirit of pure research: he did not believe that she would have got the same kick out of exploring cupboards with Adelaide.

Cecilia sat musing with her arms round her knees,

her eyes on the tossing sea below. Far out, a shaft of sunshine made a brilliant patch upon the water.

"Fornication," she said at last, very mournfully.

Roy yelped with laughter.

"Excuse me," he apologised, "it's your long words. You do like finding very long words for very simple things."

She was really rather sweet, he decided, forswearing the thoughts that had just occupied him. They had better put an end to this broad-minded conversation.

He said, "But we've got something much more important to discuss. Where did Cope get all this—about the novel, and Katy in the Cupboard. Did he say at all?"

"Oh no. He made it up. It's his theory."

"Theory my foot. He's got a wonderful imagination in some ways. But he couldn't make up a thing like this if he tried till the cows come home. You know I think it's probably true."

"Oh do you?" she said startled.

She had never supposed that he would take much interest in Cope's theory.

"It fits onto everything I've been thinking myself. It fills in all the gaps. And . . . this is funny . . . fits what Adelaide thinks. In fact we're both right."

"Miss Lassiter!" exclaimed Cecilia, in manifest contempt. "Surely she believes in nothing but her play?"

"I don't think she does now. But where did Cope get it from? Has he seen anything, or been told anything, that proves it, I wonder? Because, if so, that would be a great help to you."

"To me? How?"

"If your father got to hear, surely he'd have nothing

more to do with the picture. He hates it enough now, doesn't he? Why . . . he might even be able to get the picture stopped."

Roy spoke wih enthusiasm, quite unaware of the horror which such a suggestion awoke in Cecilia. He would get the picture stopped, she thought. He would tell Cousin Edmund and they would get the picture stopped. *And I should never go to Oxford*. Oh what a fool . . . why did I tell him I'd do anything to stop the picture? But how could I foresee this? It can't be true. It can't. And anyway there can be nothing to prove it.

"I've thought of one possibility," he said. "It's not very promising. But what about that man Shattock?"

She started violently and exclaimed, "Why? Do you know him?"

"I ran across him in a pub, Monday night. And I noticed the name because you thought I was him, first time I went to Bramstock. When you came to the door you asked if I was Shattock. Remember?"

"Yes. But what did he say?

"He said he was Effie Creighton's grandson. Is he? He seems a funny sort of person . . . not what I'd have expected."

"I think he is," she admitted. "I know Effie had a daughter who ran away with a groom, or something like that. But what else did he say?"

"He said he had some letters Dorothea wrote to Effie. I didn't pay much attention. He was drunk, anyway. And I didn't suppose they were important. I thought important letters would be about Grant. And I thought Effie was just a kid cousin. But about the novel, and Katy, that's just what she might have written to Effie."

216

(Of course she might. Of course she did.)

"And I hadn't got so much interested in Dorothea then."

(And just why he should take such an interest in that tiresome old thing is a mystery. It's ridiculous. She isn't worth all this hullabaloo, even if Basil's story is true. It doesn't do her much credit. She should have stood up to them. Have I got to be sacrificed for her?)

"But, here's the point. Cope was there too, when Shattock was talking. I didn't think he took it in much. But he might have. What if he's been to Shattock, since, and seen these letters? What if that's where he's got it from? Did Shattock ever come to Bramstock? Did any of you ever see those letters?"

"Yes, yes. He did come," she said hastily. "On Tuesday I think. My father saw them. They weren't anything like that. They were quite commonplace. A lot of people bring or send us letters she wrote, and say they are important, but they never are. You see, nothing she wrote can be published without my father's permission. He now owns the copyrights."

"Oh."

He had been sitting up eagerly, but now he gave a disconsolate sigh and leant back against the wall.

"Then we're back where we started," he said. "Shattock's out."

Cecilia also relaxed. She had known a moment's panic but the danger was passing. The lie had been so necessary that she could scarcely regret it, although she preferred as a rule to speak the truth. There had been nothing else to say: if she admitted that no more had been heard from Shattock, Roy, in his present mood, might insist upon instant investigation. She must stave him off until she could deal with the matter herself. Shattock might have left Beremouth by this time. She must find out.

The clouds were breaking. There were now several patches of silver on the water. Roy was staring at them, thoughtful and troubled. She glanced at him anxiously and decided that there really was something distinguished, striking, about his profile. The jut of his forehead and the firm set of his mouth were more discernible. She wished she knew what he was thinking.

"What are those birds?" he asked suddenly. "Those birds whistling away all the time?"

"Curlews."

Her voice shook a little on the word, for she was beginning to feel very unhappy. This walk together had not led to the closer understanding for which she had hoped when she brought him up here. She had meant to explain, to excuse, her temporary defection on the previous afternoon. Any misapprehensions which he might harbour concerning herself and Cope must be removed before she could proceed to like him better. But now this lie, this necessary lie, stood like a wall in her path. It was all his fault. He had strayed out of his own territory and launched upon activities for which he was little qualified. It was not his business to scrutinise the facts behind *The Bramstock Story;* that was only possible for people with a cultivated background. He had said himself that his job was to 'put in the cinema'. He should have stuck to work which he understood. Had he continued to think in terms of shots, these speculations would never have assailed him. In his own way he was probably an artist: that she was

218

perfectly prepared to allow. But, without his camera, he was little better than a Yahoo.

"I suppose," she said crossly, "that your intense interest in Dorothea hasn't yet prompted you to read any of her poems?"

He responded with a broad, good-humoured smile. This governessy remark was opportune. It quenched an impulse to embrace her which had been tormenting him for the last half hour. To do so would be agreeable, nor did he think that she would object, but he was sure that it was unwise to start anything of that sort. There was no knowing whither it might take them. Dalliance had better be reserved for girls who knew more about cupboards and were less occupied with the first rate.

"No," he said. "It hasn't. You see, I can't take poetry. I never could. There's something about the look of it, straggling down the page. Of course, I realise there must be something in it I just don't get. Do you know one by William Wordsworth called *We Are Seven?* About a kid who couldn't count? I had to learn it once. And I still can't imagine how anybody ever sat down and wrote it. What went on? Did he get it wrong first and then right? How did he know when it was right?"

Cecilia laughed.

"I can tell you about that one," she said. "He got it wrong. In the first version he began it with:

> "A simple child, dear brother Jim,
>   That lightly draws its breath,
>   And feels its life in every limb,
>   What should it know of death?"

219

"But a friend told him that *brother Jim* was too awful: only put in to rhyme with limb. So he took it out."

"A poet too, this friend?" asked Roy anxiously.

"Yes, I think it was Samuel Taylor Coleridge."

She gave him a short account of these two, to which he did not pay much attention. To his vivid but untutored imagination Wordsworth and Coleridge had now become quite recognisable. He saw them as creatures like himself and Ed, mumbling to one another as they watched the rushes. *Dear Brother Jim!* You know, Bill, that stinks. You're dead right, Sam. It does. It's out.

"So what," he asked, "did he put instead of brother Jim?"

"Wordsworth? Nothing. He just left the first line short: *A simple child . . .*"

"Now that's like us," said Roy, pleased. "I mean, you know a thing is wrong, and cut it out, and tie yourself in knots trying to think of something to use instead. And then you realise what was wrong was having anything there at all: no place for it in the general set-up."

He pondered and said; "I get it better when I hear it. Say some more. Say some of hers."

"I'll say some more with pleasure. But really, Roy, with the whole of English literature to choose from it's rather a waste——"

"No. you said yourself that I ought to know something about hers, and reading them is no good for me. Please do say one."

"I don't know if I can remember any. I'll try."

She ransacked her memory while Roy watched the sea. The patches of sunlight had now run together into one broad streak which was travelling landwards. Presently he heard her voice:

> "Stranger, why dost thou walk on Westing?
> To see the Channel gleam below.
> To hear the call of curlews nesting.
> To feel the wind. Was it not so
> With thee, a hundred years ago?
>
> Ay so it is, when joyful thither
> To see, to hear, to feel, I fare.
> Death called thee hence, life brings me hither.
> Can souls, by time so sundered, dare
> An instant's bliss to share?
>
> Naught else is shared by mortals, stranger!
> Ere thou wast born I knew mine end.
> To each his own despair and danger:
> In bliss my very self may blend
> With thine, O nameless friend."

For some time he made no comment. He turned his head, listening intently, as though he might catch in the sigh of the wind, the faint call of the birds, some echo of that other voice, young, uncertain, heard here so long ago and silenced so soon.

"I'm glad," he said at last, "that she was happy sometimes. Of course she was. She must have been. If she was like . . . like other people, she must have had moments of great happiness. Somehow I've always been seeing her as sorrowful, yet that never seemed quite right."

Turning to her he added, "Thank you. You said it beautifully."

She met his look with one of pain so manifest that he

was shocked. The overtone of passion and tenderness in his voice, when he spoke of Dorothea, had been unbearable.

His heart was wrung for her. Again he saw her as the helpless girl coming down the stairs at Bramstock, the shadowy figure in his dream, wandering on the brink of despair and danger. His imaginative compassion, not yet wholly yielded to the dead, rushed out towards her.

"What is it?" he asked hurriedly. "Cecilia! What's wrong? Couldn't I . . . can I help?"

She flushed and turned away.

"Nothing's wrong," she said, "but you annoy me. You'll never begin to understand poetry if you think of it in that sentimental way. This obsession you have with Dorothea makes you think everything about her marvellous. But if you dispassionately compare that with any really good poem, you must see that it isn't."

"I didn't say it was marvellous. But . . . all right! Now say a really good poem. I'll be madly dispassionate. Give!"

"Wait a minute till I think of a good one."

What would convince him, she wondered? It must be something with a strong visual appeal. She tried to identify herself with his mind and a picture came to her which suggested the right poem. She drew a breath and began again:

"I met a traveller from an antique land
Who said: Two vast and trunkless legs of stone
Stand in the desert . . ."

He listened with a critical frown, as though determined to believe that Dorothea had done better. But gradually his expression changed. At: My name is *Ozi-mandias, King of Kings*, he wagged his head as if in resigned agreement.

". . . Round the decay
Of that colossal wreck, boundless and bare,
The lone and level sands stretch far away."

He was looking at her oddly.

"The sands?" he said. "The sands? That's . . . that's strange."

"But can't you see it's better?"

"Oh yes. I do. I do. It's in quite another street. It packs real punches. That, about the sands . . . flat boundless sands . . ."

"No, Roy. In poetry the exact words matter. The alliteration———"

"What's that?"

"Words beginning with the same letter. And the rhythm. Two syllables and one. One syllable and two. *Boundless and bare . . . lone and level*. They make a music to carry your mind away . . . away. . . ."

"I begin to get it. The words do matter. Where are these sands then? Where are they supposed to be?"

"I don't know. Egypt perhaps."

"Doesn't sound like any place Mundy could find on the map."

He looked at his watch and added, "I ought to be thinking of my bus back."

"My best way home," said Cecilia, scrambling up, "is to go straight down that road. It's not a mile from here to Bramstock."

He got up too and for a moment they paused un-

223

certainly. Then he said, "Perhaps we shan't be meeting again? Adelaide doesn't want any more atmosphere."

But he said it with a question in his eyes. If she wanted to see him again she could say so.

She made up her mind. To see him again would only cause her pain. She must forget him if she could.

"It's been very nice to meet," she said, holding out her hand. "And I wish you every possible success with your work. Good-bye, Roy."

"And I wish you a glorious time at College," said he. "You deserve to go, for you really do manage to make sense of poetry."

That sent her scuttling down the hill. She ran helter skelter towards Bramstock until she reached the first turn of the road. Then she stopped and looked upwards. He was walking away along the skyline. She waved, but he could not have seen her, because he did not wave back.

Her heart gave a last warning tug. It told her that the focus of her existence had now shifted. It bade her call to him, bring him to her, and confess the truth.

With a strangled sob she turned and ran on.

The unfenced track led up to the crest of Westing, past some wire and derelict huts which had once belonged to the radar station. Roy walked slowly, pausing at every few steps to look at the sea, glad to be alone. The whole Channel was now in sunshine although the hill remained in shadow. He knew that he ought to hurry, if he was to catch his bus, but he lingered, dreamily enjoying the prospect, the glittering distance, the sombre foreground. The light was now on Hodden Beach, turning it from grey to yellow. Field after field sprang into warmth and colour.

The river gleamed among the reeds. And then the travelling ray touched the hill.

With its arrival ecstasy broke over him, a happiness which he had encountered once or twice in his life, but never in such full measure. It was his defence against the aghast desolation through which he sometimes travelled: of late years he had thought that it had deserted him.

As always, he knew that it was not merely his, but felt by others. He was not alone. He was less alone than anybody. For ever, for a moment, he had found release from that prison cell in which each man lies solitary from the cradle to the grave.

PART IV

Honest Collins

Maiden, a nameless life I lead,
A nameless death I'll die.

Scott

1

May Turner had gone into Beremouth to cash a cheque, lunch, and do some shopping. She came back in the middle of the afternoon looking so much distressed that Alice hardly dared to ask what was the matter. The wonderful Roy must be at the bottom of it: nothing else could discompose her to such an extent. She flopped down into a chair by the fire and sat there, brooding miserably, while Alice hastily got her an early cup of tea.

Yet when, inevitably, the name of Roy came up, it was coupled with the usual boast. Alice was asked to guess how much he earned.

"You've been seeing him then?"

"Oh yes. I met him in the bus. He gave me a lovely lunch. At Badger's. What he earns a week! I was surprised. Guess!"

"Ten pounds?" guessed Alice, who thought that far too much.

"Twenty-five."

"No!"

"And he said, They don't pay us well, in Scripts."

Never, in the course of their hard and useful lives, had May or Alice earned as much as this. Alice found it difficult to conceal her annoyance and said that he ought to dress better.

"That's what I told him. But he says he's saving. He has no car and he eats at the cafeteria in the studios, and his digs . . . well, he boards with a van man's family. But I told him that he really ought to tell his poor mother how well he's doing. She'd be so pleased. He promised me he would, if I . . ."

May paused and her friend pounced.

"If you? What did he want? Not *money?*"

"Only to lend him £10 till he can get it out of the P.O. He's got £300 saved. But it takes three days and he badly wanted the money this afternoon. So we got it at my bank. I know he'll pay it back."

"What did he want if for?"

"I don't know. He was in a great hurry. It was something that costs twenty, and he only had ten."

"I'd have made him tell me before I came across with it. Now you think it must have been something silly."

"No I don't. Why should I?"

"You're looking very rueful."

"Oh not over that. It's something else. I'm afraid I've made mischief."

May rose, took her teacup over to the fire, and sat down with her feet on the fender.

"You see . . . when we were in the bus . . . no . . . it was because of what happened before that."

"Better begin at the beginning," suggested Alice.

"Well! This morning, when I was in the garden . . . but that's not really quite the beginning either."

"Better start with you being born in Macclesfield."

"Well, you know I've always rather worried over what might happen to Roy if he ever got seriously interested in a girl."

"No? Well! Fancy that. I'm surprised."

"He'd take it very hard," said May, to whom Alice's jeering comments had always been a tonic. "I was afraid some girl might take him in with a hard luck story. That would be his weak spot, because he's so imaginative. I used to be afraid he'd marry some little tramp, going to have a baby, because he was sorry for her."

"I don't see him doing that, I must say."

"You don't know him. I do. So I was in the garden this morning, and who should I see, waiting for the bus outside the post office, but Cecilia Harding."

"Good grief! You aren't going to tell me——"

"Wait. Listen. There was something about her. I looked at her. I thought: she isn't waiting for the bus. She's waiting for somebody in it. You know how a girl looks, waiting for her boy?"

"Never seen one waiting for anything else."

"Sort of . . . solitary . . . and as if she couldn't get on with her life till he comes. It quite surprised me. Cecilia, I thought. And then the bus came in and out jumps Roy. They'd arranged to meet. That was plain. They hardly said a word. They just set off together and took the lane up to the hills."

"May! What a fusspost you are! Can't he go a walk with her? And anybody less like a little tramp going to have a——"

"So I thought, then. Well! Come midday, I was sitting in the bus, and Roy comes rushing up and jumps in, just as it starts."

"Alone?"

"Yes. She'd gone the other way home. He told me that later. Well, so when he saw me, he came and sat beside me. I could see he was wildly excited. Like he used to be when he was little: deliriously happy over nothing. *Up and away!* I used to call it. He pretended not to know me. He said: You've made a mistake Madam. My name is Ozi-something-or-other. Sheer nonsense. Till I really began to think something must have happened on the hill. So we fixed this lunch together. And I cautiously brought up her name. And at first I was rather reassured. He seemed to like her, but he didn't talk about her as if . . . until . . . I was perfectly astonished! He said how hard on her this picture was, and how she hated it, and how she'd tried to persuade her father not to let it be done at Bramstock. I couldn't believe my ears."

"Where on earth did he get that idea?"

"From her."

"No! Oh the little fibber! Fancy his believing it, though."

"He wouldn't know what people are saying."

"But her mother is telling everybody."

"Only Mrs. Wallace. It was Mrs. Wallace told everybody."

"So that's her hard luck story. I never! I hope you undeceived him."

May shook her head sadly, and admitted that she had.

"I felt so furious with her, I couldn't hold my tongue."

"Was he shocked?"

"He wouldn't believe it at first. He said it was only old cats gossiping. But then he got very worried and thoughtful. And then he suddenly said there was somebody he had to go and see. I was to meet him at Badger's at 1:15. And he went rushing off as soon as the bus got in. And I did my shopping. And all the while I got more and more sorry I'd said anything."

"Oh why? Why shouldn't you?"

"I remembered her, waiting for the bus, looking . . . rather touching, somehow. Rather pathetic."

"Pathetic? Cecilia? She's as hard as nails."

"No, Alice. I kept remembering what old Miss Paton said about her, once, when we were all pulling her to pieces. She said she always felt sorry for that girl, the only clever one in the family, and sent to a silly snob school, where the teaching was wretched. Any education she's got she's given to herself; can you wonder if she's a bit conceited and egotistical? She got that scholarship by sheer determination and hard work. And then those spineless people said they couldn't afford the rest of the money, though they throw it about on the silliest things. That sister of hers had a Season in London that cost the earth. No! That child has had quite a row to hoe. By the time I got to Badger's I was feeling quite bad about it. I waited till 1:30. I thought Roy was never coming. And then he rushed in and asked me to lend him £10. And I have a feeling this person he'd been seeing had told him something. Because, later on, I tried to say something about Cecilia—how I felt there were excuses . . . and he shut me up. He just looked black and said: No. She's a liar, that girl. And I take back what I said about old cats."

"Well, May. He'd have heard it sooner or later."

"I'm sorry he should have heard it first from me. Waiting for that bus . . . I don't suppose when first she told him, she realised . . . I daresay she doesn't quite realise it now. But I do think she cares about him. And someday she might feel like screwing up her courage to tell him the truth."

"Not necessarily."

"Perhaps not. But now she's lost the chance."

Alice rose and took the tea things into the kitchen. When she came back she said firmly, "Now May! Don't be soft. Those two would never suit. Even if there's a passing attraction it could never come to anything. They wouldn't be happy."

"I'm not thinking of happiness. It might do her good to be unhappy, if she learnt to know herself better. But she'd be such a much nicer girl, for ever after, if she loved him enough to tell him the truth. Oh dear! One should never interfere between young people. They are so very good for each other, if one leaves them alone. Even if they hurt each other."

"There's some truth in that," agreed Alice. "I see what you mean. But don't worry too much. You haven't broken up anything that mattered terribly."

May tried to think so, but she could not put the business out of her mind. She took up her knitting, put it down, smoked half a cigarette, undid the parcels she had brought from Beremouth, pottered about the room, and pottered into the garden, although there was nothing to be done there. The four o'clock bus rattled into the village, turned round, and rattled off again. Nobody was waiting to meet it this time, yet it seemed to her that a vulnerable young creature, hovering perhaps upon the brink of destiny, still haunted the scene. That moment in time was already six hours old and travelling away into the past.

The village street was quiet and empty, now that the bus had gone. She leaned on the gate, listening to the rooks in the churchyard elms. She hoped that Cecilia would not have to be very unhappy. She thought that unhappiness is not the worst misfortune that can befall us. She told herself that it would probably be all the same a hundred years hence. She wondered why people use that phrase, and whether there is any shadow of justification for it.

2

The effect of Bramstock atmosphere upon Adelaide's script had been lethal. When she returned to work on Friday morning she discovered that her sparkling, sinful Doda had been ousted by a spinster aunt. Strive as she would she could not reanimate the one or dismiss the other.

As the day wore on she grew so miserable that a request from Mundy for a word or two was almost welcome. He might serve as a stimulant: he might annoy her into a positive frame of mind. She asked him to tea and stipulated that he should not bring Cope with him.

He came, and she had never seen him so polite. He told her all about the Dorbridge Assizes which were to open on the following Monday. There would be a picturesque Assize Service in Dorbridge Abbey Church on Sunday morning, with a procession from the Judge's Lodging, Trumpeters, a special Bidding Prayer, and all the Dorbridge almsmen in traditional costume. She might like to see it. He would engage a car and they would drive over together. It was exactly the kind of pleasant jaunt to which she had looked forward when she came to Beremouth and she would have welcomed the invitation with enthusiasm, could she have felt quite at her ease with him. But she was oppressed by a suspicion that all this civility was merely a prelude to something else, nor was she surprised when, at length, he said abruptly:

"By the way, I want to talk to you about Collins. His behaviour lately . . . I don't know if you know . . . ?"

So this was it! A party was forming against Roy. She did not want to join it, but she could not feel that he had been right to knock Mundy down, whatever the provocation.

"You mean yesterday?" she faltered. "I knew there was a . . . a disagreement, but not what it was about. I was very sorry."

"Has he talked to you at all about some letters, papers, connected with Miss Harding, which have turned up lately?"

"No. Not a word. You mean new letters?"

"Yes. I only heard of them myself this week. Letters written, I understand, to Effie Creighton. And part of a manuscript. A descendant of hers wants to sell them. I doubt if they are important but I thought I'd better secure them; Cope was negotiating the business for me. I went to collect them today and found that Collins, posing as a representative of B.B.B., had demanded them and taken them away. He's got them now. I rang through to his room and told him to hand them over. He won't. It's monstrous. I am the research expert on this Script. He must give them up!"

"It's very odd of him," she agreed reluctantly. "Had you told him about them, then?"

Mundy hesitated and then proceeded with great fluency, "No. What happened was this. Collins and Cope

237

were together, in some bar, when they first heard of this material. Cope told me and I instructed him to buy it. But there was some delay. The owner asked too much: he thought it was more valuable than it is. He didn't realise that he couldn't sell the copyright, because he hasn't got it: the Hardings own that. And then he wouldn't take a cheque. It wasn't till today . . . but the papers are legally mine. They were promised to me. Collins has no interest in them whatever."

"Oh dear! But if you hadn't discussed it he mayn't understand all this. He may have thought he ought to get these papers for B.B.B."

"I don't know what he thought. But I've told him all this over the phone, to his room. If he hasn't come to his senses by tomorrow morning I shall ring Hobart. His behaviour at Bramstock I might be willing to overlook, but this is the last straw. Either Collins comes off this script or I do."

"Oh dear!" repeated Adelaide.

She would have liked to support Roy but she could not see that there was much to be said for him. Letters and manuscripts were not in his department. She offered, very reluctantly, to speak to him herself. This, it seemed, was what Mundy had come to request.

"I don't want to get the boy fired if he'll come to his senses. He might listen to you."

She crossed to her telephone and rang Roy's room. A sharp agitated voice, which she scarcely recognised, answered, "Who's that?"

"Adelaide. Roy! Could you come down here for a minute or two? It's rather urgent."

"Mundy with you?"

238

"Er . . . yes."

"He been saying I've pinched some papers of his?"

"Yes. And, you know, I really think——"

"Because I haven't. I bought them and paid for them and I've got a signed receipt."

"But, Roy, all that part of our work is Mr. Mundy's business. Yours is to take care of the continuity. Besides, these papers were promised to him first. He made an offer."

"Did he? How much?"

"I don't know."

"Then ask him."

The question did not please Mundy, but he admitted that he had offered fifty pounds. Roy laughed when Adelaide passed on the information.

"Did he? I paid twenty. It's on my receipt. Who'd take twenty from me if Mundy had offered fifty?"

"I'm sure there's some mistake. But you must let him see them. They might be important: he wants to know."

"What? He offered fifty pounds without knowing if they are important?"

"Mr. Cope was acting for him."

"Then Cope will have told him what's in them. But I promise he shall see them. So shall you. So shall a lot of people, as soon as I've had copies made. Just now I'm reading them, and I'd rather not be disturbed. Sorry. I'll tell the office to disconnect my phone."

Roy's receiver clicked as he replaced it.

"What was he saying," asked Mundy anxiously.

"He gave twenty pounds."

For a moment she feared that Mundy might be going to choke. She was not, by nature, quick to suspect double dealing, but it occurred to her that Cope had misled his patron as to the amount offered, with the intention of making thirty on the deal. That Mundy should have employed so unreliable an agent, instead of conducting the business himself, was not easy to understand. A number of vague conjectures crossed her mind.

"Mr. Mundy," she began timidly, "you must think these papers important or you wouldn't have offered so much. Are they . . . are they likely to make any difference to our story?"

"Oh no. I doubt if they will affect your script. What else did Collins say?"

"He's going to send copies to a lot of people."

"He can't do that! He's no right to do that!"

Mundy began to walk about the room.

"We have to consider," he exclaimed. "There is, after all, a great deal of money concerned. If false rumours got out, which might have an adverse effect. . . . Your money, Miss Lassiter! How do you stand in this? Forgive me for asking."

"Oh I've got my money," said Adelaide placidly. "They've paid for the rights; it's not dependent on the picture being made. My agent insisted on that, because Miss Fletcher is so liable to change her mind."

This information seemed to depress him. He continued to walk about,, went to the window, surveyed the sea, and then said, "Personally I've a perfectly open mind. The diary may have been misleading. Grant may not have been the man."

"Not Grant?" gasped Adelaide. "But . . . but . . . who . . . ?"

"That remains to be seen. There was *somebody*.

240

There must have been. The poems in themselves are warrant enough for that."

Adelaide made no reply. She was quite stunned by the evaporation of Grant.

"That girl," he almost shouted, "had had sexual experience. With somebody. You must agree?"

She was about to do so when an unexpected doubt raised its head. She surprised herself by saying, "Well, I don't know. If it's only the poems. I don't see they prove anything like that."

"My dear lady! Passionate love poems. A perfectly inexperienced woman could never have written them."

This annoyed her. She had been writing passionate love scenes all her life with perfect confidence, although her experience had been limited to an occasion in 1906 when a horrid man in a bus had pulled the ribbon off her pigtail.

"I don't know what I agree," she said in affronted tones. "If a woman has imagination, that's all that matters."

"Imagination!"

Across Mundy's face flashed the incredulous fury which the idea of imagination can sometimes arouse in those who have it not.

"Imagination wouldn't take her far!"

"We creative writers have it," said Adelaide complacently.

> "If thine the guilt and mine the bliss,
>   'Tis I alone must pay for all,
>   If mine the pain . . ."

"I don't call that one passionate anyway. I call it sad. And in any case, Mr. Mundy, that's beside the point.

If the man was not Grant, what do we do about this picture?"

"Oh, I don't think your picture need be affected. This material can't be published without Harding's consent, and it's entirely to his interest to keep mum about it. Even if some rumour gets out I don't believe B.B.B. will worry. No, I think your picture will be all right."

"But you wouldn't allow it if the story turned out to be quite untrue?"

"Allow? It's nothing to do with me. It's a picture of *your* play. Which took, as I may remind you, great liberties with many known facts."

"Aren't you employed to see that the script is accurate?"

"In period detail. I've never regarded myself as responsible for the story. That yarn is entirely yours."

Not entirely, she thought wildly. Not entirely. But not entirely his, either. Oh how unfair!

"You can't," she cried, "put it all onto me!"

"I'm not putting anything onto anybody. It's Collins who seems to be out for trouble. If we can shut him up I don't see that there need be any."

"But we can't . . . just say nothing."

"That might be the best thing for everybody concerned. A great many people would suffer if the present story was demolished. And would anybody be a penny the better for it?"

A torrent of contradictory ideas hurled Adelaide this way and that. It was some minutes before she found sure ground beneath her feet.

242

"But I couldn't go on writing the script."

"No?" He looked genuinely surprised. "Why not?"

"I couldn't believe in it any more, you see."

"Is that necessary?"

"Of course it's necessary," she told him sharply. "An artist has to believe in his work. Surely you know that?"

"An *artist!* Yes . . . possibly."

The insult could not wound her because she had never supposed that anybody could regard her as other than an artist. She had begun to suspect that Mundy thought poorly of her work, but that he should doubt her good faith was inconceivable.

"Yes," she said innocently. "I'd have to throw up the script and I think I ought to tell B.B.B. why."

"You'll look very foolish if you do."

"No, I don't think so. I shall say that I was misled by your book. If anybody looks foolish, it will be you, Mr. Mundy."

"Oh . . . very well . . . very well."

He set off for the door, and then turned to stare at her as though she had been some strange creature encountered in the zoo.

"I had no idea," he said at last, "that you took yourself seriously."

He had been gone for some minutes before she grasped his full meaning. When she did so she grew very pale: it was as though he had spat in her face.

"But nobody . . . nobody at all," she said aloud, "has the right to say that! He could say my work is bad, if he thinks so. But to say *that*. . . ."

She rushed to the telephone, intending to ring up Roy and assure him that, whatever happened, she was on his side. The Office informed her that Mr. Collins was taking no calls.

3

The electric fire in Roy's room faded and went out. Sitting at the table in the window he gradually realised that he was cold. He looked round and saw the black bars; another shilling ought to be put in the meter, but he had not got one and it was too much trouble to go down to the office for change. He took the eiderdown from his bed, wrapped it round his legs, and went on reading.

All the Clone material, the childish scrawls supplying fresh instalments concerning Gabriel and Edward, enquiring after Bruno, lay fastened together with an elastic band. The novel now joined them.

He thrust it away, thinking it too short to be of any value save as a nail in Mundy's coffin. Yet he paused to ponder on it before taking up the next paper.

The form of the narrative had irritated him. Three chapters had been devoted to a consumptive, a tiresome, sententious fellow, the narrator, wintering for his health, in a villa upon the slopes of Vesuvius. His daily walks

245

took him past a curious momument on the hillside. Peasants, when questioned about it, crossed themselves. One day he struck up an acquaintance with a mysterious stranger whom he had several times observed in the vicinity. In the course of far too much time this person obligingly confided the story of his life to the invalid, who confided it to the reader. Such a roundabout way of telling things struck Roy as unnecessary. The story broke off before anything happened, although an eruption of Vesuvius seemed to be on its way. Yet the whole was presented in a wild weird light, like the light on thunder clouds, which he had accepted as natural while reading, but which haunted him as soon as he put the manuscript down.

He told himself that she did not know the ropes. Had she gone on she would have learnt how to announce that these people existed, in a simpler way. And then he remembered, with a shiver, that she had gone on. She had achieved a ghastly virtuosity in learning the ropes.

He took up the letter to Effie which was pinned to the manuscript. As he read it he preserved his mind, as far as he could, from the agony which had inspired it; he was trying to consider all this material in the light of evidence, to estimate its effect upon a detached reader who had hitherto accepted Mundy's version. He thought that it was conclusive.

The remaining letters were in a large envelope upon which was written: *Effie's letters from Bramstock. 1889. To be kept with the Harding papers. G.G.10/1/1896.*

He took them out of the envelope and began upon the first:

246

My Dearest,

You will be relieved to hear of my safe arrival, although I fear it will be some time before you do, if the stories we hear of snowdrifts in the North are true. The roads may be closed to the post carts. I was lucky to travel before the bad snow. It is very cold here, but not deep. I sent you an account of my journey to London from Green's Hotel this morning. My journey here was quite as comfortable. I had a footwarmer all the way and my nice seal skin kept me very snug. I was thankful not to have the long cold drive from Dorbridge. It is nothing of a drive from Beremouth.

Here it is all very sad. I still cannot forgive Esther and Pip for not sending for me, and for leaving it to a servant to write and let me know that Thea was asking for me. I remember now all about that maid—Molly Shaftoe. She used to be in service at the Rectory, but she got a bad heart. Thea took her to Bramstock as a sort of personal maid. That is one of the difficulties. Poor Molly is not qualified to be a sick nurse: she was only a scullery maid. But I love her for writing to beg me to come.

I am trying to like Pip and Esther, since you told me not to be unjust and prejudiced. But I have found it hard not to hate all the Hardings, for years. I feel they have always treated Thea so badly, continually trading on her goodness and unselfishness. But of course Philip and Selina were the most to blame for that, also, I suppose, my uncle. It was their doing that she was turned into such a drudge, and could never be spared to come and stay with us when we asked her, and never allowed any life of her own. It had all become a settled thing by Pip and Esther's time. And she should have stood up for herself more.

247

I really think that *now* they are doing all that they can for her. They *talk* of her with pride and fondness. It is her choice that she will have no nurse save poor Molly. She has a horrid room, but that again is her choice. They tried to persuade her to take a better one, long ago, when she grew so famous. But she said that she had got used to the other and would not trouble to change.

The children are nice well mannered little things.

Katy is infinitely better than I had expected. Quite presentable. She is thirty-six! It suits her better not to be young. The heavy look is more natural. She is very, very stupid, to be sure, but hardly more so than many people who are supposed to have their wits about them. It is all Thea's doing. Her life work has been to make the best of Katy and to bring her on. I believe that it is owing to her cleverness and patience that Katy can talk properly, and feed herself, and appear to be a sensible person in many ways.

But oh that cupboard! It is still quoted. I shall try to persuade Esther that it was probably all Selina's imagination. I remember Katy before the cupboard affair. There was always something very wrong with her.

You will be wondering why I do not write about Thea. I keep putting it off because I do not know how to write without crying. I loved her so much, long ago.

It is not because she is dying. We must all die someday. It is her life which seems so sad, which is strange when one thinks of her famous books. But I cannot think that she got very much pride and pleasure out of them. I think of her as she used to be, when we were girls. You must remember her at the wedding, how pretty and lively she used to be? That was the last time. I did not see her again until Grant's funeral, and then she was quite altered. I hardly knew her, such a stiff, grim woman, and she was not twenty-five!

248

Time must change us all. But when I think of my happy, happy life, and compare it with hers, I do not know how to bear it. I wish you were here. I wish I could soon get a letter from you. This is the first time that I have felt very wretched when you were not by. I do not know how to endure sorrow, away from you. We have been lucky to have been parted so seldom, in our life together. Is it selfish to hope that, when we *must*, I shall be the first to go? You are stronger than I. One is obliged to think of these things, at such a time.

I sat with her for a while this evening. We talked a little. Her face is shrunk to be very small, like a child's face. She was wandering at first, though she recognised me and seemed pleased that I had come. She said she had a message for Bruno. I think she meant you, from what she said later: I do not know why she called you that. Later she became quite collected and explained why she had sent for me. She is anxious about Katy's future. She is afraid that they will put Katy away somewhere. She says that Katy must always be Miss Harding of Bramstock. It is pathetic, as though she were determined that Katy should have everything she ought to have had in the normal way. She is leaving everything to Katy to ensure this, except for a legacy to Molly Shaftoe, which I am glad to know of. And she has named you an executor of her Will, because she says she feels that she can trust you to see that it is all done. She says she trusts nobody else. The other executor is her lawyer. She meant to write to you and ask if you would consent, but kept putting it off. She said she felt shy, feeling that it was much to ask of somebody whom she did not know very well. She asked me if I thought you would consent. Dearest, I hope you will not be vexed. I told her I was sure you would. If you had been there, and heard her, you would not have hesitated for a moment.

I did not stay long for she grew drowsy. I am writing this in my room before I go to bed. Goodnight, my dearest love.

Ever your own Effie.

p.s. Esther has just been in to know if I wanted anything. She hung about for a little and I could see that she wanted to know if Thea had said anything about her Will, but did not like to ask. I pretended not to understand.

Are all families so selfish? Perhaps they are. Perhaps we all have some blind spot which is quite apparent to others. I know now that I was very selfish to Anthea, and that other people thought so. I was so happy at home. I hated going away. I should have roused myself to take her for visits, or for a Season or so in London. I think that it was boredom at home that made her go off with Alfred Shattock. E.

Bramstock, Jan. 15th

Dearest Love,

I have had no letter from you. But I did not expect one, as the newspaper is full of accounts of the blizzard, in Cumberland particularly. Many places quite cut off etc. So many sheep lost. I shall be quite anxious until I hear. I trust Lewthwaite got them down in time. I keep thinking of the poor creatures, upon the fells. I am so much afraid that you are there too, helping to dig them out. I shall be very vexed if you are. It is work for younger men. You will be laid by with lumbago for the rest of the winter.

Here nothing is changed. It is very dreary. Thea was unconscious most of the day. The doctor came. They give drugs.

The curate came, but she was not able to see him. He seems to be quite a nice young man but not quite a gentleman, I think. Did I tell you that Mr. Winthorpe is said to be very ill? It is sad that he cannot be with Thea at this time, when they have always been such friends. I never liked him, I do not know why.

Esther has been talking about Katy. They certainly mean to put her away as soon as they can, would have done so long ago, had it not been for Thea. I must say I sympathise with Esther. Katy is very tiresome and utterly wrapped up in herself. She said to me: When Aunt Thea dies, who will mend my stockings?

She bullies the children. Whatever they do, she forbids it. I could not bear to live with her myself.

One must not blame the poor thing, for she cannot help it. The others could. They are all bone selfish, the Hardings, and the women they marry grow just like them. The only one of them with any heart has been poor Thea, and woefully has she suffered for it. She began, I remember, by being rather selfish until Mary married, and, upon my word, I am sorry that she ever reformed, for she went much too far the other way. Even Mr. Winthorpe thinks so, Esther tells me, and he was a perfect martinet for duty. It seems he does not approve of her sacrificing herself so entirely for Katy and for years has remonstrated with her about it, but she would not listen to him. He thought Katy ought to be put in an establishment.

I told Esther what I thought about the cupboard. She said that it is a story which ought now to die out. I hope it will.

One thing has surprised and vexed me. Anthea and Alfred called here last summer! They were taking a holiday in Beremouth. They stayed at The Old Ship, and drove over and left cards. The name Shattock conveyed nothing to Esther, but Dorothea realised that it must be my daughter, and insisted upon returning the call. How strange of Anthie not to tell us! I suppose she knew we should not think it quite the thing. She had never met Thea, and I am sure that she called out of vulgar curiosity, in order to inspect her famous cousin. Our son in law would not be likely to restrain her.

I shall be anxious until I hear that you forgive me for promising that you will be an executor. I expect the lawyer here can do most of the work. I forgot to tell you that I said to Thea that she ought to tie the money up in some way so that unscrupulous people will not get it out of Katy. Thea smiled and said there would be no danger, that Katy has a strong sense of property and can be trusted to look after what is her own.

Later. Molly came and said Thea was awake and asking for me. I went up. But she was wandering. She talked about Clone—a place we invented when we were children. I think I have a lot of letters from her about it somewhere, written ever so long ago. She asked if I had kept them and seemed pleased when I said I had. But then she became distressed. She asked if I knew that Clone had fallen to the enemy? The treasures of Clone, she said, were all despoiled. And then she said, very angrily: There was but one survivor at Thermopylae, and he had no honour! Where is the wretch who told all those lies? For a moment she looked quite like her old self. I suppose she was thinking of her last book.

It seems very strange that she should have written those books, for they are so unlike her. Yet there is something of her in them. I know that you have always laughed at them. But I remember even you allowed that parts of *The Children's Crusade* are very striking. I remember you exclaimed over it when you read it—the part about the mad priest preaching through the villages, and the poor children running away from home to follow him, and how they all believed a children's army might win back the Holy Land and the terrible description of them straggling over the Alps, and dying, and getting lost, and the few that ever reached the sea all taken and sold as slaves to the Turks. You said then that parts were so good as almost to compensate for holy little Ulrica converting so many Turks. I know that it is not true, and that no children are supposed ever to have escaped from that dreadful expedition. But nobody would have wanted to buy the book if it had been as shocking as that, and it would have been a waste of Thea's time to write a book that nobody would buy. I am sure they would all have been furious with her here, if she had done so. Little Ulrica dying was sad enough, though I never minded it much, and could not cry over it as some people did.

Do you remember how we suffered when Anthea read the book? At about thirteen, I think, and she went through an extremely priggish phase, meekly reproving us for everything we did. And you said: Effie! We must make up our minds to it. Just at the moment, Anthea is little Ulrica, and we are Turks.

Ever your own E.

Bramstock. Jan: 16 1889.

Dearest Gerald,

There is nothing new to tell you except that Mary has arrived, and means to stay until it is over. Esther wrote to her. They have not seen much of her since her second marriage. She is very much altered. I do not think I should have recognised her. Very stout and with a domineering manner. Even Katy quails before her. She used to be such a gentle girl.

She does not seem to be greatly distressed. She went to look at Thea, who has been unconscious all day. She came down and said calmly: I fancy it will not be many more hours.

253

But, Gerald, she has told me such a very strange thing. Yet it will not altogether surprise you. It seems that Mr. Winthorpe *did* want to marry Dorothea! We have always wondered why he did not, when they were such close friends.

But it is all very strange. Mary believes that Thea never had the least inkling of it. About a year after Mary married, he confided in her, and asked if she thought that Thea could ever be brought to care for him. She says that he was dreadfully agitated—quite unlike himself. He said that a refusal from Thea would be more than he could endure. He would never speak rather than bring such a thing upon himself. Mary undertook to sound Thea. She did not, of course, betray him, but one day she brought the conversation round to him. She said what a pity he did not marry, and what a good husband he would make, did not Thea think so? Thea said she could not imagine him married and that the thought of him as a husband made her shudder. She was sure that he was very good, and respected him, but, *as a man,* she thought him very disagreeable. So much so, that she disliked having to shake hands with him, although she strove to conquer that feeling because it was uncharitable.

I know what she meant so well. I felt it myself. It was the same sort of dislike one has for earwigs and spiders. That is strange, because he was quite handsome, as you will remember? He could never inspire in me that feeling—I cannot think of the right word for it—perhaps *kindliness* would do? It is what a girl feels towards any agreeable man, and a man, I suppose, towards any pretty girl. Do you know what I mean? It is not love, but a readiness to please and to be pleased. I do not think that love can grow up without it. I believe that I felt it oftener *after* I was married. Pray do not laugh at me! I mean that I felt more affectionate towards the whole male sex, because one man had made me so very happy. I think all happy wives must feel that kind of friendliness to men.

So Mary told Mr. Winthorpe that there was no hope. She did not of course, repeat Thea's words, but she gave him to understand that he would have less chance than anybody. She says that he was fearfully cut up and, she thought, extremely angry. But he must have forgiven Thea, later, or he would not have helped her so much with her books.

I am wondering how you are off for food. You should have plenty, even if you are snowed up for weeks. There is plenty of flour, salted butter, pickled eggs, several barrels of apples, and all the hams, bacon etc., in the stone kitchen. If you want more blankets, there are two chests full, in the sewing room. Mrs. Toombes should know this, but will you remind her? If I am not there she is quite capable of letting the poor maids freeze.

Ever your own loving wife.

The light had grown so dim that Roy could barely decipher the last lines of this letter. He unwound the eiderdown from his legs and went across to the switch by the door. As the central ceiling light flashed on, the grey window darkened to a deep blue. The small bright room became an isolated box, containing him and his activities; it was no longer an extension of the falling night outside. The change made him uneasy. Before reading any more he sat for a while, looking at the sea as it tossed darkly behind the Esplanade, and listening to its faint racket. Then he took the next letter.

Bramstock. Jan. 17, 1889.

My Dearest,
It is all over. Molly came to call me at about two o'clock this morning. She told me that she thought it was

the end. I suggested calling the others. She said no. Thea wished nobody to be roused, if the end came in the night. I went with Molly.

It took two hours. We supported her in turn. She never said anything. The funeral is to be on Friday.

When it was over we laid her down. Molly stood twisting her hands and crying a little. She said: Beneath are the Everlasting Arms. I was glad that she was able to say this. I could say nothing.

Your own E.

Roy put the letter down and consulted a list which he had got from Shattock. No statement was made as to the number of letters written by Effie from Bramstock. He then picked the sheet of paper up, folded it into a spill, lighted it, and held it over the ashtray until it was burnt and lying in charred fragments among his cigarette stubs. Nobody need ever know that one letter was missing.

He then took up the last.

Bramstock, Jan. 21st.

My Dearest,

At last! A whole bundle of letters from you! Oh I am so much relieved about the sheep. I might have known that Lewthwaite would bring them down in time. If all shepherds were as weatherwise as he, fewer sheep would have been lost, all over the country.

Here there is hardly any snow left, but the wind very cold. We all were chilled to the bone at the funeral.

I had not been in Bramstock church since Mary's wedding. Thea and I walked down the aisle last time as bridesmaids, and our lives seemed all to be beginning. How little I thought that next time I should be following her coffin, after thirty-three years! It was quite a crowded affair; people from all over the county, and the church quite full. I suppose because she was so famous. Not even room for the Bramstock servants. I was vexed that no place had been found for Molly. She was standing outside with the villagers.

Henry looked very well in his lawn sleeves. Mr. Winthorpe is said to be very ill indeed. I saw Mary's second husband. He seems to be quite nice. Bob was there; rather to everybody's surprise. Esther had said frequently: We must not suppose that Lord Harding will condescend to come! But he looked more cut up than most of them.

Several 'lions' turned up and a representative of Thea's publishers, Messrs McFarren; quite a gentlemanly person with a beautiful wreath. I talked to him a little at the house, afterwards. He said that the Queen is very fond of Thea's books and has them all. I think that should have been mentioned in *The Times* obituary. Did you see this? We all thought it a little disparaging, as though Thea's popularity had only been a sort of fashion. Pip was very angry. He means, I believe, to write a little Memoir about her, in which he will mention this about the Queen.

As you can imagine, they are all quite furious about the Will. Even Molly's legacy annoys them. There is no talk *now* about putting Katy away. Henry, if you please, has asked her to stay with *them*. He thinks it 'might be pleasant for Pip and Esther to get her off their hands for a while'. It has taken him a great many years to hit upon this grand idea. Pip and Esther will not let Katy go, if they can stop it.

Katy is in high feather. Somebody must have told her that everything is hers now. She is busy dragging everything she can lay hands on out of Thea's room to her own. Books, clothes, papers, odds and ends of rubbish! There is not much that anybody could want—all poor Thea's things so plain and shabby. I doubt if she ever spent sixpence on herself. Katy said to me in her loud flat voice: It is all mine. Nobody can have it but me!

How I long to get back to you! I feel so old and sour. I don't grieve for Thea. I am glad she has got away. As soon as I hear from you that the line is clear, I shall set off, spending the night again at Greens.

Gerald, it is so like you to remember something about her that I had forgotten. The saying you quote in your last letter: Where is my scoundrelly Bible? When did I tell you that? I had quite forgotten. Yes, it is exactly like her, *once*. I expect, at the time, I thought it irreverent. My mother took such a grave view of life, I think my spirits were quite overpowered until I married you and came to see that we can laugh at things, yet take them quite seriously. It was a revelation to me when you explained those Latin words: *Ridentem dicere verum.*

I never learnt Latin. Thea did, and Greek too. But she never had anybody to explain anything to her. I do not think a great education is of much use to a woman unless she has a husband. And if she has a husband she does not need an education. She can ask him.

Your loving wife,

Effie.

P.S. Word has just come that Mr. Winthorpe is dead.

4

In prehistoric days, before the invention of Technicolour, an amorous couple fell off the roof of B.B.B. studios. Upon which the roof became taboo. A notice was put up forbidding access to it and nobody ever went there except Mamie, who climbed the stairs daily to look after the Script Supervisor's rabbits. These were snugly established in a little hut behind a chimney stack and were supposed to be a great secret. Hector Fraser could not bear to see all that space going to waste, especially when his wife would not let him keep rabbits in his own garden. Everybody liked him the better for this little piece of illegality; that he should be getting away with something proved him to be human. Etiquette forbade any overt reference to his rabbits, but messages from all over the building poured into the Script Department when, one day, Mr. Hobart was reported to be on his way to the roof to watch something happening on the lot. The rabbit hut was boarded up when he got there, and garnished with notices saying: DANGER! HIGH VOLTAGE! KEEP OUT!

Mamie found the stairs trying as her baby grew heavier. When she toiled up on Saturday morning she thanked heaven that only a fortnight more of it lay in front of her, though what would happen to Fraser, the Script Department, and the rabbits, during the following six months she could not imagine. It was only because she could not bear to abandon them that she had stuck it for so long, waddling about in a smock, and trying not to know that Fraser's office was now called The Antenatal Clinic. Her husband was quite annoyed about it.

She was panting by the time she got to the hut, and her pale freckled face was flushed. To find Ed Miller waiting there was the last straw. She knew why he had come, but asked crossly what he wanted.

"I'll wait till you've fed the bunnies," he said. "I can't stand the smell."

He handed her a box of liqueur chocolates and retired to the parapet, which gave a fine view of the lot. S.P.I. was making a picture down there. Some licentious soldiery, in very clean ruffs, sacked a convent. Terrified nuns rushed up and down in a plywood cloister. More nuns, not wanted in this shot, sat smoking in a motor coach. Ed's attention was concentrated upon a single figure, wistfully hovering on the outskirts of all this activity.

"Look at Elmer," he said, when Mamie joined him. "Did you ever see anything so pathetic? He can't help hanging around. Why does nobody ever let him sack a convent?"

Mamie could never be cross for long. She laughed, sat on the parapet, and began to eat her chocolates.

"About Roy . . ." began Ed.

"Roy?" She opened her eyes wide. "What about Roy?"

"My grapevine tells me he's in doghouse."

She shrugged her shoulders and adjusted her smock.

"Your grapevine! I believe you've got every line in this building tapped. I believe the cutting room is full of mikes."

"Could be. What's Roy been and gone and done?"

"Any business of yours?"

"Sure. If there's ganging up——"

"There isn't," she said quickly. "Nobody knows but Mr. Fraser and me. It's that man Mundy, on *The Bramstock Story*, down at Beremouth. He was trying to get Mr. Hobart."

"And couldn't. Because Hobart's at Gerrard's Cross."

"If you know it all, why ask me?"

"My grapevine went dead when the call was put through to Hector. Due to certain precautions always taken by you, darling. But I do know what he said before they could persuade him that Hobart isn't here. He wants Roy's head. He's having Roy up for assault unless we fire him."

"If you know that much," sighed Mamie, "I might as well tell you the rest. What's happened we don't know; only what this Mundy says. If it's true, Roy's gone crackers. He's knocked Mr. Mundy down. He's knocked Mr. Mundy's secretary down. He's pinched some important papers. And he's saying he means to wreck the picture."

They looked at one another.

"Roy?" murmured Ed. "Roy? You're talking about Roy? Sure? But what was the trouble about?"

"A disagreement over the story line."

"A *disagreement?* Roy! He disagrees?"

Ed shook his head feebly.

"So what happens?" he asked.

"We've written to Roy about it," said Mamie demurely.

"Written him a letter?"

This was unusual. Letters were not often written at B.B.B. It meant that Fraser was playing for time.

"And does Hobart get to hear about this?"

"We hope not."

Mamie looked regretfully at her box of chocolates as if deploring her own greed. She took another.

"Actually," she confided, "Mr. Fraser's rather pleased. Only that mustn't get round to Roy. If you breathe a word about it to Roy, I'll never tell you anything again."

"Sure. But . . . pleased? For the love of Mike, why?"

"I can guess. So can you."

Again they exchanged glances.

"It might be good news," agreed Ed. "As long as the silly little bleeder doesn't get himself fired."

"Mr. Fraser will do his best to stop that."

"Will he? I thought Hector never had much use for Roy."

"He didn't. Though he thinks Roy is brilliant, mind. But too much of a yes-man. Never sticking his neck out for anything or anybody except himself. He always said Roy's marvellous career would turn out to be interesting to nobody except Roy."

"I've thought that myself. Told him so, once."

"Roy may be in the wrong. But it's better to be in the wrong than nowhere, which is where he's been ever since he got into Scripts. I mean . . . not here really. Just living in a pipe dream about what he's going to do someday."

"A pretty common pipe dream around here."

"Yes. But, meanwhile, he thinks everything's a rat race. And the best thing to do is to turn himself into a super rat. But Mr. Fraser says super rats don't really make very good pictures, and we've got enough yes-men around already."

"He's dead right. And that goes for the whole Industry. I must say, I'm glad to know that Roy can blow his top off, regardless of the consequences. For his own sake, I hope he won't do it often. But I'm glad to know he's got it in him. Aren't you?"

"I'm fond of him," said Mamie, with her mouth full.

"You! You're fond of everybody, you soft-hearted creature. What's Roy ever done for you?"

"He's going to look after the rabbits while I'm away."

"He is? You are trustful! How many do you expect to find when you come back?"

"I've told him," said Mamie, getting up. "Double the number I've left. In any case, Mr. Fraser's going to take Roy off this script, and put him onto a documentary. Tin miners."

"That'll larn little Roy."

"Officially he's in disgrace. Mr. Fraser thinks he'll probably need snubbing for some time to come."

"I get you. If Roy once got it into his head that it pays to be Honest Collins, no studio would hold him. Might as well feed him to the bunnies."

"He does overdo everything," agreed Mamie. "Well . . . thank you for the candy."

She turned to go, but Ed had by no means done with her.

"So what's cooking at Gerrard's Cross? Trouble with Kitty?"

"How would we know if there is?"

"Thought Hector might have heard something."

"When do you think about cutting? That's what I sometimes wonder."

"I heard a rumour the Sales Department aren't so happy over *The Bramstock Story*. Bad reaction to advance publicity. That could worry Kitty."

This was launched at Mamie's retreating back. No more was to be got out of her, although he strongly suspected that she knew all. If Roy's misdemeanours were to be kept from Hobart, some revolution must be in the wind which would put *The Bramstock Story* off the map. Mundy could ring up till Kingdom Come, once Hobart had lost interest in the project. Nobody would ever be able to remember who he was.

Ed wandered into the room of a friend who had a girl friend who typed most of the contracts. He wandered out again having discovered that a contract had been rushed through for a book called *Those Early Days*, by a David Kerr. The telephone book furnished several possibilities. Ed tried one in Chelsea and was informed by an excited female voice that David Kerr had gone to Gerrard's Cross.

"*Bramstock Story's* off," Ed told the cutting room. "News will probably break on Monday. Kitty thinks the Harding girl wasn't famous or important enough. They've got a new picture. Hobart, Kitty and the author are in conference, right now, at Kitty's place. *Those Early Days.* David Kerr. Ever heard of it?"

"God no!" said a colleague. "What's it matter?"

"Not much. Same thing in the end. Dirty story about a famous girl, till Hobart takes a gander. Clean as a whistle by the time it goes on the floor. Crinolines, I wonder, or farthingales?"

Unable to rest until he had got this detail, Ed wandered down to a basement cubby-hole where the madman Issachar was busy with designs for Elmer's railway station. This Issy was no yes-man; his genius for designing sets enabled him to say *no* to everybody, which he daily did. His top was permanently blown off. It was a perpetual grievance to him that so many of his beautiful sets were never used.

At the barest hint that *The Bramstock Story* was off he began to break up the furniture.

"Hold your horses," advised Ed. "Why not ask Elmer? He's on the lot, wandering about like Little Orphan Annie."

Issy rushed from the room. Ed, while waiting for his return, inspected some charcoal drawings which lay about. Most of them were first sketches for sets in Kitty's pictures. When Issy's cupboards got too full he would make a bonfire of those which were no longer needed. They were exquisite; nothing that the public would eventually see would be half as sensitive and imaginative. The little figures were highly dramatic, indicated by a line or two, and perfectly placed in their setting. They remainded Ed of Tiepolo, an artist on whom he doted. Issy had the same power of creating a soft, round face by

265

a single line, with four blobs for mouth, nose and eyes. Occasionally Issy would give one to a friend, but Ed had never been so favoured.

In this collection was one which he could not place. A long room ended in a mirror over a fireplace. Three windows at the side threw cross lights. By the fireplace, leaning against the mantel, stood a girl at bay. A man in black stood half way down the room, his face faintly reflected in the mirror.

Issy returned in a more pacific mood.

"Is all right," he reported. "In de odder picture is also railway station. Elmer on dat is insist."

Ed nodded and, pursuing a surmise of his own, said, "Stockton and Darlington line, it'll have to be then. I say, Issy! What's this? What picture was it in?"

"Set for *Bramstock Story*."

"But you haven't got any sets yet? Only the station?"

"Is Roy. He is ringing me, midveek, about dis bloddy station. He is telling me he vant dis room, long, long, *mit Spiegel*, and man's face reflected so."

"I see. Makes me quite sorry the picture's off. You aren't going to scrap it, are you? Why don't you give it to Roy?"

Issy looked doubtful.

"I am not knowing Roy so well," he objected.

"I think you ought. He'd be pleased. He's all burnt up over this picture. I begin to see why."

"That I don't believe. Roy is never geburnt."

"I tell you he is. Knocks down anybody who disagrees with him."

"Knocks?" enquired Issy, suspecting some unfamiliar slang.

266

"Like this." Ed demonstrated. "Ker-blam!"

"So? Good. I keep it for him. Is *kunstlich* how he tell me about de room."

"Thanks Issy. Bye-bye."

Up in the cutting room Ed announced that *Those Early Days* must be Victorian.

"My guess is that it's too early for crinolines. But Kitty will wear one, if I know Kitty."

5

Out on the sands a fresh wind was blowing and the air was full of noise, the din of waves and the screaming of gulls. Adelaide's room, when Roy went back to it, was too quiet and too warm for his mood. He lingered in the doorway, half minded to resume his chilly, aimless wandering.

"Come in or go out," said Adelaide. "But shut the door."

He came in. She was sitting by the fire, where he had left her two hours before, with the Creighton papers spread on a little table in front of her. Her eyes were red and her cheeks were puffy.

"You've been crying," he said accusingly.

He would have been angry with her, had she not cried. Now he asked what good it would do.

"I always cry when I'm sad. I don't see why I shouldn't."

"It's a good thing somebody is sad after all these years."

"Effie was sad."

"Effie! She couldn't see what was under her nose."

"You can't blame her."

"I blame everybody," announced Roy.

His mood was such that he was inclined to blame the sea gulls, and the dogs, scampering and barking on the beach, for their callous indifference.

"It's a waste of time blaming people," said Adelaide. "We must consider what's to be done."

"There's nothing to be done. I see that now. I thought I could do something. I thought I'd been clever. But I can't do anything with those bloody—sorry!—Hardings sitting on the copyrights, and thinking of nothing but their £500. I might just as well have never bought the stuff."

"At least you stopped Mr. Mundy getting it."

This seemed to cheer him a little. He sat down beside her.

"Have you seen him this morning?" she asked.

"Yes. He's offered me £50 . . . or else! I told him where to put it. Now I suppose he's rung up B.B.B. He hopes he'll get me fired. It's possible. But I couldn't let him have it, could I?"

"No, Roy. You couldn't."

"It's all lies, his saying he made an offer. I know what happened. Cope went and saw Shattock Tuesday, and read it all. And then he started needling Mundy, dropping hints, but never telling him where the stuff was. Mundy probably didn't take it seriously until I scared him, talking as I did, in the graveyard."

"Why? What did you say in the graveyard?"

"Oh nothing much, really. But then he thought he'd better get hold of the stuff, only he must have haggled so long over Cope's rake-off, for telling him where it was, that I got in first. He hasn't a leg to stand on. And as for knocking Cope down I never touched him. It was the Lower Upcott Football Team touched him. He's an awful mess this morning, but if I'm fired for that, I shall appeal to the Screen Writers' Union."

"But when did all this happen?"

Roy's gloom abated a little. He replied, with some zest.

"Last night, in The Plymouth Packet. When I'd finished reading . . . *those* . . . I went out. I walked about a long time. I went along by the sand dunes. I don't know where, quite. And when I was back in the town it was late, so I got some fish and chips, and then went for a drink. And I had one or two. And then Cope came in. He pretended not to see me. He said something off the record to Josie. That's the barmaid. She didn't like it. I said: Don't mind him. He's a grampa. So he went for me."

"No, no! You must have said more than that."

"I didn't. That's exactly what I said. He may have a reason for not liking it, if he really has a daughter in Australia, twenty years old at least. Might cramp his style a bit. So he went for me, and I dodged and he crashed into a swing door, and batted this football team that was coming in, and they got annoyed with him. I've done nothing to Cope except tell all the barmaids in Beremouth that he's a grampa."

"You're being very childish. This won't get us anywhere. If we can, we want to get this picture stopped."

"Adelaide, old dear, we can't. B.B.B. couldn't care

270

less, so long as nothing's published. I don't suppose they'd worry much if it was: their audiences wouldn't know. And nothing will be, thanks to the four-letter-word Hardings."

"But we don't quite know, do we, what the Hardings will do when they hear about these papers?"

"I'll tell you. They haven't made me an offer yet, but they will. Perhaps they'll go higher than Mundy."

"You shouldn't jump to the conclusion——"

"I haven't. Miss First-Rate rang me up this morning. Said she'd tried to get me last night but my phone was disconnected. Oooh! She talked so fast I couldn't get a word in edgewise. So you know, when she got home yesterday, she found she'd made a *mistake!* Her old man *hadn't* seen those letters after all. She must have got them mixed up, somehow, with all the others people keep offering. Wasn't it *silly* of her?"

Roy's voice shot up into a contemptuous falsetto imitation of Cecilia on the telephone.

"So this conscientious girl, she rushes off to the Old Ship, as soon as she can. Too late! She finds Shattock just paying his bill; he was beating it home to Brenda, and getting a bit tired of telling people he'd done a deal with me. And oh! She's *so* relieved to think they're in safe hands! If I come out tomorrow, three P.M., I can hand 'em over. They've got a cousin coming to lunch who's just crazy about stopping the picture, and he'll be terribly interested."

"So what did you say?"

"Didn't say anything at all. She said all this without drawing breath, hardly, she was so afraid what I'd

271

say if she stopped. But at last she had to. I just said nothing. *Roy! Are you there?* I said nothing. At last she hung up."

"But you'll go, won't you?"

"Go? Certainly not."

"I think you should. This cousin might be helpful."

"I don't believe in him. It's just a trick to get hold of those papers, so they can quietly burn them. You don't know that girl, Adelaide. Any other girl who pretended to be sore, because her family was getting £500, would have given me a laugh. But this one . . . she had this line about Wordsworth and Shelley and how important it is to be first rate, and I fell for it. I really believed what she said."

"But you shouldn't leave it to her to tell her family what's happened. With artful people you have to be a bit artful yourself."

"Not when you're on the level."

"Oh yes. It isn't enough to be in the right. You've got to be just as artful and cautious as if you were in the wrong, if you're dealing with people like that."

This was a new idea to Roy. He could be extremely artful, and was by habit cautious, but he had always associated these accomplishments with self interest. An honest man, in his opinion, has no chance whatever in this wicked world. His integrity renders him helpless, and, though he may succeed in making a nuisance of himself, nothing can be hoped from this save a tonic to his spirits. To plague the enemy was Roy's only plan of campaign, which was why he had told all the bar maids in Beremouth that Cope was a grandfather.

He was too furious and too wretched to hear reason.

When the luncheon gong rang it was Adelaide, not he, who took the precaution of locking up the papers before they went down to the dining room.

The sight of Cope's black eye, as they passed the enemy table, was too much for him. He began loudly, "I say, Adelaide! Did you ever hear about the door that started knocking the younger generation?"

Cope jumped up, but was restrained by Mundy. Adelaide was almost trembling by the time that she had got Roy safely to their table.

"You might be ten years old," she complained. "I'm so worried and upset, and you're the only friend I've got here."

"Yes. It'll be drear for you, darling, if I'm fired. Parked with Mundy and the haunted Grampa."

He brooded for a while upon fresh moves in the nuisance campaign and then said, "I think Mundy ought to do a little work for his money and translate that Latin in Effie's letter. I wrote it down."

He fished a piece of paper out of his pocket and gave it to the waiter who brought their soup, with instructions to take it to Mundy and ask for a translation.

"If only I could be sure what I ought to do," mourned Adelaide. "I want to do what's right. I think this picture ought to be stopped. I can't bear the idea of it, when I think of her sad life . . . that something so unlike the truth . . . I want to start a great outcry."

"So how do you mean to do that?" asked Roy gloomily.

"I know a lot of distinguished literary people . . . at least, I've met them . . . I belong to several societies. I thought, if you would let me have copies that I could show to people, I could get letters written to the papers demanding the truth."

"Nobody starts yelling for the truth unless there's something in it for them."

"But I'd have to be sure first that the Hardings wouldn't do anything. And then there's the money."

"What money?"

Adelaide did not answer because the waiter had returned with Roy's slip of paper.

"Gentleman says he's sorry, sir. He can't."

"Would that be because he doesn't know Latin?" speculated Roy. "Or because he's sore about something? Oh well."

He handed the paper back to the waiter with a lordly gesture, "You get this translated, will you?"

"Yessir!"

The waiter, looking a little stunned, took it off behind the service screen.

"You can't expect him to do a thing like that!" protested Adelaide.

"Why not? This hotel boasts of its service and we pay enough. What money were you talking about, Adelaide?"

"The money I was paid for the rights. It doesn't seem honest to sell them the rights, and then do everything I can to stop them making the picture. If I try to start a great crusade, I ought to give it back."

"You couldn't do that! Thousands of pounds!"

"Not so much, because of Inland Revenue. If you sell screen rights they tax you as if you earned that every year. I haven't spent it yet. But, if I give it back, I must

274

do it before April sixth, or else it will be another financial year, and that would be dreadful. So I must decide quickly."

"I don't get you," said Roy, startled and sobered.

"Because of Inland Revenue. If I give it back in this financial year, it need never appear in my returns, and I wouldn't be assessed on it. But if I'm paid it in one year, and give it back the next, I might. I don't believe Inland Revenue would care a thing about poor Doda. They're so inhuman, I always think. And I really couldn't afford to give it all back, and then pay Inland Revenue what I would have had to pay, if I hadn't given it back."

"Adelaide! My dear old thing! You can't possibly give back all that money."

"I don't want to, naturally. But what ought I to do?"

"It wasn't dependent on the picture being made."

"No. If *they* shelved the picture. But to sell them something, and then try to stop them using it . . . I do feel I have a duty to that nice Mr. Hobart."

"Nice! Have you ever met him?"

"Oh yes. Why? Isn't he nice?"

Roy, who had always thought of Hobart as an incalculable natural phenomenon, could not answer.

"I had lunch with him and Miss Fletcher, at her lovely house at Gerrard's Cross," said Adelaide. "We discussed the picture. They couldn't have been kinder."

He could imagine it. He could see Kitty's dazzling smile as she explained how crazy she was over that lovely, lovely play. And Hobart, with his old world courtesy, would have pulled Adelaide's chair out for her, and made her feel as though she were a duchess. Was she really unaware that, at any moment, they might throw her lovely, lovely play into the ash can, and ask some other author to lunch?

He looked across the table and met her toffee-coloured eyes, beaming earnestly behind her strong glasses.

"*Because* I feel I must keep faith with Doda," she said, "that doesn't mean I can break faith with them."

An uncertain creak was all the answer that he could give her, until he had taken it in more fully.

That she might really surrender the money he found himself obliged to believe, although the fact stunned him. He had come to like her and had trusted her with his precious documents. But he had always thought her an incomparable goose; in spite of a dawning admiration he must continue to think her that.

The emotional hurly-burly in which he had tossed, for many hours, began to subside. The Creighton papers had plunged him into despair and rage against the human race, its greed, inertia, callousness and self deception. Dorothea's lot, her wasted, joyless life, he saw as thrust upon her by several respectable people of whom few, if any, could actively have wished her ill. Many of them must have been aware that she owed nothing to Katy, but it had suited nobody to say so. Even Effie, who saw it all clearly, had been content, in the secure happiness of her distant home, to exclaim occasionally that it was a great shame. And Winthorpe, who came nearest to being the villain of the piece, had raised a demon beyond his power to control: he had been driven to protest against a self sacrifice to which he must originally have thought that he

276

could put limits, when it had served his private purpose. That it had all been needless suffering, a mistake which some energetic and disinterested action might have put right, was, to Roy, the intolerable part of it.

Poor old Adelaide, energetic and disinterested a hundred years too late, might be pathetic and slightly ridiculous, but she was a challenge to his angry condemnation of humanity. He did not believe for a moment that her literary acquaintance would abet her appeals for a crusade on behalf of the unimportant Dorothea. And her notion of "Doda" was probably as far off the mark as her idea of Hobart and Kitty. All three were creatures of her imagination. But keep faith with them she would, at any cost to herself. If somebody like that had been around at Bramstock, he thought, everything might have been different.

Or would it? Not if the rest had been unwilling to play ball. It might have happened, from time to time, that one or other of them had felt guilty, would have been willing to do something had the rest agreed, but nobody else, just then, was in a co-operative mood. The suggested amelioration could easily be dismissed as untimely or unpracticable, and the whole dreadful business thrust once more into the limbo of unacknowledged wrongs.

So I think Adelaide's crusade is cockeyed, he thought. So that lets me out. So I can go on saying there's nothing to be done except keep ribbing Mundy and Cope? Well . . .

He leant across and, with one finger, tapped her hand.

"I'm sorry," he said, "I made that crack when you

cried. I'll do anything you want. You want me to go to Bramstock? O.K. I'll go. What exactly do you want me to do?"

"Find out if they really don't mean to publish."

"Right. I think I can do that."

"Tell them how you feel about it all."

"Couldn't do that. They'd never believe it. Who would?"

"I do."

"They wouldn't. If they could, they'd have done something long ago. No. Besides, I wouldn't really know how to explain to anybody how I got into this. I'll just find out what's cooking and report back to you. I don't hand over anything, I take it?"

"Goodness no. Unless you take copies you could give them."

"Hardly time to get copies made. Saturday afternoon."

"I've got a typewriter and we've got twenty-four hours. I won't go to Dorbridge, to that service, tomorrow. We'll just keep at it. When one gets tired, the other can type. We could get a lot done, though we might have to make an abstract outline of the novel."

The waiter was again at Roy's elbow, smiling broadly and proffering a slip of paper. Roy took it and read, *"Ridentem dicere verum.* To speak the truth with a smile. Horace. First satire."

"Who did it?" he asked.

"Scullery hand, sir."

"How come he knew?"

"Student, sir. Takes a vacation job here."

278

"Thank him, will you? Could he use a pound?"

Roy got out his wallet and gave the waiter a pound. The man rushed off with it, as though anxious to get out of the room before he exploded.

Adelaide said, "You aren't as frightened of waiters and people as I am."

"Frightened? Why should I be? But can you beat it? Here's Mundy paid the earth to put some class into our script, and when we want to brush up our Latin we have to send out to the scullery. I shall put that pound on my expense sheet and mark it: Due to A. Mundy's ignorance."

He was determined now to do what he could for Adelaide, whom he had got into this quandary and who had never reproached him for it. If, by some unlikely chance, he could bounce, bully or blackmail the Hardings into publication, her problem would be solved. She would not have been concerned and could keep her money with a clear conscience. He meant to do his very best to bring this about, but he had by no means lost his infantile zest for a nuisance campaign against Mundy and Cope. During the meal he thought of several other ways in which he might annoy and disconcert them.

"You'll never grow up," sighed Adelaide, when he confided them to her. "I can't make out why you bought those papers. Why did you?"

"Can't make it out myself," confessed Roy. "It's a funny thing, Adelaide. I believe it's the first time in my life I ever did anything without knowing why. I must be losing my grip."

"Grip on what?"

"Myself. My career."

"They aren't the same thing. Your career isn't *you*."

"Isn't it?"

He pondered, sighed, and added, "Twenty pounds! I believe young Katy would have had more sense."

6

That Cecilia should be waiting by the ruined playhouse was no surprise to Roy. He had expected to find her in that melancholy ill-omened spot. He gave her a genial grin as he came up.

His grudge against her was much diminished. She was a jungle prowler as astute as any he had ever encountered, but he had only himself to blame for not perceiving this sooner. He should not have been misled by the unfamiliar. His chief illusion had been the pathos with which he had attempted to endow her, but she had known nothing of that; it had been a case of mixed identity. He did not mean to let her bamboozle him again. He felt no particular animus against her.

She hurried up to him, chattering with nervous eagerness.

"We got your telephone message . . . so very glad you could come . . . you've brought them?"

Her eyes strayed to a handsome pigskin brief case which he carried, lent to him by Adelaide.

"Cousin turned up?" he asked.

"Oh yes. And it's all wonderful. He's quite brought

my father round. And he's so thrilled about these papers. Ever since the poems were published, in 1902, he's been sure that some explanation like this. . . . When I told him what I thought it was, and that we might be able to prove it, he nearly went through the roof."

"Excitable old party! His name Harding?"

"Yes. He says of course it needs careful handling. It isn't headline literary news. But he knows people. He can pull strings. He hopes to get a lot of publicity. He wants to start with some articles in a literary magazine, striking a blow at what he calls Mundyism. We got properly together over that. You know? Treating all poets like case histories, and all poetry like some kind of cryptic mumbling on a psychiatrist's couch."

"You and he must be"—Roy crossed his fingers—"just like that. Take me to him."

This she seemed to be in no hurry to do. She paused and said, "I . . . I wanted to explain . . . just one thing."

"Only one?" murmured Roy.

"I . . . I didn't mention Basil Cope. He's not really relevant."

"Isn't he?" said Roy, sitting down on one of the walls. "So who told you all this about Gabriel?"

"Oh you did."

"Me? When?"

"When we went that walk on Friday."

"So why did we go this walk?"

"Because you wanted to tell me about it."

"But I never . . . oh well! Carry on. We won't argue over what really happened. What did you tell Cousin at lunch?"

"You didn't tell me then that you'd bought the papers," she said quickly.

"I'm glad to know I didn't tell you such a cracking lie."

"But I explained that you are as anxious to stop the picture as I am. How we both feel about Dorothea."

Roy felt his temper slipping.

"Please cut your feelings about Dorothea," he begged, "or I might say something really rude."

"But Roy, you know I've always——"

"Oh go feed yourself to the swans! No . . . sorry! Let it ride. So you gave me a very good character, in spite of my fishy behaviour."

"I don't think it was fishy."

"But Cousin does, doesn't he?"

Her silence answered him.

"Cousin thinks you're a confiding little thing, who doesn't know a crook when she sees one. Cousin thinks I cornered the stuff before anybody else could, so as to sell to the highest bidder. You've stood up for me like anything, but they don't believe you?"

"I'm sure . . . when you've talked to them . . ." she murmured.

There was some admiration in the look which he gave her. Such dexterity in securing credit was uncommon, even in his experience. In B.B.B., he thought, she would get right to the top in no time, unless somebody had the sense to knock her on the head at the start. Cousin must feel proud of her. Then a new idea struck him.

"He rich, this cousin?"

"Yes. He's very well off. He wants to buy——"

"Could he be sending you to college?"

She flushed scarlet.

"Why on earth do you say that?"

"I was just wondering how you'd get there, if your father throws up his contract. Because you are going, aren't you?"

"The two things aren't connected at all."

"Cousin, he might think it tough this brave little girl should suffer. Not so many girls would think their auntie's reputation mattered more than their careers. Perhaps Cousin says he'd like to take care of that?"

"Roy! That's a monstrous thing to say."

He laughed and shook his head at her.

"I haven't promised to hold my tongue about Cope. Why should I back up this fairy tale of yours, just to save your face? I don't feel inclined to unless I know how important it is to you. Is Cousin sending you to college? If he is, then I'll do my best not to get you in wrong with him."

The struggle between self-respect and self-interest was violent but brief. He watched her and decided that he would not give her away, whatever she said. He did not much mind what Cousin thought of him. But he rather hoped that she would take a chance and refuse to crawl to him. When, at last, she nodded, he stifled a sigh.

"O.K.," he said. "I won't spill the beans. Cope's out. You deserve to get to college. Not everybody would do what you've done, to get there."

"It's kind of you," she muttered. "I don't know what to say."

284

"Say a piece out of Wordsworth."

He rose and walked away towards the river, thinking that she had better recover countenance a little before they went up to the house. He had much to consider, and very little time. Cousin existed, apparently. He might be an ally. But it was impossible to take Cecilia's word for anything.

She had wandered away along the fence into the wood, where she was absent-mindedly picking celandines. To own up had been very hard, but that bad moment was now behind them, and she was conscious of considerable relief. He now knew everything. He did not seem to be so very angry. She could only account for his lenience by supposing that he really understood her, and knew that this lapse was not typical or in character. He must be aware that, actually, she was an upright and lovable person. He must see her misdeeds as she herself saw them: they were not exactly hers, but wrought by some changeling with whom she could never be confused by anybody who really understood her.

Now that he knew all, she need no longer raise any defence against the thought that perhaps she loved him. The days of running away, of denying it, were over. She need never again be afraid to listen to her heart.

She turned to look fondly at him, as he strolled among the reeds, and waited for him to come back to her, standing by the gate into the wood. When he rejoined her something passive, submissive, in her attitude, struck him. He saw her as his aunt had seen her, when she was waiting in Upcott for the bus. Briefly, and for the last time, he felt sorry for her, telling himself that she would

285

have to go through a lot before she got wise to herself. He looked at the flowers she held, and spoke in a gentler voice than he had ever used to her before.

"Pretty little primroses."

"They're celandines," she told him.

"We'd better go, hadn't we? That's a pretty name. Celandines. . . ."

They said nothing as they went through the wood. He was wondering about Cousin. She was too full of happy confusion for speech, and waiting—waiting for him to say something more.

7

There were no flies on Cousin. So much was immediately apparent when Roy surveyed the two men who rose from either side of the drawing room fireplace to scowl at him. Mr. Harding was evidently thinking in terms of horsewhips, but Roy could meet his glare with tolerable fortitude. Cousin might be short and spare, he might have the face of an elderly sheep, but his sharp eyes were a great deal more disconcerting.

Nobody offered to shake hands. Introductions were not considered necessary. Mr. Harding indicated a chair and gruffly told Roy to siddown.

Roy did so, selecting a chair with its back to the light, a manoeuvre which, he was sure, had not escaped the notice of Cousin. Cecilia retired to a window seat. They had probably told her not to talk.

Cousin opened the proceedings.

"We understand that you have acquired some documents, the copyrights of which probably belong to Mr. Harding."

"That's right," said Roy, slapping his brief case. "I brought copies of them. They prove Mr. Mundy's book to be all erroneous."

Acquired, he thought, was a very good word. It sounded much more refined than bought.

"Have you informed Blech Bernstein British?"

This was a poser. Roy had never thought of such a course.

"Not yet," he said. "I was waiting for some reaction to what I told Miss Harding. But of course . . . I have the Company's interests to consider."

He said this very piously, perceiving that it was not a bad line. It might give him a perfectly respectable reason for being involved in this affair. He should have thought of it before. He now did so, while giving a brief description of the papers.

"Can you tell us how they came into your possession?"

"I bou—acquired them off a man called Shattock."

Cousin was an adept at asking questions. He took Roy so smoothly through the meeting with Shattock at the Lord Nelson that he might have been handling this sort of thing all his life. Then he abandoned Shattock to explore Roy's position at B.B.B. and the terms of his employment. Which he wants to know, thought Roy, but he'll go back to the papers when I don't expect it. He'll get me off my guard and then pop up with something tricky. He'll ask why I bought them, which is just what I can't tell him.

Those calm and steady eyes were beginning to get on his nerves. They reminded him of somebody else, but, busy as he was, with answering questions, he could not

288

place the impression. He had seen eyes like these, when he was on a job, not so many months ago.

"But you did not, at the time, think Shattock's information important?"

"He was drunk. I thought he was just nattering."

"What made you change your mind?"

"Working on the script. Nothing in the story seemed right somehow, when I saw it in close up."

"So you went to Shattock and saw the papers?"

"That's right. I hadn't bought them when I talked to Miss Harding, Friday. But that afternoon I saw Shattock again, and he said there was another party after them. I thought I'd better get cracking. Actually it was Mundy after them."

"You thought it was your duty to get hold of the papers?"

"Yes, my lord."

There was a stir in the room. Both the men were staring at him and then they cast a brief, enquiring glance at Cecilia, who shook her head. Roy blushed and hastily said, "I mean . . . yes."

He remembered now where he had seen eyes like those. In the autumn he had gone to the Old Bailey several times, when at work on a script with a court scene in it. His mind was stored with detail. The judge's eyes had particularly struck him. They were different from the eyes of anybody else. He's out for the truth, was the thought which flashed through Roy's mind. Even if it doesn't suit him. That's what's the matter with his eyes. Not so good for me.

"And why did you think it was your business?"

Here it was. But duty to B.B.B. was a most opportune line. These papers might, he explained, create a lot of awkwardness if they turned up in the hands of a person out to make trouble after the picture had gone on the floor. He explained what the floor was. His intention was to hand them to the Script Supervisor, who would doubtless pass them on to Mr. Hobart. He explained Mr. Hobart, and disentangled him from Elmer Simpson. Honest Collins, the conscientious employee, devoting himself to the company's interests, began to take shape as quite a convincing character, if only he could keep it up, and Cousin would swallow it.

"What line would you expect Mr. Hobart to take?"

Roy had not the least idea. Nobody could ever be certain of the line that old perisher would take. He thought of saying that he hadn't a clue, but rejected it as out of character for Honest Collins, a respectable youth working for people of the highest integrity. It smacked too much of the rat race.

"I don't know," he said, "but I expect, if he thought the story was all erroneous, he might call the picture off."

"Why? His company would be safe from any embarrassing publication, as long as the papers were in their hands. They can only be published, you know, by agreement between Mr. Harding and the owner of the documents—yourself, at the moment."

Roy assumed an expression of reproachful surprise.

"I don't think Mr. Hobart would like to take advantage of that to slander a lady. Mr. Hobart is . . ."

He stared at the ceiling as though seeking the right word and produced it at last rather dubiously. His manner implied that they might not have heard it before.

"A gentleman."

Which could be true, he thought, for all he knew to the contrary. In any case the roughest neck in the rat race had a better right to the title than those Hardings.

He could feel that the shot had gone home and began to enjoy himself, which was imprudent.

"In that case," observed Cousin, "Mr. Hobart would not object to publication."

"Oh no. If I turn in these papers to B.B.B. I daresay he would be willing to come to some agreement about that."

Mr. Harding could contain himself no longer, although he, too, had probably been told not to talk.

"What?" he shouted. "D'you mean to say you're not offering them to us after all this palaver?"

"I didn't want any palaver," said Roy. "I didn't come here to offer them to you. I came because you asked me to come. If you'd wanted them yourselves you could have had them weeks ago. But Shattock said you weren't interested."

"Let's get to business. How much are you asking?"

Cousin moved as though to intervene and then sat back without saying anything. He suddenly seemed to have decided to leave negotiations to Mr. Harding.

Some witnesses will give themselves away more readily when examined by a fool than when fencing with an astute opponent. They become overconfident. The temptation to score assails them. Roy did not know this, and relaxed as he faced Mr. Harding.

"If Mr. Hobart thinks I did right," he said, "he'll

repay me the twenty pounds I gave for them. I'm pretty certain he'll think I was right to let him know."

"We'll let him know. D'you suggest we shouldn't?"

"You might do. You might not. I don't think Mr. Hobart would be pleased if I merely handed the stuff over to somebody who *says* they'll let him know."

"Are you saying you don't trust us?"

"Not to do anything on the dot, Mr. Harding, considering how little you've bothered about it in the past. How do I know you won't delay for months, and then publish something just before the premiere? That could really be awkward for the company. I'd be fired, if it came out that I could have stopped that happening."

"We want to publish as soon as we can."

"Oh? Neither you nor this other gentleman have said so. You want the papers, it seems; you don't say what for."

Mr. Harding leapt out of his chair shouting, "What kind of people do you think we are?"

Roy also rose, swept away by a sudden, unexpected recurrence of rage. His glee in baiting these people collapsed. The whole tribe of them rose up before him: the conceited extravagant old father, Philip, Henry in his lawn sleeves, Lord Harding turning up at the funeral, Pip and his *Memoir*. He thought of their women, of Selina, Esther and Mary, gathered to prey upon a creature too fine to defend herself. And here they were still, a weak, blustering man, a rapacious woman, and a crafty girl, miserably scheming over the final pickings.

"I only know one thing about you," he said.

At the change in his voice, an unguarded intonation, there was a movement from Cousin.

"You didn't mind taking money for a dirty picture about a lady . . . a lady . . ."

The voice shook. Roy controlled himself and went on.

"A lady who was your relation. She did a great deal for you, and saved your house for the family. She's dead. But some people, in your shoes, might have felt grateful. Even if they thought the story was true, they might have tried to shield her. If they couldn't stop the picture being made, at least they wouldn't have . . . stooped so low as to take a rake-off."

"You think the family treated her badly?" murmured Cousin.

"Badly!" Roy turned on him. "I don't know about you. I don't know what relation you are. But these Hardings here have lived off her for a hundred years, and they seem to think that's all right because she was only second rate. Perhaps she was. But she never got much chance to be anything else. She never wanted to write all those stories. She was forced into it, because they needed money. No money in poetry, which was what she wanted to write. Not an hour to herself, not even a room to herself, until they thought they could cash in on her. It says so in that *Memoir*. You didn't need any new letters to tell you that. She didn't stop writing poetry, when Mary married, for any far-fetched reasons, but because they turned her into their slave. All these new letters prove is how she suffered, how terrible her life was, how lonely. Even Effie didn't understand, though she was fond of her. Even Effie didn't know why she died, crying for Clone, and calling herself a traitor. I suppose you think that's ridiculous, because you've decided she wasn't a good poet."

"It's the poetry then? It's the poetry?"

Cousin's eyes were no longer impartial. They were glittering with enthusiasm.

"So rarely do I meet anyone who is fond of it," he exclaimed.

Roy shook his head.

"I don't know anything about poetry. But it was her work, that she wanted to do. And I know how hard it is for anybody young . . . to be young, and want to do your own work, when the whole world seems to be saying: 'You can't. You never will.' And she was very young. She was only a girl . . ."

He had again to master his voice before he could go on.

"That's why I got into this. That's why I bought the papers. I think enough money has been made out of her. I wish I could stop this picture. I wish I could get something printed. But I don't count on any help from you. I don't expect you to believe me. My best chance might really be to go to Mr. Hobart."

Picking up his brief case, Roy turned to go but had only got half way to the door when he was arrested by a shout from Mr. Harding, so incomprehensible that he paused and gaped.

"You've insulted the Queen. You've insulted the Queen."

"What Queen?" demanded Roy.

"The Queen of England. You have accused her of conspiring to defraud you."

294

"I never said a word about her."

"Insult my family if you like. But you can't speak to the Queen like this. You have been addressing your Queen."

Before Roy's inward eye flashed a shot of a grave girl in Guard's uniform, on a horse, taking the salute as a cinema audience stood to attention. He looked wildly round the room as if asking where she was. Cousin, who had, in muttered undertones, repeatedly commanded Mr. Harding to shut up, now explained.

"I don't think we need worry about that. In theory, when I am on Circuit in this county, I *am* the Queen, but——"

"What?" cried Roy. "Are you really a judge?"

"Yes. I am Sir Edmund Harding. But I don't really——"

"On Circuit? What? Are you the judge that went to church in Dorbridge this morning?"

"Don't pretend you didn't know," bellowed Mr. Harding. "You called him *my lord*."

"It was an accident. I never thought . . . I'm sorry your ma . . . I mean my lord. I honestly didn't know. It slipped out because you reminded me of the other judge."

"What other judge?" asked Sir Edmund sharply.

Roy explained about his expeditions to the Old Bailey.

"And then, when you were going on at me like a judge, I suppose I got this feeling I was in Court."

"Going on?"

"Cross-examining me. Bullying me."

"Bullying?" repeated Sir Edmund testily.

"Oh you know what I mean. Keeping on at me till you'd got the truth."

"Which I got?"

"Yes. But I don't expect anybody to believe it."

"I don't wonder. I find it very difficult to understand. You say the poems had nothing to do with it? What put you on to it then? What made you feel that the story was all wrong?"

Roy looked blank and shook his head.

"It was the shots," he said vaguely. "I started seeing it in shots, and they didn't fit anywhere. Her by the river with the swans . . . couldn't see that unless she was alone. Her and Winthorpe in here. Couldn't make out what was wrong with it, till I found out he wasn't old. Couldn't see a single shot with this Grant in it."

"Shots?" ruminated Sir Edmund. "You mean camera shots?"

That he could possibly have meant anything else was so astonishing an idea that Roy shut up. A silence fell which was broken by Mr. Harding, who demanded whether they were ever going to get down to business.

The brief truce between Roy and the judge furnished no answer to this. But the situation had undoubtedly altered.

That a Harding could be the Queen was difficult to believe. Roy wavered, not at all sure that all judges were men to be trusted. Judge Jefferies, according to *Lucy Walters*, Kitty's last picture but one, had been a proper old bastard. Yet that girl on the horse was unlikely to pull a fast one on her subjects, and would, surely, fire anybody who said they were her, and in that capacity, behaved like bastards. There could be something in it.

"If you were in my shoes," said Roy, turning to Sir Edmund, "what would you think you ought to do?"

"Leave these copies for us to look at, and send others to your Mr. Hobart. Nothing need be decided this afternoon. You don't have to hand over the originals to anybody unless you like. We could publish with your permission."

This sounded both safe and sensible. It would be a load off poor Adelaide's mind. But Roy began to regret his rash improvisation of Honest Collins. He had no wish at all, now, to send copies to Hobart, who might be very angry indeed at the obscure screen writer who had stirred up this hornet's nest. If only Cecilia had mentioned that Cousin was a judge, a great deal of trouble might have been saved. Trust her not to play anything straight. He threw a glance towards her window seat and saw that she was not there any longer. She must have slipped out of the room unnoticed.

While all these thoughts passed through his mind his face grew longer and longer. Sir Edmund, watching him with a slight smile, added, "Of course, if you prefer not to appear in the matter, and are perfectly satisfied with my word for it that we'll inform your company immediately, and mean to lose no time in publishing, you might decide to let us have the documents."

The tone was bland, but it disposed of Honest Collins. Roy perceived that his bluff was called and that this praiseworthy youth had never cut any ice.

He grinned and said, "Well yes. If I . . . I'd just as soon not come into it really, if we could make some other arrangement. I mean, it's always better not to stick your neck out. You could say you got the letters direct off Shattock, couldn't you?"

A very severe look reminded him that he was advising his Queen to tell a lie. He blushed and added, "Or . . . or something."

"Let's see the documents anyway," suggested Sir Edmund.

Roy began to take them out of the brief case and pile them on a table, apologising for the typing, and explaining that he and Adelaide had made these copies in a great hurry.

"Miss Lassiter?" exclaimed Sir Edmund. "Does she know about this? She must feel pretty sold over that play of hers."

"Miss Lassiter," said Roy, "she . . . well, she puts all of us to shame really. I haven't heard her say one word about how hard it is on her. She's so keen to get it put right, and the picture stopped and the truth published, she even talks of giving back all the money she got for the rights, if there's no other way."

"Good heavens! Why?"

Roy felt that it was his turn to bestow a severe look.

"Because she read this," he said, selecting a paper from the heap. "It's the most important. You'd better read it first."

It was the letter which Dorothea had sent to Effie, with the manuscript. He gave it to Sir Edmund and came to a decision. If that letter upsets him as much as it ought to do, he thought, I'll trust him. But if he can start yapping about it, as soon as he's read it, I must watch my step. After all, he's a Harding.

Sir Edmund read the letter in silence. Mr. Harding

meanwhile snatched up some of the Clone letters, of which he could not make head or tail.

"War?" he exclaimed. "What war? In 1849. Here's Dorothea writing that war has been declared. What war would that be?"

"Just a war she made up," explained Roy.

"What for? Why? And who's Edward? Never was an Edward in the family that I know of."

"Oh, Mary made *him* up."

"Extraordinary thing! But this Fountainhall, she writes about. They couldn't have made that up. We've got a picture of it."

"Oh yes they did," said Roy.

"You mean to say there's no such place? But there's a picture of it."

Mr. Harding stumped over to stare at the blue fantasy, which hung between a view of Bramstock Church and one of the river.

Sir Edmund had finished Dorothea's letter. He went to the window and stood with his back to them, staring out into the garden. Roy glanced at his watch. He wanted to know exactly how long it would be before this Harding could turn round and discuss what he had read. Two minutes, he thought. Two minutes, or over, and I do a deal.

"Mary?" Mr. Harding was muttering. "Mary? I'd always heard that Mary Baines was a very sensible sort of woman. *She* wasn't a writer."

"It doesn't look so like a place," said Roy, joining him in front of the picture. "Did you ever see a place like that?"

"And frame it!" continued Mr. Harding. "But no

. . . I believe it wasn't in a frame. I think Cecilia found it in a portfolio in the library, and put it into this frame. No. We framed it. And we hung it up. Of course we thought it was a place."

He took a suspicious stare at some of the other pictures as though asking himself whether they were places or not.

Two minutes were over and Sir Edmund still stood with his back to them, gazing out of the window.

8

Cecilia lay upon her bed, sobbing, not from grief but from sheer intensity of feeling. Roy's voice, when speaking of Dorothea, had been too much for her.

Not that she had paid any close attention to what he had said; it had been his tone which overset her. They could settle what they liked about the letters. She had lost interest in that business which was but a tedious interlude before she could be alone with him again. She was impatient for the future, for the days ahead, when they would wander through the woods together, wander over the hills, troubled by no reservations or misunderstandings.

She was in that state of euphoria which knows no anxiety, for which the mere thought of love carries its own reassurance. He might not have discovered this miracle yet; she had only just acknowledged it herself. But that it involved them both she never doubted, for she could not imagine herself loving yet not beloved. It seemed to her inevitable that he would, someday, speak to her in that voice which she had now heard twice: on

Westing Hill, and today, in the drawing room. On each occasion he had been speaking of Dorothea. Had any living woman moved him to that tenderness of utterance she might have trembled. But she felt no fear of the dead and merely recognised in those tones a promise of happiness to come.

After a while she stopped crying but still lay upon her bed, tired, and too happy to move. She could still scarcely believe that all her fears had been groundless, and that she need not have run away from him in a panic when they parted on Friday. He knew everything, and it had made no difference. He understood.

She began to smile. At some future time she would have to acknowledge all the comedy of this extraordinary attachment, trace its history, and explain it, if she could, to her astonished friends. But that was a diversion to come. She must get used to it herself first. Nobody would believe that he was good enough for her. His idiom, his accent would disconcert them, and for these she did not mean to apologise to anyone. Nobody would applaud except perhaps his aunt, who obviously thought the world of him but who could never have hoped to see him make so astounding a conquest.

At last, still smiling, she got up, bathed her face and powdered her nose. She wanted to be down in the drawing room again when Roy took his leave so that she might stroll some of the way back with him and hear him say something, she did not much care what. They had plenty of time.

On her way along the passage she was waylaid by her mother who peered round a bedroom door and asked, "Has he gone?"

Now that Edmund had undertaken to pay Cecilia's college fees, Mrs. Harding was as ready as anybody to disclaim all connection with that tasteless picture. She had thought it more dignified to remain out of the way while Roy was in the house.

"Not yet," said Cecilia.

"Is he giving a lot of trouble? I've been thinking. I've had an idea. If that young man is very difficult, and wants a great deal of money, why not get hold of that nice Basil Cope?"

"Basil Cope? Oh no, Mother!"

"He knows these people. He came with them on Thursday. I can't think why we never mentioned that at lunch. I'm sure Edmund knows his uncle. He might help us. He might know if there was anybody at those studios that we could appeal to . . . somebody more one's own class, you know, who talks our language."

A door closed downstairs. Footsteps crossed the hall. Cecilia started forward, but her mother seized her arm.

"Edmund should consult Basil Cope before . . . he shouldn't pay the earth for those wretched papers . . . it's a mania! And I suppose the more they cost him, the less . . ."

Cecilia broke away and rushed downstairs. In the drawing room she found her father and cousin studying Roy's copies.

"Has he gone?" she cried.

"Yes," said Sir Edmund. "And we've done a deal. He thinks he can trust us. I'm sending him a cheque for twenty pounds. He's sending me the original documents. We're sending copies immediately to the mysterious Hobart, explaining that we mean to publish."

"When is he bringing them? Tomorrow?"

"He's posting them direct to me in Dorbridge. We've settled that I'm to handle the whole business on your father's behalf."

"If that fellow ever shows his face here again," grumbled Mr. Harding, "I'll shut the door in it. I can't think why you allowed him to be so insolent, Edmund."

"As I imagine he would say, we'd bought it," said his cousin. "But I must admit, I was staggered. I knew he wasn't speaking the truth at first. I believed that he had invented the aristocratic Hobart on the spur of the moment. But when we did get it . . . my hat! I believe it though. For some reason he's completely cracked about my great aunt. If she hadn't been dead for more than sixty years, I'd have said he was in love with her. Wouldn't you, Cecilia?"

She was gone. It was only a couple of minutes since she had heard him cross the hall and he could not have got far. She might, if she ran, catch him in the wood. See him again she must, so as to arrange another meeting.

He was not in the drive. He was nowhere in the wood. She ran on and came to the river valley. There was the cottage among the reeds, but no sign of Roy. He must have walked very fast. She stared round wildly and began to run again, crossing the foot-bridge, so that she could see the whole way along the river path. He was nowhere. He had vanished from the world.

For an instant she knew complete despair; she was sure that she would never see him again. Then common sense reasserted itself. Such a calamity was impossible. She turned back over the foot-bridge, mocking at herself for taking a small disappointment so seriously. He would come back, today or tomorrow. If she could only know which day, she might call herself perfectly happy.

The swans, flying down to their nests, answered her unspoken question, but their wings told her nothing, nor could she have believed that answer, any more than another girl had believed, hearing it, a hundred years ago, in this same sad place.

Slowly she took her way back through the wood. It was spangled with small golden flowers. Their name had been the last word which he spoke to her; to look at them was to recall, perfectly, his face and his voice.

She thought, with joy, how year after year the undaunted spring would bring back these flowers to remind her. She was young and she expected nothing evil from time. She feared neither its anguish nor its solace. She had still to learn that it may, at the last, erase all—that she might, after many springs, reach one when she wondered why she had always detested celandines.

9

A green track led through the woods to join the Dorbridge road. It had been given up, as a carriage drive, in
Pip's day. The gate at the end was, as usual, tied with
rotting rope.

Roy climbed it and drew a breath of relief as he got
out of the Bramstock domain. He had chosen this way
back to Upcott because he had had enough of that dismal
river valley, and never wished to see it again.

The metalled road ran up the hill in two sharp
curves; he made a face as he surveyed it for he disliked
climbing. Then he set off on the long plod, rising above
the trees and gaining a gradual view of the sea, Hodden
Beach, the fields, and, at last, the reed beds. His thoughts
were turning to the future. Now that the problem of the
Creighton papers was settled, so well settled, he was able
to consider the effect of this episode upon his own position at B.B.B. He had, in a fit of excitement, declared
that he could not care less about this, but his temper had
changed. He did not now want to be thrown out, just
when a job in the cutting room was so nearly within his
grasp.

He did not exactly regret the brief delirium which had seized him in Bramstock churchyard, but he must face the consequences. He was in a scrape for which he could remember no precedent, if Mundy had really complained to Mr. Hobart. Employees in the Script Department might assault one another occasionally, but Production never got to hear about it. The victim uttered no official complaint; he awaited an opportunity to get his own back. No screen writer, so far as Roy knew, had ever knocked down a highly paid literary adviser. Should he be recalled to London he must have some plausible story ready, or suffer for it.

There were several alternative defences. He reviewed them all as he trudged up the hill.

He could deny it. There had been no witnesses. Mundy had been drunk and tripped over a gravestone? Mundy had suffered from sudden vertigo? Mundy had delusions? Mundy had been misbehaving himself in so glaring a manner that strong measures were justified? Mundy had been knocked down by somebody else?

The verdict would depend upon Hobart and Fraser. Should they disagree, Fraser's support was the more vital. A screen writer in Fraser's black books would never survive for long. There might be outward compliance with Hobart's views, but the delinquent would vanish, for some quite unconnected reason, as soon as Hobart had forgotten the affair. Whereas a writer whom Fraser wished to keep would probably survive, although he would not be in evidence during the period of Hobart's displeasure. He would be despatched to the other end of nowhere on some obscure documentary.

If the same story were likely to go down equally

well with both men the task would be comparatively simple. But this was improbable. Hobart was reputed to be emotional and easily scared. Justice was all that could ever be expected from Fraser; a bid for sympathy in that quarter would be worse than useless.

If possible a joint interview must be avoided. Hobart must be tackled first and then Fraser; all manoeuvres must be directed to secure that. And with Hobart the best approach would probably be one of inarticulate embarrassment. *Yes . . . I did hit him. . . . I can't possibly say why. . . .* Some minutes of this sort of thing might intimidate Hobart into asking no further questions.

One promising factor could be taken into account. Mundy himself would be in the soup as soon as Hobart received copies of the Creighton papers from the Hardings. Whether the picture went on or not, Mundy's incompetence would be manifest; he had been paid to supply accuracy and he could not have been more wrong. Mundy fired would be Mundy forgotten, and the enquiry might never be held if it could be postponed for a week.

By the time that he had reached the second curve of the road Roy had almost determined upon a convenient indisposition. He possessed an infantile talent for being sick whenever he liked; he had never mentioned it to anybody because he had always thought that it might turn out to be useful. It might prove as effective with Hobart as with Fraser. He would go back to London looking very yellow, would creep, retching, into their offices, and begin upon his story, only to be checked

with: No, Collins! Not here! Go home! Go to bed. We'll
have to discuss this later.

And to bed Collins would go until Mundy was forgotten. It was a hazardous proceeding, but it might work.

At the top of the hill he took the unfenced track
round to Upcott. The wind was sighing, the curlews
were calling, but there was no gleam upon the sea. Today
it was in a prosaic mood and stretched away towards a
hard horizon, a grey, wrinkled, uneventful floor across
which stocky coasters went about their business. He
paused and viewed it with calm pleasure but without the
exaltation of Friday morning. That he did not, and
could not, expect to recur. Twice or thrice in a life-time
would be as much as any man could ask. He did not suppose that those others had, in their day, known it often.
Perhaps, for them too, it had only been once.

To nobody in the world could he have told the true
story of this tremendous week. He had no wish to do so.
For the one person to whom he had communicated some
part of it, few words had been needed. Issy's excited
voice, over the telephone, had exclaimed: *Ja! Ja! I do
that*. As though the entire image had been transmitted
over the wire by a couple of sentences from Roy. And if
Issy had drawn that picture he would have got it exactly right, in a few strokes of charcoal. He would have
flown through time and space. He would have been
there.

Nobody but Issy could draw her so well, thought
Roy, because they got him down, just as they got her
down. Poor Issy! We'll never know what happened to
him before he escaped to England, but he'll never get

anywhere now. He hides in that hole and earns his dinner and draws things and burns them. And she never got anywhere. And I shall probably never get anywhere either. And there are so many more of us than there are of people who do ever get anywhere. There must have been, ever since the beginning of the world.

The thought of these lost legions filled him with a fortitude more enduring than happiness. His own success or failure seemed to him, just then, of little significance beside his fellowship in a battle, ever renewed yet as old as time. His strength came, as he now knew, from his comrades; he shared it with his nameless friends among the victors, the defeated, the casualties, the survivors, the renowned and the forgotten, the living and the dead.

www.vintage-classics.info

Visit www.worldofstories.co.uk for all your
favourite children's classics